ROBIN BURCELL

COLD CASE

AVON BOOKS
An Imprint of HarperCollins*Publishers*

This is a work of fiction. Names, characters, places, and incidents are products of the author's imagination or are used fictitiously and are not to be construed as real. Any resemblance to actual events, locales, organizations, or persons, living or dead, is entirely coincidental.

AVON BOOKS
An Imprint of HarperCollins*Publishers*
10 East 53rd Street
New York, New York 10022-5299

Copyright © 2004 by Robin Burcell
ISBN: 0-06-105377-5
www.avonmystery.com

First Avon Books paperback printing: February 2004

Avon Trademark Reg. U.S. Pat. Off. and in Other Countries, Marca Registrada, Hecho en U.S.A.
HarperCollins® is a registered trademark of HarperCollins Publishers Inc.

Printed in the U.S.A.

10 9 8 7 6 5 4 3 2 1

To my three girls,
I love you, I love you, I love you.
I said it first!

A portion of the author's royalties will be donated to COPS in memory of the men and women who have given their lives in the line of duty. COPS, Concerns of Police Survivors, provides resources to assist in rebuilding the lives of surviving families of law enforcement officers killed in the line of duty.

COLD
CASE

1

"**O**fficer down! Officer down!"

The panicked words echoed in my ears just as the shots had seconds before. My partner, Sam Scolari, dragged me toward the stairs out of the line of fire. My back hit the wall and we both fell.

"Anyone see the gunman?"

"What the hell happened?" came another shout.

I wasn't sure myself. We were on the second floor of the Twin Palms Motel, assisting Narcotics with a drug raid, on a case we hoped would lead to information on the homicide of Fiona Winchester, a woman killed at this very same motel. They, Narcotics, were on the first floor, and had made their arrest, while Scolari and I had gone up the stairs looking for evidence that might tie into Fiona Winchester's murder, as well as a case against suspected mob boss Nick Paolini. He owned this building. Supposedly ran drugs from it.

"Where the hell is the goddamned ambulance?" someone shouted.

The surge of adrenaline had drained me completely as Scolari and I supported each other in the stairwell of the dank motel. Armed officers rushed past us. One of them stopped.

"Jesus!"

I looked up to see a rookie female officer, her face-paling as she stared at Scolari.

"What?" he asked her, his voice gruff. "You never seen a little blood before?"

I shook my head at him, wanted to tell him she'd probably never been in a shooting before. Never realized the emotional impact, the way it slowed and fragmented one's thoughts. But I turned, saw Scolari's face, white as the officer's. Saw the blood covering his raid jacket. My stomach roiled with nausea.

Scolari met my gaze. He tried to smile. "You okay, Kate?"

Yeah, I wanted to say, vaguely aware of a siren wailing. It grew louder, but strangely seemed farther away. "What about you?"

He didn't answer. I don't know if he heard me.

The female officer was speaking into her radio and I couldn't hear a sound.

I realized then what had happened.

Looked down, saw the blood spreading on my shoulder.

I was the officer down.

2

Three years later.

If someone had told me when I graduated from the police academy over a decade ago that I'd be sitting here, searching for a killer from the Cold Case file in front of TV cameras on *San Francisco's Most Wanted,* I doubt I would have believed them—especially considering I'd spent the last two years of my career avoiding TV cameras. And not doing a very good job at it. I'd had some high-profile cases that brought some bad publicity to the department. Which has something to do with how I ended up with the Cold Case files to begin with—an attempt to keep me out of trouble, I suppose. It was not the elite job of choice in the Homicide Detail at SFPD, but it was a damn sight better than being booted back to patrol, so I took my knocks, vowed not to bring any more dubious publicity to the San Francisco Police Department, and dutifully set about repairing my career so that I could get called out in the middle of the night to look at dead bodies like all the other homicide inspectors.

Then again, maybe this wasn't such a bad deal after all, I thought as the lights from the TV camera blinded me.

"Three, two . . ." I saw someone point at the TV reporter, a petite, dark-haired woman, who happened to be my ex-husband's girlfriend.

"Good evening. I'm Beth Skyler, and you're tuned into *San Francisco's Most Wanted,* our once-a-month look at crime in the city, brought to you by Channel Two News. With me is Homicide Inspector Kate Gillespie, who is hoping that you, our viewers, can help with a case that has remained unsolved these past three years. Can you tell us a little about the case, Inspector?"

Smiling at Beth, I tried to remember my instructions not to look directly at the camera—as if I could even see it behind the blinding lights. I had two minutes to give my information, which didn't seem like nearly enough time to discuss a woman who had been killed and then forgotten by the rest of the world. I could only hope it was enough time, that one person would give us the break we needed, the break I hoped would solve two cases at once, which was one of the primary reasons I had chosen it, perhaps even a bit selfishly. "Three years ago a woman named Fiona Winchester was shot and killed as she exited the Twin Palms Motel. The only evidence found at the scene was a rose, though we have no idea if it is related. The murder occurred shortly after Fiona left work from her waitressing job at Etienne Reynard's and drove to the motel." Etienne Reynard's was an exclusive restaurant near the Embarcadero—and happened to be the other reason why I'd pulled the case. The restaurant had made Sunday's paper because the owner was helping to raise money for a women's shelter. I hoped the double whammy of my appearance and the publicity surrounding the fundraiser this coming weekend might generate some new leads.

A photograph taken from Fiona Winchester's driver's license flashed on the screen, or so I was told, since we couldn't see it behind us. After that I made the announcement of a thousand-dollar reward. About a minute later the segment was over. Beth and I stood at the same time.

"Thanks for airing this," I said.

She had to look up at me, since I happened to be about a head taller than her five-two frame. "Not a problem," she said. "I'm hoping tomorrow we can get one of your robbery guys to appear about the diamond heist. I heard the total was something close to a million . . ."

The dollar amount of the diamonds stolen from a gem show was closer to six million, but I knew better than to comment. The true value wouldn't be released to the public, and since I didn't work robbery, and Beth was fishing for her next scoop, I merely smiled and said, "Well, good luck."

We both walked off the sound stage where my ex-husband, DA Investigator Reid Bettencourt, stood waiting. "You were great," he told Beth, giving her a kiss on the cheek, just before handing her a bottle of water.

She smiled, then took a sip, and Reid turned to me. "Not bad, Kate, except the hair. You might want to wear it different next time."

My shoulder-length hair, not quite as dark as Beth's, was pulled back in a no-nonsense ponytail. I liked it that way, and refrained from saying that the show wasn't about me or how I wore my hair. It was about catching a killer and serving justice. So I simply thanked Beth again and got the hell out of there before she could corner me on the diamond robbery, and before my ex could criticize anything else about me.

I'd pretty much put the whole interview from my mind by the time I returned to work the next morning. Unfortunately, my coworkers, being typical cops, had not. My desk was decorated with fake Academy Awards in honor of my brush with fame.

"Yo, Gillespie." This from my current partner, the short, stocky Rocky Markowski. "What's it feel like being famous for five whole minutes?"

"Yeah," Felix Shipley said, pausing as he typed on his computer. "Some Hollywood type called. Wanted to know if you had an agent. We told him you weren't accepting anything below six figures."

"Six?" I said, taking off my tan blazer and hanging it on the coat rack, then pulling my holster and weapon from my belt and placing it in my top drawer. "It's seven or no deal."

Which was right about the time that Gypsy, the Homicide Detail secretary, walked in the door handing me a single red rose wrapped in cellophane. "This just came for you," she said.

"Nice," I said, opening the small envelope attached to the ribbon with the name "Kate" written on it. "Maybe I should appear on TV more often."

"Secret admirer?" Rocky asked.

"I guess so," I said, turning the card over, as my phone rang. "It's blank." I didn't miss the connection to the case, but before I could figure out which one of my coworkers had sent it, Gypsy popped in again to alert us·that the tip calls were starting. By lunchtime, we'd had our share.

"All in all," I said, hanging up my phone just as Rocky's rang again, "some pretty poor leads."

Rocky nodded. "Nothing like a little reward money to bring the nutcases and entrepreneurs out of the woodwork," he said, answering yet one more call. After a few seconds he covered the mouthpiece. "You gotta hear this. It's classic Madame Korsakoff."

Madame Korsakoff was a drag queen psychic, who made it a point to call in a prediction whenever a reward was offered on a crime, on the off chance that it came true and that she—or he, depending on how you looked at it—could collect.

Shipley and I both leaned forward to listen, in hopes of catching part of her call. Ed Zimmerman, in his usual grumpy mood, stood and grabbed his radio. "Don't know why you even bothered going on TV. All these things do is generate dozens of fake leads that you gotta sift through, just to maybe even find one."

"Gee, what was I thinking?" I said.

Shipley watched Zim as he headed out the door. "He's just jealous, because Madame Korsakoff never called when he had his big moment on TV."

Rocky waved for us to be quiet, then hit the speaker phone. "I'm sorry," Rocky said. "We had a bad connection. What was it you said?"

"I am sensing that your killer is very near," came a rather deep, though somewhat feminine-sounding voice with a feigned accent that ran the gamut between Haitian and Russian.

"No kidding? Any idea where?"

"I am sensing on a street corner by a bank."

"You wouldn't be sensing a street name, would you?"

"Not yet."

Rocky shook his head. "Maybe a suspect name?"

"No," came Korsakoff's answer. "But he will come to you shortly out of the past. Not yours, but someone else's. I am sensing this. Maybe in the next couple of days. You must be careful. Especially near money. How do I get my reward?"

"Tell you what," Rocky said. "You sense me a name and location of a suspect and we'll discuss the reward."

"I am sensing you don't believe. That wouldn't be wise."

"You work on that info. We'll hold the reward money."

Rocky disconnected and said, "Makes you wonder. What if she really was psychic?"

"Shoulda tested her," Shipley said. "Ask her who stole all those diamonds. The robbery detail would pay the reward from their own pocket."

"Forget the damn diamonds," Rocky said. "Ask her where lunch is. Pizza and salad bar is what I vote for. You in?" he asked me.

"I'm in," I said, pulling open my drawer to get my car keys and weapon. My phone rang again.

"Let it go to voice mail," Rocky said. "We haven't received one solid tip and I'm starved."

"Maybe it's Madame Korsakoff, sensing the name of our suspect," Shipley said.

"In that case," I replied, "we wouldn't want to miss out." I hit the speaker-phone feature, then said, "Gillespie, Homicide."

"Are you the officer on TV last night?" Definitely not Korsakoff, no accent, and at first I couldn't tell if it was male or female, since the caller spoke low and the connection sucked. Cell phone I figured. Even so, Rocky and Shipley sat on the edge of their desks to listen to the call, undoubtedly hoping it was as entertaining as our drag queen.

"Yes," I said. "Who is this?"

"I'm calling about the woman who was killed. I know who killed her."

"Go ahead. I'm listening."

"I-I don't want to tell you on the phone. Can we meet? Somewhere else? I'd rather not go to the police station."

"Do you have a place in mind?"

She hesitated, named a cross street, then added, "By the bus stop. Monday at one."

"I have an appointment then," I said. I didn't, but I figured she wouldn't know. "How about today?" I asked, watching Rocky shake his head no, undoubtedly worried I'd cut into his lunch time.

"I-I can't. It has to be Monday."

"If I'm going to meet with you," I said, "I'll need something more. Something that tells me you're legit. Like a name and a phone number."

"Loo—I mean, Jane . . . Doe. No number."

"That's original," Rocky whispered.

I ignored him and said, "Jane, I'm going to be honest with

you. I have a problem about meeting someone on a street corner, when I don't know what's going on or anything else about that person. You do understand, don't you?"

". . . I know who killed that woman."

"And allegedly so do fifty other people who have called today. What makes you any different?"

A muffled sound, then, "He's, um, the same person who had you shot at the Twin Palms Motel."

Her answer caught me off guard. Apparently Rocky and Shipley, too, judging by their faces. But I recovered quickly and told her, "And that person is dead." Or so we believed . . .

"No. He's not," she said. "He's still alive. The man who *had* you and the woman shot. I can give you his name."

I hesitated. Told myself that this was obviously another opportunistic call. A lucky guess. Someone looking for reward money. Antonio Foust had long been the only suspect in my shooting, though nothing was ever proven—other than our suspicions that he'd been working for mob boss Nick Paolini at the time. Foust was dead now and Paolini had denied all involvement as well as any knowledge of the crime, but that was to be expected. Most criminals never admitted their crimes unless confronted by irrefutable proof, and even then it was a stretch to get them to confess.

"Maybe so," I finally said, as Lieutenant Andrews walked into the office, listening. "But I'm going to need something more. Something that tells me you know what you're talking about."

She was quiet a moment, and Shipley gave a sharp nod, as though to say: *We knew she was another flake.*

Right about then, we heard the same muffled noise on the other end of the phone, as though she had covered the mouthpiece, and then, "I know you were pulled from the hallway by a tall gray-haired officer. An older man."

The room went quiet. I know my heart stopped, then

started up again in loud hard thumps at her words, and I was sure the others could hear it. For a second, I couldn't even talk or move, and I felt as if someone had suddenly dropped me back into the Twin Palms, because I could see my partner at the time, Sam Scolari, dragging me out of the line of fire, then into the stairwell.

She couldn't have known—unless she was there, or someone had told her.

It was a moment I would never forget.

A moment that didn't appear in any reports.

Just the shooting, then the aftermath . . .

"What else can you tell me," I finally said.

"If you meet me, I'll give you the proof you need Monday at the bus stop. I'll be carrying a red rose."

"I'll be there, but—"

She disconnected before I could question her further, and the dial tone filled the room. I hung up, staring at the phone for I don't know how long, until Andrews said, "Is it legit?"

"I have no idea. We purposefully didn't make a connection on TV to the Fiona Winchester case and my shooting. She brought it up."

Shipley sank into his chair, looking as surprised as I felt. He'd been there that night. "How could she know about Scolari?" he asked.

"I don't like it," Andrews said. "It's been three years. Why now?"

"Because," Rocky said, "Gillespie was playing movie star on *San Francisco's Most Wanted*. Whoever she was saw an opportunity for money."

"What if it is legit?" I asked.

He didn't say anything at first, his dark gaze on my phone, as though he'd find the answers there. When he looked at me there was determination in his eyes. "Only one way to find out. Call Zim. I want the four of you to scope out the place today. Monday, Gillespie and Markowski go to the meet.

Shipley and Zim will set up in the area, keep an eye out for anything that doesn't look right."

"Check," Shipley said.

As soon as Zim returned to the office, we grabbed hamburgers to go, then headed to the intersection. The bench at the bus stop was located on the corner in front of a bank. Across the street was a grocery store, a hair salon, and a few shops, as well as a small office complex where Zim decided he could set up. Shipley would sit outside the espresso shop on the opposite corner, keeping an eye not only on us, but on the BART train station, accessed via escalators that led down to the belowground train. That done, we combed the area, which was crowded with pedestrians, tourists and locals, all taking advantage of the balmy spring day, walking instead of hopping on the train or the bus. And who could blame them? Billowing white clouds scudding across the blue sky in the mild breeze made it a tempting prospect to linger outdoors.

We, however, didn't have that luxury, and eventually returned to the Hall of Justice to make our operation plan. We needed to ensure that we had everything covered, including a few radio cars as we called them, that would set up a couple blocks away out of sight, ready to respond Code Three in case they were needed.

The mild weather carried over to the night as I drove home to my Berkeley Hills apartment, and I went over every detail of the call, replaying the phone conversation in my mind, wondering if there were any subtle clues that I might have missed, hoping the call wasn't a hoax. It couldn't be, I told myself. How could they know that Fiona Winchester's murder at the Twin Palms was related to my shooting?

Needless to say, I didn't sleep well that night, never mind the rest of the weekend, and before I drove into work that Monday morning, I stopped for a double mocha, my new drink of choice, before fighting the traffic on the Bay

Bridge, which was its usual nightmare. When I got into work, I was ready for the day, ready to meet this woman, find out if there was any truth to what she said. What I wasn't ready for was the nasty voice mail from some unknown male caller, and I listened to it again, not sure I heard it right, or even what it was about.

"You stupid, goddamned cops! What the hell do you think you're doing? Trying to get me and what's left of my family killed?"

That was it. No name, no reason, no reference to anything else. "Nutcase," I said, pressing the buttons to archive the call, just in case something came up a few days or weeks down the road.

By 1200 hours that afternoon, we were driving to our assigned locations, making sure we were there ahead of our would-be informant.

We were sitting in our car, which was parked about thirty feet from the bus stop, watching, appreciating why this woman picked this location. Cars pulled in and out every few seconds, people walking to the store or the bank. It was impossible to keep an eye on everyone, but we did our best.

"How's Torrance doing?" Rocky asked me as he sipped on a Coke we'd picked up from a drive-through en route.

"Not bad, I guess." Mike Torrance used to be the lieutenant in charge of Internal Affairs until he left the department to join the FBI a few months ago. I suppose you could consider him my on-again, off-again *almost* flame, primarily because we'd never seemed to get our so-called flame lit at the same time. Even so, he'd telephoned about once a week to update me on his progress at the FBI Academy, and deep down I still held out hope that we might actually make things work once he returned. "He should be back this week—" I said, stopping when Rocky nodded at a woman who walked up to the bus stop and sat on the bench.

She stayed there for thirty minutes reading a paperback

novel, until a bus pulled up and opened its doors. I saw her speak to the driver, then shake her head. She did not, however, get on.

"Maybe that's her," Rocky said into the radio.

"No red rose," Shipley radioed back. "I vote we hold off. A lot of buses stop at that corner. Maybe it wasn't hers."

"You think she'll show?" Rocky asked a while later.

"Who knows," I said, looking at my watch. "Ten minutes left. Let's go."

I called Shipley and Zim on the radio to let them know. We got out and stood by our car. He watched one direction, I kept an eye in the other. At precisely 1300 hours, a white female, wearing a bright blue scarf around her neck, carrying a single, long-stemmed rose, exited the grocery store, moving our way, looking around, even behind her, as though worried she was being followed. "That's gotta be her," I said to Rocky, as she weaved around the cars through the parking lot, then crossed the street, walking in our direction. I continued watching her, figuring she might be late thirties, early forties. Hard to tell since she was wearing large-framed dark glasses, never mind the scarf around her neck, something a lot of women did when they wanted to hide their age. She was tall, big-boned, wearing form-fitting clothes that showed off what the guys I worked with would clearly call a rack job, and she had short red hair that seemed to absorb the sunlight rather than reflect it.

"Jane Doe's got a wig on," I told Rocky.

"Goes with the name."

"Yeah, well let's hope her info isn't as fake as everything else." I keyed my radio to speak with Shipley and Zim. "Possible contact heading our way."

"Got her in sight," Zim radioed back. "Big woman, but definitely a looker."

A few seconds later when she was just a few yards from us, Shipley came on the air. "Got a WMA, baseball cap, gray beard, red and black Pendleton jacket, blue jeans, moving through the parking lot, your direction— Disregard. He's going into the bank."

Rocky and I glanced toward Bay Trust Mutual as the white male adult they had seen reached the door, then strangely hesitated, looking in both directions before entering, the sunlight catching on what looked like an earring in his left ear.

". . . see that?" Shipley radioed.

But I couldn't answer right off, because the woman we'd been waiting for walked up just then, and I was struck by the knowledge that I'd seen her before. Unfortunately, I couldn't place where. Her long fingernails were painted bright red, though one, her left index finger, was broken, and she wore two very large cocktail rings on each hand, gaudy, but on her they fit, perhaps because she was big-boned.

She gave us a nervous smile. "Are you Inspector Gillespie?"

"Yes," I replied. "And you are?"

"Um, Jane. Jane Smith—I mean, Doe."

Right. Jane didn't sound too sure of her name. The only thing real on her face seemed to be the mole by her upper lip. "You have some information for me?"

"Um, yeah. You wanted to know about the shooting at the Twin Palms?" I wanted to give her my complete attention, I wanted to know where I'd seen her before, but my glance strayed to Bay Trust Mutual and the man I'd seen walking in.

"Keep an eye on the place," I told Rocky. To the woman, I said, "What can you tell me?"

"The man you're looking for is going to be—" She stopped, as we heard two loud pops from inside the bank. She turned that direction, her face paling.

"Jesus," Rocky said.

I grabbed the woman, pulled her behind our vehicle with one hand, drew my weapon with the other.

She started sobbing.

"Don't move," I told her.

"Shots fired!" Rocky called on the radio. "Bay Trust Mutual!"

Before we could do anything else, the suspect burst through the door.

And ran straight toward us.

3

The wail of sirens grew louder. "We have contact with the bank," the dispatcher said. "Confirmed gunshots, one man down."

"Suspect coming our way," I radioed, over the frantic muttering of our informant.

Rocky tugged on her arm, got her behind the car. He and I steadied ourselves. Took aim. "Shit!" Rocky said. A woman, oblivious, exited her white van, walked toward the bank.

"Police!" I yelled. "Get down!"

Too late. The suspect grabbed her, dragged her against him. Used her for a shield. My heart thudded in my chest when he pointed the gun against her head. His other hand gripped the green bank bag as he held her around her waist. "Come near me, I'll shoot her!" he called over her screams.

"Suspect has a hostage," I radioed. He dragged her around the corner, out of our view. "You see them?" I called on the radio.

"I got them in sight!" Zim radioed back. "He's taking her across the street, behind the office building."

Several radio cars called in their arrival. Fire and ambulance were still a couple minutes away. "Son of a bitch," I said, my glance straying to the woman who had met us in the lot. She was crumpled on the ground, tears streaking the heavy foundation on her face. She would survive.

I only hoped the woman taken hostage had a chance. "You have enough for a perimeter?" I radioed.

"Affirm," Zim called back. "Got it covered. Go ahead and take the bank."

I nodded to Rocky. We were joined by a uniformed officer and edged our way to the bank. It would need to be cleared for safety—make sure no suspects remained behind. First aid would be rendered. I called into dispatch, let them know we were about to make entry.

"Ten-four," the dispatcher replied.

We entered. Found the victim, a white male, late forties, sprawled on the floor. The officer ran up to him, as Rocky and I made sure there were no more suspects in the building. I heard someone crying, someone hiding behind one of the desks. It was several minutes before the paramedics arrived to assist, too late for our victim, the bank's CFO.

His name was Earl Millhouse, shot dead as he walked out of his office on his way to lunch at his usual time, carrying a bank bag, according to one of the clerks, though they were confused as to why he had it or what was in it. What they weren't confused about was that the suspect grabbed the bank bag from him, then shot him point-blank. As much as I would rather not have looked, he wore a wedding band on his left hand, and I wondered about his wife and if he had children and how old they were. Rocky interrupted my thoughts when he said, "It looks clear. Let's go find your informant."

We exited the bank and discovered that the woman I'd hoped would help solve the more personal case from the Twin Palms was nowhere to be found.

"Hell," I said, eyeing the parking lot, wondering where she could have gone. Not even the rose she'd been carrying was left behind. I was feeling slightly nauseous from the adrenaline that had invaded, then left my body. A man dead, and for what? A few thousand dollars?

"Hell," I said again, and this time it had nothing to do with not being able to find my informant.

"Maybe one of the uniforms got her name as a witness," Rocky said, misinterpreting my comment.

"We can only hope." But that was not the case. No one had a record of her, and then we were caught up in the aftermath of the robbery investigation—assisting with the perimeter, as Shipley and Zim found the hostage, safe, thank God, accompanying her to the Hall for a statement. It was a good couple of hours later that we were finally released from the search, the suspect nowhere to be found. My guess was that he made it to the BART station, catching a train out of there.

Shortly thereafter Rocky and I finally found the time to canvass the shopping center, hoping to find someone who might have seen or remembered not only the suspect, where he came from, but also our mystery witness, our Jane Smith-Doe. Eventually we made our way into a small beauty salon called Hair Designers.

We showed our IDs and the stylist, a tall blond-haired man, looked up from the woman whose hair he was cutting. "I bet you're here about the robbery?"

"Good guess," I said, recognizing that he was trying to lighten the mood, and truly appreciating it. He gave his name as Chuck Deeter. "Did you see what happened?" I asked him.

"Not till it was all over," he replied, combing out the woman's wet brown hair, then snipping the ends, letting the wisps fall to the floor. "One of our regulars works at the bank so we called her. Said her boss was killed."

"I'll probably go to hell for saying this," said the manicurist, a woman named Renée. She filed the nails of a young woman seated in front of her. "But she told us he was one mean son of a bitch. Made everyone miserable, including his wife. I have a feeling there won't be too many people sorry to see him go."

"Other than that," Chuck said, "there's not much to tell. We didn't really see anything, just heard the sirens, not that that's so unusual around here."

"Actually," I said, "we were also wondering if you happened to see a woman, maybe in her forties, red wig, hanging in the area just before the robbery."

"Couldn't miss her," he replied, snipping more hair. "She walked in here, wanting to get her broken nail fixed."

"She seemed real nervous," Renée said, working the nail file on her customer. "She didn't want to wait thirty minutes."

Chuck laughed as he combed out his client's hair. "It was going to take a lot more than thirty minutes to fix what ailed her. The first thing that needed to go was the red wig—not with her skin tone—"

"At least she had good taste in cars," Renée said.

"She was driving a green Jaguar—" Chuck looked out the plate-glass window, pointing with his scissors to the parking lot. "At least I think it was her Jag. It was parked right there and she was standing next to it."

"I thought I saw another lady out there with her," Renée said. "A blonde. Didn't really pay attention, until Chuck pointed out the wig lady. It *definitely* didn't come from *our* store. All I know is that the blond-haired lady walked in the other direction and wig lady walked in here."

"Where'd she go afterward?"

"Wig lady? I guess to the grocery store. It was a good half hour before the bank was robbed, maybe more. After that?" She shrugged. "Who knows? We probably didn't notice her take off because of all the action at the bank. Sorry."

"Not a problem," I said, taking one of my cards and putting it on the counter by the door. "Do me a favor? If you see her again, get a license plate and give me a call?"

"Sure."

"So much for my cold case," I told Rocky once we'd left. "If you're lucky, she'll call again."

But there was no message from her when we returned to our office, and so we finished our reports, then filled out our overtime requests. It was close to eight in the evening by the time I made it home to my Berkeley Hills apartment. The phone was ringing when I stepped in and I raced for it, hoping to catch it before the answering machine picked up.

"Hello?" I said, over my recorded message.

The beep sounded and then, "Kate? It's Mike."

"Hi," I said, sinking into the couch, thinking how nice it was to hear him say our first names, not Gillespie or Torrance like when we were working together. "You're back?"

"I flew in this afternoon. I heard you had a robbery?"

"Unfortunately the suspect got away," I said, then told him what had transpired, including the part about my missing informant on the cold case.

"We may be working the robbery," he said. "I don't know yet." He was quiet a moment, then said, "What are you doing Friday night . . . ?"

"Gee, let me check my social calendar."

"You interested in dinner . . . maybe a movie?"

Be cool, I told myself. What came out was, "A real date?"

"I figured that would be safer."

I smiled into the phone, though it was a self-deprecating smile. Torrance had been shot the night after he posed as my date on a case we had worked together several months ago, before he'd left for the FBI. "I'd love to go," I said.

"I'll pick you up at seven."

By the time Friday morning rolled around, I was more than ready for a relaxing evening with Torrance—though what I was envisioning in my mind was *anything* but relaxing. First, however, I had to get through my day, and I checked my voice mail in hopes that my alleged informant had called again. Three messages, not one from her.

"Any luck?" Shipley asked.

"No," I said, hanging up the phone, then pulling the file from my desk. "Looks like it's back to square one."

Rocky was making a fresh pot of coffee. "You see the report on our shooter? I put it on your desk."

"Haven't looked at it yet," I said, picking up the file. I took a couple of minutes and read through the report on the suspect. Older guy—not your typical bank robber. Gray hair, beard . . .

Rocky looked over at me. "What's on our agenda this morning?"

"I was thinking we might head to the Twin Palms again."

He glanced up at the clock. "Maybe about ten?"

Trying to roust anyone from their roach-infested beds in that place any earlier would be useless—the effects of crank or heroin and drinking all night. "Ten's good," I said, since that would give me time to review my case—again.

My victim, Fiona Winchester, was thought to have been a wrong-place, wrong-time sort of thing, as she was shot walking out of the building. Apparently she was a frequent visitor there, more than likely present to buy drugs, which gave us some clue as to her background. It was either prostitution, drugs, or both. But her criminal history didn't match up with her behavior. I flipped through the case file to make sure we hadn't missed something.

"What's up?" Rocky asked, perhaps reading my perplexed expression.

"According to this, Fiona Winchester had no criminal history."

"So?"

"So she was supposed to be a prostitute. I find that a little odd."

Shipley looked up from his computer screen. "I remember Scolari commenting on that," he said, referring to my previous partner, who had recently retired. "He thought it was odd, too. But we couldn't find anything that said otherwise. She had a purse full of condoms and had just made a drug buy from the guy on the first floor. No one at her apartment seemed to know her for the simple reason that she was never there, and her roommate was even less help. No bank accounts, no cars registered to her."

I pulled out the enlarged copy of her driver's license, studying the colored photograph of a smiling strawberry-blond twenty-one-year-old female, who at first glance did not fit the profile of the typical Twin Palms clientele. Finely boned features and a dusting of freckles across her nose gave her the perfect mixture of stunning beauty and innocence. And the knowledge that driver's-license photos were notoriously bad, and she looked great in hers, told me that she was—or had been—extremely photogenic. It also made me wonder what had happened in her life that had sent her down such a rocky path.

"What's with her family?" I asked, since that section of the report took up little space, the family saying nothing about her—almost as though they didn't know her.

"Weird," Shipley said. "Both of them—father and daughter. Getting information out of that clan was like being a Hatfield and dealing with the McCoys. No doubt in my mind why Fiona turned to prostitution. Wanted to get the hell out of there."

My curiosity was piqued and I changed my mind about where I planned to go first. "Get your radio," I told Rocky. "I want to go talk to these people."

Twenty minutes later we were pulling up in front of the Winchester home, a dilapidated wood-sided house that, judging from the few flakes of paint left on the structure, might have been white at one time.

A window facing the street had plastic wrap duct-taped across an expanse of broken glass, and the second step was missing from the three that led to the porch. We carefully stepped over it, knocked on the door frame, then stood to one side of the door. A moment later, we heard hollow footsteps as someone approached and then the unmistakable sound of a shotgun racking.

Rocky and I drew our weapons, jumped from the porch and stood on either side. I shouted, "Police! Put down the gun."

The door opened and someone peeked out at us through the screen. "How do I know?" a man called out.

"We've got ID. You can call nine-one-one and ask, or you can come out and look. Put the weapon down, open the door, and let us see your hands. Both hands."

"I'm going out," he said to someone inside. "If it ain't the cops, call them."

Rocky was radioing for backup, and I aimed my weapon at the door with one hand, held my star out with the other. A second later, the door opened the rest of the way and a man stepped out, his hands up in front of him, holding the shotgun by the end of the barrel. He set it against the side of the house, then kept his hands out. Though he was a good twenty or more years older than Fiona Winchester, I could see a resemblance. Same strawberry-blond hair, though flecked with gray, and same freckles, thin face, but unlike Fiona, a broken front tooth. His gaze narrowed as he eyed the star, then called out, "It's the cops, Lizzie." Then to us, said, "Don't worry. Gun's unloaded."

I nodded to Rocky and while I covered him, Rocky went up, checked the shotgun. "Yep. Unloaded."

"Who else is inside?" I asked.

"My daughter, Lizzie. No one else."

"Why the gun?"

"How'm I supposed to know you're who you say? I already had one daughter murdered. You don't think that's enough? Especially after you go blasting on TV about what happened? Stirring up that hornet's nest all over again?"

That was when I recognized the voice. "You're the one who left me the message?"

"You're goddamned right. I saw you on TV. It's bad enough I lost one daughter because you cops ain't smart enough to figure out what's going on right beneath your goddamned noses, her running drugs for the mob, not even figuring it out 'til I tell her you don't earn that kind of money delivering takeout. But then you gotta go and put it on TV and remind my other daughter. Last thing I need is for her to go traipsing off, thinking she's gonna bring home a million bucks like her sister, all so she can get killed, too."

"A million bucks?"

"Figure of speech," he said. "Don't try to turn the tables on me. Just ask your goddamned questions and leave."

"May we come in?"

He shut the door. I took that as a no.

I signaled for Rocky to keep an eye on the place, and I holstered my weapon, then opened my notebook. "What can you tell me about her?"

"Ain't nothing to tell. She ran away from home the moment she turned eighteen and took up with some fellow who promised her he'd make her rich. Running drugs is what I figured."

"You're sure about the occupation?"

"She might notta known, but there ain't no doubt in my mind. What else you gonna do to send home that kind of money?"

"She sent home money?"

"Few hundred bucks a week."

"Do you have the name of this man she . . . was working for?"

"Jones. James. I don't know. Always driving a fancy car. Met her at that restaurant she was waitressing at. That hoity-toity place that was in Sunday's paper. Picked her up one day and that was it. Wanted to take Lizzie to go live with her, but I told her she could go to hell. Guess that's what she did."

When he couldn't offer any further information, I asked, "Mind if I talk to Lizzie?"

"Do you got to?"

"Yes."

He turned toward the door and shouted, "Lizzie! Get your backside out here. The cops want to talk to you."

There was a shuffling inside, then a moment later a girl, maybe seventeen, came out the door to stand next to her father, and as I studied her face I realized that other than the braces—something I found unusual considering the unkempt appearance of the exterior of the house—this girl was even prettier than her deceased sister, despite her baggy T-shirt and jeans, and her short, almost hacked haircut.

"Lizzie Winchester?" I asked.

"It's really Elizabeth. Everyone calls me Lizzie."

I looked at her father and said, "We would like to take a statement from her alone. Would that be possible?"

He glanced at his daughter, who didn't meet his gaze, then shrugged and went inside.

"What can you tell us about your sister?" I asked, once he'd shut the screen door.

"I don't know," she said, hopping down the steps, easily skipping the missing one, without seeming to think about it. "She was hardly ever here."

"Do you know what she did for a living? Or who her friends were?"

"Don't know about any friends," she said, kicking at a weed growing through a crack in the sidewalk. "Least not any she brought here. She wasn't exactly eager to show off where we lived. She graduated high school and my dad said college was a waste of time for a woman, so she went out and found herself something she could do. Got herself a rich boyfriend. Then her and my dad got in a fight, because he told her the guy was using her to run drugs and she was going to get herself killed, but she promised him . . . promised she wasn't." Lizzie shoved her hands in the pockets of her jeans, looking down at the ground, and I could see her eyes welling with tears.

"You ever see who she was with?"

"This guy. Waited in the car when she came in to drop off some things for me. Clothes and stuff. It was weird. He looked at everything first, like he didn't trust her. She wanted to get some pictures to put in the place she was sharing with her roommate, but my dad wouldn't let her. He told the guy to get the hell off our street and if he ever saw him again, he'd kill him. Guess the guy believed him, because he paid for her coffin, but didn't even go to her funeral."

"You don't happen to know his name, do you?"

"Her boyfriend? No. But if you want to find out, you ought to ask the girl Fiona was living with. Kyla Greene."

"They did," Rocky said, eyeing the narrative of the report he'd brought along. "She told us she didn't know the guy."

Lizzie crossed her arms. "Then she's lying."

"What makes you say that?" I asked.

"Because the guy happens to be Kyla Greene's brother."

4

"**H**ow the hell did they miss a lead like that?" I asked, as we drove off. "Fiona's roommate is the sister of the guy Fiona dated?"

"Easy. Like the kid said, the roommate lied. Obviously protecting her brother."

"From what? Being a murderer?"

"Or a drug runner."

I pulled over about a block away and opened the case folder to run the roommate's driver's license to determine if she was still listed at the same address she had shared with Fiona Winchester. She was and we drove out there.

The apartment was typical of many in the city, several units atop retail space. The area, however, surprised me, fashionable Noe Valley, a place I often thought of as nouveau hippie. If this is where Fiona Winchester was living and sending a few hundred dollars home each week, then she was no ordinary waitress, and definitely not some street hooker. "You sure she wasn't a call girl?" I asked.

"Hell if I know," Rocky said. "I'm not the one that did her victimology. Zim did."

"That explains things," I said. Zim was known for cutting corners, and if he did the background check on Winchester, he undoubtedly overlooked plenty.

It was close to ten; Rocky and I stood on either side of the door as he gave it a sharp rap. A moment later it opened, and Rocky's jaw literally dropped, his gaze fixed straight ahead. I followed it and saw a striking blonde, thirty-something, looking anything but virginal in a floor-length white silk robe that clung to her perfect figure. I had to do a double take. She looked very much like the woman from the bank parking lot, but the hair was wrong—blond, definitely not a wig . . . and she was far more delicate, fine-boned. Definitely not the same woman, but I couldn't get past the sense of familiarity. Maybe I was seeing things. I'd thought the woman in the parking lot seemed familiar, and now this woman here . . .

She ran her finger down the neckline, parting the robe far enough to expose a good portion of her right breast. Just as she reached the sash, looking as though she might be intent on revealing more, I cleared my throat and said, "Are you Kyla Greene?"

Her hand froze as she glanced my way, undoubtedly seeing me for the first time.

"Who are you?" she asked.

"Kate Gillespie, Homicide Detail, and the man you were . . . about to show off to is my partner, Rocky Markowski."

"I-I thought he was someone else."

"Apparently," I said, and Rocky shot me a glance that I chose not to decipher. I wondered if he'd noticed the resemblance—if he'd even gotten past her neckline. "Do you have any ID?" I asked her.

"Yes. Wait here, I'll get it." She stepped in, closed the door, then returned a moment later with a temporary copy of a driver's license that identified her as Kyla Greene.

"You don't have something with your picture on it?"

"Someone stole my purse. I'm supposed to get the permanent copy in about ten days. What is it you want?" she asked, pulling her robe tighter and glancing from me to Rocky, perhaps in search of an ally.

She struck gold. Rocky stepped forward, smiled at her and said, "I'm sorry to inconvenience you, ma'am, but we're here to discuss the Fiona Winchester case."

"Oh," she replied, leaning against the doorframe, smiling back at him. "I'm not sure what help I could be. That was . . . so long ago."

"We understand," Rocky said, and had I been a lesser person, I would have rolled my eyes right about then.

As it was, I was beginning to see some of the major flaws in the case, one being: siren versus male. Hard to discern legitimate information if one can't take one's eyes off the witness's thinly clad breasts. I sighed inwardly, cleared my throat once again, and said, "What we are looking for is any information on who Fiona was seeing. Male companions."

"I wouldn't know, even if I could remember that far back."

"Try," I said.

She gave me an annoyed look, turned to Rocky and said, "You must be the one in charge. Surely you can tell her I have no idea—"

"Do you have a brother, Miss Greene?" I asked.

She stiffened. "Um, why do you want to know?"

"Just wondering."

She hesitated, then with a sigh of resignation, stood aside. "Come in. I'd rather not do this out here." We walked into a lavishly, and, if my opinion meant anything, garishly furnished apartment of chrome, glass, and white leather. Definitely expensive stuff. A faint odor of tobacco hung in the air. "What do you do for a living?" I asked.

"You don't know?"

"Humor me."

"I'm a professional escort," she said, walking over to the coffee table in front of the couch. There was a pack of cigarettes on the table and she picked it up, shook one out, and lit it with a crystal lighter. "I get paid big bucks to escort men who don't want to go stag on trips or to various functions."

"Tell me about this brother who was dating your room-mate."

"Oh," she finally answered, seeming relieved. "You mean Jim. For whatever reason, when she was killed, he said it was important that he not be associated with her."

"Nice guy," Rocky said.

"Makes you warm and fuzzy just thinking about it," I replied, wondering about her demeanor. Something was off. "Any particular reason why he'd distance himself from her?"

"Business, plain and simple," she replied. "He sells cars and Fiona was killed outside a place known for prostitution and drugs. He said it would tarnish his image."

"And you didn't have a problem with that?"

"He keeps this apartment for us to use and pays my bills when it's slow. What do you want?"

"The truth would have been nice."

"He didn't kill her. What difference would it make?"

"Do you know who did? Or why?"

"Why?" She sat on the couch, crossing her legs, then tapped her foot impatiently. "I expect because she was in the wrong place at the wrong time. Twin Palms, wasn't it?" she asked, pausing to take a drag off her cigarette. She turned her head, blew out a stream of smoke, then said, "She was naïve. Too naïve. Let people walk all over her."

"Like who?"

She shrugged. "We didn't share client lists."

"Your brother knew she was doing this?"

"Knew?" She laughed. "He practically recruited her. Met her at this restaurant he always hangs out at. His friend owns it. An attorney. If you want to find out more about who she . . . dated, ask Jim yourself."

"We'll do that. Maybe you can provide us with his full name and address?"

"Easy. Jim Greene. He runs the used export lot in Daly City. Maybe you've seen the commercials? You want a lean, mean machine, buy from Jim Greene?"

"He wouldn't be the Jim Greene who was under investigation a few years ago for—what was it, Markowski?"

Rocky forced his gaze from Miss Greene's legs, looked at me and said, "Huh?"

"The car dealer from Daly City."

"Cocaine?"

"Something like that," I said, watching Kyla.

She took one last drag from her cigarette and stubbed it out. "I wouldn't know anything about that. I don't use drugs. If you want his number, look it up in the phone book," she said, standing.

"One more question," I said, since she seemed intent on dismissing us. "Do you have a sister?"

She hesitated, then smiled, not quite the reaction I would expect. "No. Only my brother. If there's nothing else . . .?"

"At the moment, no," I said, taking out a business card and leaving it on her glass coffee table. "But if there is, we'll be in touch."

"Get your fill?" I asked Rocky as we walked down the hill, past a small restaurant to our car. The smell of fresh baked cinnamon rolls drifted from within, and I glanced into the window and saw several people sitting at small tables.

"Fill?" Rocky said. "Don't know what you're talking about."

"Can you say: couldn't take my eyes off her? She's a call girl, for God's sake."

"And a good-looking one, too. Makes you wonder if that's how Zim sorta overlooked a few pertinent facts in the case."

With Zim it could be anything, but I didn't waste my time commenting on that. "Was it my imagination, or did she remind you of the lady in the bank parking lot?"

"Yeah, I guess she did," Rocky said. "But better looking."

I glanced at my watch. It was ten-thirty. We drove out to Jim Greene's Big Bay Imports, home of the lean, mean machine, but Mr. Greene wasn't in, so, we returned to the Hall.

When I walked in, Gypsy looked up from her computer, saw me, and said, "Someone here to see you, Kate." She nodded toward the lieutenant's office, where I saw Mike Torrance and a tall woman with shoulder-length blond hair. Both stood with their backs to me, and were conversing with Lieutenant Andrews, who was seated at his desk.

I knocked on the open door as I walked in. Torrance and the woman turned around, and as much as I hate to admit it, the first thing that crossed my mind was that Torrance was cancelling our first official date, something, knowing him, that he'd do in person, not over the phone. He had a code of ethics so strong it made the massive metal sculpture out front of the Hall of Justice look like a pile of paperclips.

I smiled tentatively, not sure who the woman was or why she was with Torrance. "What's going on?"

The lieutenant motioned me in. I glanced at Torrance, but before either of us could say a thing, the woman he was with held out her hand. She was my height, beautiful and thinner, with a figure that any model would want. "You must be Inspector Kate Gillespie. I'm Mike's partner, Jackie Parrish." Her handshake was firm, her tone all business. I don't know why, but I got the feeling she didn't do a lot of smiling.

"Nice to meet you," I said, a bit envious that she was now working with Torrance—and I wasn't. He still looked the same, not that I expected anything different. Tall, thin, dark hair, dark eyes, dressed in a black suit that reminded me of his days in IA.

"Hi," I said, suddenly feeling unsure of myself, how I should act around him. True we were supposed to be going on a date tonight, but I didn't know how he felt about anyone else knowing our plans. He was an intensely private man.

"We're here about the bank robbery," he said, answering

the question of how I should act. Definitely business. "The FBI has been interested in Bay Trust Mutual for quite some time. A possible informant had been discreetly looking into coming forth as a witness."

"And?" I asked.

"She made some phone calls, but that was as far as it went. She said she was in a precarious position, since she was married to our now-dead CFO, who, among others, would have good reason to harm her if she did."

"The informant was Mrs. Millhouse?"

"Yes, though she is not aware we know her identity— something we'd like to maintain. We've had some information leaks—nothing serious—"

"Actually," Parrish said, "We think we've traced it to a clerk. It may not even be intentional, but this case has some far-reaching implications and we don't want to take any chances."

"What sort of implications?" I asked.

Torrance said, "It may give us the evidence we need to shut down Nick Paolini's operation—or at the very least, put him out of business."

"At least that's what we're hoping for," Parrish said. "Unfortunately, we're missing one particularly important player in all this. Someone who, until the bank robbery, escaped our notice."

"Who is that?"

"Lucia Paolini."

Lucia Paolini was Nick Paolini's ex-wife, but that was as far as my knowledge of her went. I'd never met her; they'd met, married, and divorced several years ago, back east somewhere. Nick Paolini happened to be the man I long suspected was responsible for the scar on my arm from an attempted hit—one that occurred right after Paolini's arrest for the narcotics case that I had worked, and our probing into the murder of Fiona Winchester.

True, the actual shooter was believed to be dead, but in reality the case was never solved, the questions about who had orchestrated the hit never answered.

"Paolini's ex-wife?" I said. "You think she's involved in this?"

"To what extent," Parrish said, "we don't know. But we're very interested in finding her—"

"Her attorney," Torrance said, "contacted us, saying that her life, as well as that of Earl Millhouse, the man she'd been sleeping with, wouldn't be worth a damn if Paolini found out."

"And now," I said, "Millhouse is dead—hence your sudden interest in her?"

"That and the fact she is missing," he replied. "Her attorney delivered us a letter spelling out her fears about Paolini, and that he would undoubtedly try to kill her if he discovered her intimate involvement with Millhouse, as Paolini has much to fear by their gathering of minds, so to speak."

"The attorney," Parrish said, "suspects foul play in the sudden demise of Earl Millhouse and the disappearance of Lucia, since he has been unable to contact her, and she would never leave her son."

It took me a moment to digest what they were telling me . . . "You're saying the robbery was a hit?"

"It appears that way," Torrance said. "Though we're not releasing that information publicly. The suspect who killed Millhouse hasn't been found or identified, and we'd rather keep the public perception that it was simply a robbery gone awry."

I sank into one of the chairs, unable to believe what I was hearing—primarily because of the implications of my own involvement—the possibility that I was purposefully brought into this. "A setup?"

"Yes."

"The woman who met me . . . ?"

"We're not sure. It could have been Lucia. Maybe some-one could have told her what to say. Get you there to witness what is supposed to look like a real bank robbery—remove any suspicion that it was not."

"We'd like you to work with a sketch artist," Parrish said. "In the meantime, we're bringing Paolini in for questioning, regarding the missing-persons case Lucia's attorney made on her."

Ten minutes later, I was sitting across from a young woman with a sketch pad and pencil, the woman asking me to describe who it was I saw in the parking lot. I'd seen it done several times, but never sat on this side of the sketch pad. It was quite a different matter being the one to have to remember what someone looked like. I could well em-pathize with the witnesses, and I realized how faulty mem-ory could be. "I don't know. She had a wig on and dark sunglasses. There's not much to describe."

"You saw her nose and mouth? The shape of her face?"

"There was a mole," I said, pointing on my own face to where it would have appeared. I watched, fascinated, as the drawing began to take form, a give-and-take process. I de-scribed, she sketched. Round face, strong chin, regular nose, but on her, on the drawing, it seemed to fit. Not stunning, definitely good-looking. The artist showed me what she'd done, and I told her what to change. Too wide, too thin, a lit-tle fuller. An hour and a half later, we had a complete draw-ing, and frankly, I was amazed at how closely it resembled the woman in the parking lot—but also how it resembled this Kyla Greene . . .

When we were finished, I took a copy of it and gave it to Rocky. "Definitely the woman from the parking lot," he said. "Minus the cleavage. You couldn't have had the sketch artist draw just a little farther down?"

"Somehow that wasn't the feature that stood out in my mind, go figure," I said, just as Torrance stepped in.

"You have a minute?" he asked.

"Sure," I said, following him from the room.

He indicated I should accompany him down the hallway, and, if truth be told, I was hoping he'd bring up the subject of our date. Apparently that was the farthest thing from his mind. "We'd like you to help on the interview with Paolini," he said as we walked. "He's asked that you be present. We would prefer it."

"What for?"

"He hasn't been exactly forthcoming with anything relating to his ex-wife."

"Let me guess. He denies knowing anything about her or the robbery at the bank?"

He glanced over at me, smiled, and for a moment as his gaze held mine, I felt as though he hadn't really left for several months for the FBI Academy, that his office should still be upstairs . . .

Something told me that I should tell him right then and there that I'd missed him, but before I could say a word, his partner popped her head out the door of the interview room. "There you are," she said, opening the door for us to enter. I glanced in, saw Paolini through a window of one-way glass, sitting at a table by himself, waiting. He was handsome, early forties, dark hair, combed back, olive-skinned, and looking more the part of a CEO than a crook.

"We haven't had much luck," she said. "Torrance told me you had a rapport with him."

"I'm not sure about that, but I can try. Anything in particular you want me to ask?"

"What we'd like is to be able to find at least one photo of Lucia, and learn what names she used. We're coming up blank. Not even her attorney has a photo."

"Anyone check with the DMV?"

"Dead end," she said. "I'm guessing she was using an aka. We'd like to know what it was. And what Paolini knows about the Bay Trust Mutual robbery," she said, handing me a list of questions. "As you can see, we're approaching it as a simple robbery. In no way do we want it released that we believe it is anything but. This is what we've covered."

"And," Torrance added, "what he has denied having knowledge of."

I looked over the list, then walked into the room. Paolini, always the gentleman, rose as I entered. "Inspector Gillespie," he said. "You are looking lovely, as usual."

I ignored his greeting. I knew firsthand that he could lay on the charm—quite simply because I had dated him. Granted, I was working undercover at the time, posing as the sister of someone who was buying drugs from one of his suspected dealers. And any dates we had were in very public restaurants or bars, heavily chaperoned by undercover officers pretending to be diners and bar patrons.

But even after we arrested him and he found out I was a cop, he let it be known that his attraction to me was still there. Which is why I was careful in my dealings with him. I did not trust him. I knew what he was capable of.

"Mr. Paolini."

"Call me Nick."

I gave him a bland smile instead, then took a seat opposite him, trying to decide how best to proceed. "It seems, Mr. Paolini, that we're at something of a stalemate. You have information we need. We have the DA's ear. I'm sure the DA would take into consideration any cooperation you gave us when he decides what charges to file."

Paolini steepled his fingers, his gaze direct. "Even if I believed you had enough to file the smallest of charges, Inspector, you would have to admit I have been exceedingly cooperative."

"How?"

"I'm here. I have not asked for my attorney, which I'm

sure he'll berate me for later. Trust me when I say that I, more than anyone, would like to know Lucia's whereabouts."

"And why is that?"

"She has something that belongs to me."

"And that would be . . .?"

He merely smiled.

"You know, it would help in our search if we had a photo of her."

"Unfortunately I have none. She had a strong aversion to cameras."

"Had?"

"Has."

"Not even a wedding photo? Driver's license?"

"None."

"What names did she use?"

"Lucia Greene, when I met her."

I kept my expression neutral as I said, "Greene? Any relationship to the car dealer?"

"Yes. Her first husband."

I tucked that bit of information away for now and decided to strengthen my bluff. "Lucia's attorney seems to think he has proof of your involvement in her disappearance."

"If that is true, then someone is setting me up."

"Who?"

"I have no idea. But as I explained to your . . . friends, Lucia will be at a function going on tonight. A fundraiser for the women's shelter. She helped put it together, and the people involved with it are, coincidentally or not, also involved with the bank that was robbed."

"Where?" I said, though I knew without asking.

"Etienne Reynard's," he replied.

"Nice thought, but getting in would be a bit of a problem, don't you think, never mind trying to blend in."

"There will be at least a hundred people present, not to

mention that I am in possession of four tickets, three of which I would be willing to let you have."

"Why give your assistance?" I asked.

"You distrust me, Inspector?"

"Let's just say I have a healthy suspicion." And for good reason. I wanted into that restaurant because of the Fiona Winchester case. This seemed way too easy.

"As I said, Lucia has something that belongs to me. And if her attorney has this alleged proof that I am behind her disappearance . . . I have every interest in wanting her found. Since I know for a fact she'll be there tonight, who better to clear my name than you, Inspector? And if you'd like even more of an incentive, there's a photo of her on the wall at the restaurant. I'd be glad to point it out."

I stood. "Will you excuse me a moment?" I asked, then left without waiting for an answer, closing the door firmly behind me. Torrance and his partner were standing just outside the door, having witnessed the entire conversation via the speaker and the one-way glass.

I wasted no time in giving my opinion. "I don't trust him."

Parrish said, "Let's do it. It's perfect."

Torrance crossed his arms. "I need to speak with Inspector Gillespie alone."

Parrish looked from Torrance to me, then said, "I'll be outside in the hallway." She closed the door behind her.

Neither of us spoke at first, and I glanced at Paolini through the glass. "Let me guess," I said, trying to sound light. "Our date tonight's cancelled?"

"Not exactly," he said. "We'll be going out . . . but not with each other—*if* you'll agree."

"Why do I get the feeling I'm not going to like this scenario?"

There was a slight hesitation, then, "Because I need you to be Paolini's date."

5

I stared in disbelief, certain I'd misunderstood what Torrance had just told me. I wanted to investigate Fiona's case, but I had certain limitations on what I was willing to do—or rather who I was willing to do it with. "Paolini's date? Tell me you're kidding."

He said nothing.

"You're not kidding . . ."

"No."

"And what will you be doing?"

"I'll be posing as my partner's date."

"Just out of curiosity," I said, "is there some reason why *she* can't pose as his date?"

"You know him, she doesn't. You'll have a better chance of creating a cover story."

I smiled, though somewhat sarcastically if I had to admit it. "What happened to dinner and a movie?"

"I'm sorry, Kate. If I could do things differently, I would."

Great. I was being petulant over something beyond our control, though I couldn't help but think they'd planned this whole thing before I even got here.

Torrance opened the door to let Parrish in, and I took a breath, told myself to stay calm—and then came up with the perfect reason why I couldn't go. Ironically it was the very reason I wanted to go. "I just appeared on TV for the Fiona Winchester case. Everyone will have seen it."

Parrish questioned me about the case. When I'd finished giving her the details, she asked, "What made you pull that particular homicide?"

"I saw the newspaper article about the fund-raising efforts at Etienne Reynard's, and figured since it was going to be in the public eye, why not remind that same public about the Fiona Winchester case?"

"How'd you get it on TV so quick?"

"The newscaster is my ex's girlfriend."

"I'm not worried about it," she said. "The case is three years old, and you didn't mention the restaurant on TV. Besides," she said, eyeing me with what could only be described as a cool, detached look. "You get dressed up, do something different with your hair . . . who would recognize you?"

I refrained from asking her if she'd been talking to my ex-husband, primarily because I wasn't sure if she'd catch the humor. "I'll go tell Paolini."

"I'll do it," she said. "You two go on ahead." She moved past us into the interview room.

"Your partner always so warm and fuzzy?" I asked Torrance once she was out of earshot.

"I like to think of her as . . . efficient." He glanced over at me as we walked down the hall toward my office. "You okay with tonight?"

If truth be told, I was a bit peeved that I was to play Paolini's date, but didn't want to come right out and admit it. Nothing wrong with the roundabout way. "You were bringing him in for questioning," I said. "How the hell did it turn into a social event?"

"He told Parrish the same thing he told you. That if we are looking for Lucia, she'll be present tonight at the fundraiser for the women's shelter."

"Why bring me in here at all if you'd already set this up?"

"I was hoping you'd have better luck with the other details. We have some evidence on him, enough for a weak money-laundering charge. It wouldn't make it through court, but it's enough to hold him."

"Quite the twisted ethics in this. You're asking Paolini to help find the one woman who can put him away."

"In essence," he said. "Of course, if she's already dead, he may feel he has nothing to worry about."

Obviously I was spinning my wheels in trying to get out of this. "What time and what mode of dress?"

"Six. According to Paolini, the women favor designers."

Unfortunately my budget doesn't, I thought, as he left. I figured I'd have about an hour to type up my notes before I hit the stores. Finding a designer dress on a cop budget wasn't easy, but I was resourceful if nothing else, and I knew a few good consignment shops that I'd used in the past for operations.

Rocky took one look at me when I walked into my office. "What's the matter with you?"

"Don't ask."

He gave a shrug and I sat down in front of my computer, telling myself that I'd been in this profession long enough to know this happens. And long enough to wonder if it was worth it. Even so, I put aside any disappointment with the thought that as a new FBI agent, this case was important to Torrance. We'd have other Fridays—I hoped.

About an hour later, I was finishing up my paperwork, when Gypsy walked in with a large gold box, maybe two feet long, tied with gold crepe ribbon, the sort that came from a high-end store. "This just arrived for you," she said, putting it on my desk.

My first thought was that Torrance had sent this to make up for our missed date. But when I saw the label on the box, I knew it was beyond his means. I pulled the card from the ribbon, opened it and read: "For your assignment, Nick."

Because it was from Paolini, I was hesitant to open it. But I admit to being curious, and decided there was no harm in pulling off the ribbon and looking in, since it would have had to pass through security before it made it up here. I lifted the lid and saw a gown of black crepe. Exquisite was the only word that came to mind. There was no price tag, and I had to imagine that if one had to ask, one couldn't afford it. But neither was there a size. It looked right. I was somewhere around a ten or a twelve, give or take a few pounds, but who the hell knew how designer dresses were measured?

Rocky eyed the dress, then whistled as I held it up. "Secret admirer?"

"Nick Paolini."

He narrowed his gaze. "Come again?"

I gave him the *Reader's Digest* version and he eyed the dress again. "Hell if he doesn't have good taste, Gillespie."

"Hell is right," I said, replacing the dress in the box. I called Paolini's number. When he answered, I said, "The dress has to go back."

There was a moment of silence, then, "If you hope to blend in, it's necessary."

"There's a consignment store that sells slightly used designer dresses."

"And should one of these women recognize her dress from a previous occasion?"

"Point taken. But I can't accept it."

"Then consider it a loan. I'll donate it to a charity when you're finished with it. My priority is to find Lucia and clear my name."

"I'll check with the lieutenant," I said, then disconnected.

Andrews agreed to the loan, which meant I needed shoes and an evening bag to go with it. I had them an hour later, black patent leather heels and a matching evening bag, strong enough to hold a small semi-auto.

That done, I returned to the Hall, called my friend, Ginny Richardson, a Crime Scene Investigator, and asked her if I could borrow her skills. She worked wonders with a curling iron. Ginny followed me into the bathroom, wanting to see this gown.

"Damn," she said, holding it up. "Wait'll Torrance sees you in this." Ginny was one of the few people who really knew how I felt about Torrance.

"Lot of good that'll do. Our date was cancelled," I said, plugging in the curling iron.

"Cancelled? Why am I doing your hair?"

I told her the particulars as she helped me into the dress.

"Not a total loss," she said, zipping up the back. "At least he'll be there. And there's always afterward. Party can't last all night." She looked at me in the mirror as I smoothed the three-quarter-length sleeves over my arms, and then she laughed. "Your Timex doesn't exactly go with designer chic."

"It's black."

"Good try. You'll live without it," she said, holding her hand out as I slipped off the watch.

She took it, then helped me with my hair, curling and pinning it up. "For a cop, you clean up well."

I surveyed my reflection. "Too bad it's being wasted on an undercover assignment. But thanks for your help."

"You're welcome." She started out, then paused as she opened the restroom door. "And Kate? Torrance isn't likely to wait around forever. Don't do anything to screw this up."

"Me?"

She crossed her arms.

"I'll be good, I promise," I said, picking up the hairspray bottle. I had no intentions of screwing up anything with Torrance. We'd had a long discussion before he left for the FBI Academy, part of that discussion being that we'd take things slowly, and we wouldn't let work interfere—not like it had when he was working IA. Tonight was a different sort of interference, I told myself. Now that he'd left SFPD, he didn't have to worry about keeping secrets from me and I didn't have to worry about being investigated by him. The advantages of working for different agencies, I thought, as I headed back to my office to await Torrance's arrival.

At quarter to six, I was putting my weapon into my evening bag when he walked in, then stopped short on seeing me. "You look great," he said, eyeing my face and my hair, as though the dress were of no consequence.

Hell if that didn't make a girl feel good. "I've been told I clean up well," I said, noticing the slight shimmer of his suit, definitely not something a cop would wear. "You clean up pretty well yourself. Going for gangster chic?"

"Figured anyone associating with Paolini wouldn't be caught dead in something from JCPenney."

"I'm not sure I've ever seen you in something from JCPenney."

He held out his hand, indicating that we should leave. "You read the labels in my suits?"

I smiled and picked up my purse, then preceded him out the door. "It's not the labels of your suits I'm interested in reading."

He raised a dark brow, but didn't comment, and we walked in silence to the elevator, the click of my high heels echoing down the empty hallway.

"Paolini sent the dress," I said, while we waited for the elevator to arrive.

His gaze narrowed slightly as he seemed to look at the dress for the first time, fingering the material of the sleeve as though assessing its worth. "Are you saying this didn't come from JCPenney?"

"Not even close."

Suddenly he grinned.

"What?" I asked as the elevator door opened and we stepped on.

"You don't want to know."

"Yes, I do," I said, as someone called out for us to hold the door.

I glanced behind me and saw a young female uniformed officer running our way, the gear on her Sam Browne rattling with each step.

Torrance reached out, held the door, then whispered, "I'll lay odds this is one designer dress that looks better off than on."

The officer stepped in, and Torrance let go of the door, his expression almost challenging me to respond. I couldn't resist. "And how would you know?"

"At the moment, I don't," he said, his gaze never leaving mine. "But the night's still young."

6

Torrance's partner, Jackie Parrish, was waiting for us by the elevator downstairs, looking extremely elegant in a black velvet gown that set off her blond hair to perfection.

No greeting from her. Just a perfunctory, "Paolini's waiting for us outside. We've got two agents already at the restaurant, parked nearby, so they'll be able to respond at a moment's notice."

We walked outside to a black limo, near the entrance to the Hall of Justice garage. We crossed the street and Paolini slid out of the backseat.

He was holding an envelope. "Your tickets, Agent Torrance."

Torrance took the envelope, then slipped it into his jacket pocket. He eyed Paolini's car and the driver standing nearby. "We'll drive."

Paolini said, "It might seem odd if I do not arrive as usual . . ."

"Regardless. Pretend I'm your driver tonight," Torrance said, and I wondered if I imagined the asserting of power. "Gillespie rides in our car." Definitely an undercurrent of something, I decided, as Paolini nodded to his driver, who took off in the limo.

Torrance, in keeping with his new role, held the door open and I slid into the backseat of the car, somewhat amused.

Paolini slid in after me. Torrance got into the driver's seat, Jackie Parrish next to him, and he pulled away from the curb.

En route, we discussed our various roles and how we would play them. Torrance and Parrish would hover on the edges, keeping their distance from us. As Paolini's "date," I would mingle with him. He expected Lucia to be late as usual, but the moment she arrived, he'd let me know.

As Torrance neared Etienne Reynard's, Paolini took from his pocket a long turquoise-colored felt bag with the word TIFFANY printed on it, then slid a diamond choker from within. If it was real, it surely cost a small fortune. The necklace sparkled even in the dimness of the car, and I had to imagine it was amazing in light.

"This," he said, "was recommended by the woman who sold me the dress."

"She working on commission?"

He didn't reply, merely held it out, indicating that he'd put it on. I leaned forward a bit, allowing him to clasp the cold diamonds around my neck.

Perhaps I'd imagined it, but it seemed his finger lingered a moment too long, and I glanced up, saw Torrance watching from the rearview mirror.

I quickly looked away, not wanting to examine my sudden discomfort, and I reached up feeling the rough diamonds beneath my touch.

At our arrival, Torrance exited, held the door open for us, and we got out. "We'll meet you inside," Torrance said, not looking at us, but at the restaurant and the surroundings. Saying nothing more, he entered the car and drove toward the parking garage across the street.

Paolini took my hand and we walked to the restaurant, where he paused outside the door, eyeing me. "The necklace fails to do you justice."

I wasn't sure what to say, so I simply smiled, and we continued on. Etienne Reynard's was a five-star restaurant, the sort without prices on the menus, not that there were any tonight, and as he led me through the small lobby, the maitre d' greeting him by name as he produced the two tickets, I saw at once why Paolini had sent the dress and insisted on the diamonds. "Looks like a goddamned mini-Oscar ceremony," I said under my breath, looking around at the other guests, the shimmer of silks, the resplendence of jewels.

"You'll find," Paolini said, "the question most asked tonight is not *where* did you get your gown, but *who* made it."

"Like I'd even care, let alone know what the hell they were talking about," I said, then pasted a smile on my face as he led me to the bar.

"The usual?" he asked me, I assumed for the benefit of anyone who might be listening.

"Please," I said, discovering that his idea of "the usual" was a bottle of Opus, though I shouldn't have been surprised by so exorbitant a choice of wine.

He handed me a glass as he took his own. "I hope the wine meets with your approval," he said, a moment later when we were out of earshot.

"I'm sure it does," I replied. "Except I didn't come here to drink."

"Sip, at least," he said, looking around the room with that same practiced eye Torrance used. "I don't necessarily trust everyone here. They might suspect you weren't drinking for a reason."

So I sipped, discovered that I had expensive taste in wine, and wondered if I was ruined for the wine I could afford.

Paolini led me to the far end of the bar, past an icy buffet covered with prawns, crab, lobster tails, and oysters on the half shell. A large ice carving of a mermaid crowned the center and glimmered in the light, and long-stemmed red roses were scattered throughout the display.

On the wall behind the buffet was a gallery of photos,

something that appeared to be customers at various functions from the restaurant. "The photo?" I asked Paolini.

"Yes," he said, guiding me closer. "It's the second from the right. The three women sitting at the bar. Lucia, Fiona Winchester, and Kyla Greene."

I studied it, and immediately recognized the siren Rocky had been smitten with at the apartment this afternoon. Fiona sat in the middle. A third woman, dark-haired, and easily as beautiful as the other two, sat on the right. "So that's Lucia?" I asked, trying to memorize her features so I could search the guests to see if she was present.

He was about to answer when two men walked up.

"Hell," the oldest of the two said, looking directly at Paolini. He was maybe my height, snowy hair and a thick, gray mustache that covered the top of his lip. "Nick. Didn't expect to see you here, tonight. And with a beautiful woman, to boot," he said, eyeing me, then holding out his hand. "I know Nick. He won't introduce us for fear you'll have eyes for no one but me."

I shook his hand, smiled, and replied, "And if he didn't treat me so well, he might have something to worry about. I'm Kate, by the way."

"Kate," he said. "A pleasure. Where have you been hiding her, Nick?"

"Away from you, Stephen," Paolini said. "Stephen Reynard is our patron for the night and the owner of Etienne Reynard's. He is also a practicing attorney."

"You have a beautiful restaurant," I said.

"Which dims in your own beauty."

And to think I was getting paid time and a half for this. "Nick, you never told me you had such charming friends."

"How that escaped me, I'll never know," he said, as a woman in a diaphanous blue gown walked up, her gaze directed at Paolini as she linked her arm with Reynard's.

"Nicky," she said. "You should have called. Told us you were coming."

"A last-minute decision, Adriana," Paolini said, then promptly introduced her to me as Stephen Reynard's wife.

Her gaze narrowed after the introduction. "I could swear we've already met," she said. "Your face seems so . . . familiar."

Time to move on, I thought, and turned to the youngest of the group, tall, dark-haired, late thirties, and extremely handsome despite his acne-scarred face. Holding out my hand, I said, "I don't believe we've met."

He took my hand, his clasp cool. "Jim Greene."

"Greene?" I said, as though the name meant nothing at all. "And what is it that you do?"

His smile, even and white, did not reach his eyes, which made me wonder if he'd learned that I'd been at his lot that afternoon. "Car sales. Maybe you've heard my commercials? Jim Greene's lean, mean machines?"

There were a dozen questions I wanted to ask Jim Greene, and they all had to do with the Fiona Winchester case. I wanted to know how he was involved beyond what Fiona's younger sister had told me. I wanted to know if he knew SFPD had been to his car dealership looking for him, or if Kyla Greene had called and warned him. I hoped if he had found out, that he hadn't realized that I was one of the officers.

Most of all I wanted to know if Fiona's case was somehow connected to that of his and Paolini's missing ex-wife, Lucia. To have one of the key players in the former case turn up in the latter was beyond coincidental in my opinion. Unfortunately I couldn't come right out and ask, not without blowing my cover—assuming I had a cover to blow. Banking on the hope he didn't know who I was, I smiled and said, "What sort of cars do you sell?"

"Preowned high-end imports."

Stephen Reynard laughed at the description. "They're used, honey. Don't let him fool you."

Greene, however, wasn't laughing. "If you'll excuse me," he said, then walked away.

I wanted to follow him, but figured now wasn't the right time, so I turned to Reynard and said, "How do you find time to practice law and run a restaurant?"

Reynard said, "Actually, I haven't practiced in several years. I've decided to make it a point to try to keep my late partner Marcel Etienne's name alive . . ." He looked away as though the thought pained him. "Despite his problems, he was a good man."

"I'm sorry," I said.

"It was tragic," Reynard said. "Cocaine . . ."

I was quiet for a moment, trying to appear sympathetic, and wondering if it was possible that Reynard might not have known that his late partner had been dealing drugs from here.

Before I could think of a proper response, Reynard smiled, squeezed his wife's hand, and said, "We should, uh, mingle with the guests." With that they left. I had gathered that he preferred not discussing his late partner, though I wasn't at all certain whether it had to do with the loss of a friend—or something entirely different.

"Perhaps some dinner?" Paolini said, "and a chance to re-group?"

"I seem to be hitting raw nerves."

"One can't help but step on a grave when walking across a cemetery." He took my wine glass. "I'll take this to our table and meet you at the buffet."

The moment he left me, I looked around for Torrance. I didn't see him, though I found Parrish, standing near the buffet, lifting a rose from the ice, as though admiring it. I scanned the room again, this time, noticing a blond woman in a burgundy dress, her back to me. Kyla Greene. I was just about to head the opposite way, to keep her from seeing me, thereby blowing my cover, when she walked off, and I saw who she was talking to. He was thin, an older man. His receding gray hair, beard, and mustache were neatly trimmed, and he wore an earring in his left ear, something long, almost dagger-shaped.

My heart started thudding as recognition hit, and I fought to keep my expression neutral.

He was looking directly at me.

The suspect from our bank robbery—our hit man—was standing right there.

I told myself things would be okay as long as he didn't recognize me.

As long as he didn't know I was a cop.

I was in a room full of people, yet felt strangely alone, vulnerable. I looked for Torrance again. Then Parrish. Panicked when I couldn't find them.

I turned away for an instant, a mere second to check again for Torrance and Parrish. And when I looked back, the man was gone.

Son of a bitch.

7

Parrish had been near the buffet. No longer. I walked toward the lobby. She could have gone out, or made a left to the ladies' room. I decided to check there first. I pushed open the door, entering a posh, though small sitting area with a large mirror on one wall. Beyond that and around a corner were the actual restroom stalls, and I walked in, but didn't see anyone.

If not to the ladies' room, then where? I returned to the restaurant, surveying the guests, telling myself not to panic. Just because the suspect saw me didn't mean he recognized me. Even so, I needed to warn the others about his presence. I saw Paolini seated at a table, drinking his wine, watching the crowd.

Where the hell were Torrance and Parrish?

Calm, Gillespie. Be calm.

I meandered down the hallway, giving a casual glance to see if anyone was watching me, then I pushed open the swinging door into another hallway. The kitchen was to my left, the scent of garlic and butter filling the air. Someone was speaking rapid Spanish, though I couldn't hear what was being said over the rattle of pots and pans and a droning noise in the background, like a muffled engine, something that seemed out of place in a restaurant setting. I unsnapped my purse, felt for the butt of my gun, reassuring myself that it was there. As I moved down the hall past the kitchen, the noise grew louder. I followed it to the end of the hall, where an Exit sign glowed neon green.

I pushed open the door, stepping out into the cool night air, and discovered the source, a large industrial-type generator, located across the alley just to the left of a small warehouse. No sign of Torrance or Parrish.

"I'm sorry, guests aren't allowed back here."

I spun around upon hearing Stephen Reynard's voice. He'd come up behind me, but apparently I'd missed his approach over the noise of the generator, and I was glad I'd kept my weapon concealed. "I think I made a wrong turn. I was looking for the ladies' room, saw the exit and figured I'd get some air."

He looked across the alley, then at me. "We have gang problems. It would be wiser to get your air out in front. The ladies' room, incidentally, is to the left just outside the swinging door." He stood aside for me to enter.

"Thanks," I said, moving past him. I strode down the hallway. I glanced back, saw him watching me, even as I pushed open the swinging door and turned the corner to the ladies' room, where I heard a voice, low, urgent, drifting from the vent at the bottom of the door. "But who *is* she?" the woman asked.

". . . easy . . ." came a second voice, also too low to discern much other than it was female, and that only because both came from inside the ladies' room.

". . . Talking about . . . diamonds . . . ? . . . she said, 'Tiffany' . . ." then laughter.

My hand went up to my throat, lingered on the cold stones. And then ". . . don't like . . . competition. It ends . . . *tonight* . . ."

This last was said with such finality that I wondered how serious she was about ending it—and just what that something might be, especially considering who I'd seen on the premises. I pushed open the door.

And ran right into Jackie Parrish.

She looked up, saw me, surprised. There was no one else in the sitting area but her. She put one finger to her lips, and moved toward me, pushing me out the door, just as I heard, "The diamonds are still— Is someone there?"

The door closed behind us before I could see who it was.

Parrish hurried me down the hallway, back to the restaurant and the din of guests. "I think they were talking about you," she said.

"Who was it?"

"Some lady in a burgundy dress, talking to another lady in a blue dress. I think she might be the owner's wife."

"Adriana Reynard. Kyla Greene would be the woman in burgundy. Rocky and I were at her apartment today."

"Then she probably recognized you. I saw Miss Burgundy watching you, and when she walked in the front door with that guy she's been hanging with, I followed."

"Which guy?"

"The one with the gray beard and the earring—it's an enameled feather, something Native American—"

"He's our suspect from the two-eleven at the bank."

"You sure?"

"Positive."

Torrance, unaware of the nature of our conversation, walked up, held his arm out as though he'd been eagerly waiting for her all night. She smiled up at him—playing her part far too well in my opinion.

"Watch yourself, Gillespie," he said, quietly. "I've heard some talk I don't particularly like."

"What's that?"

"Your name being mentioned in the same breath as television."

Great. So much for my cover, like I even had one to begin with. I wondered if it would be catty to give Parrish one of those I-told-you-so looks. "We have bigger problems," I said instead. I told him what I'd told Parrish.

"I don't like it," he said.

"I like it even less," I replied. "I think we're in over our heads."

Parrish didn't look the least bit ruffled, though with her it was hard to tell what she was really thinking. "We have backup outside."

Torrance shook his head. "I think Kate's right. We get out now."

"I'll go tell Paolini we've decided to leave," I said, then left the two of them alone as Reynard moved to the center of the restaurant, calling out for everyone's attention, thanking everyone for their help in raising funds for the Hope Central Women's Shelter. When the guests raised their glasses, toasted, and drank, I sat next to Paolini, leaned over, and said, "We're leaving."

His gaze was on Jim Greene, who approached Reynard. Both glanced over at me as they talked quietly amongst themselves. "What's going on?" he asked.

"No time to explain," I said.

As the two of us stood, Adriana Reynard walked up and said to Paolini, "Do you realize who you are with, Nicky?"

"I'd like to think I do, since I've been seeing her off and on these past two years." His lie was smooth, but his tone held an edge I hadn't heard before, reminded me that this was not a man to trifle with.

Adriana glared at me, then said in a voice loud enough to be heard across the room, "She's a cop."

All movement in the room stopped. All attention turned toward us.

Adriana Reynard narrowed her gaze at me. "I saw her on TV," she said. "Talking about Fiona Winchester's murder."

From the corner of my eye, I saw Torrance move in closer. Paolini held out his hand to me. Then he turned the force of his stare on Adriana and said, his voice even, slow, "What is it you're implying?"

Adriana hesitated, as though suddenly unsure of herself. "I—I figured you should know."

"You're a fool to think I did not," he said, then guided me toward the lobby. I glanced back, saw Jim Greene pull out his cell phone. Torrance and Parrish followed us. At the door, Paolini said, "We need to keep up some sort of pretense of appearances. If I'm not worried, they may put it aside."

Torrance nodded at Parrish. "Stay with Kate. I'll get the car."

"Will do," she said, as he headed off toward the garage.

The three of us strolled down the walk, when Reynard came bursting out the door. "Nick, I'm sorry about my wife."

Paolini eyed Reynard. "So am I," he said. Paolini, Parrish, and I continued on, crossing the street to stand on the corner beneath the streetlamp and await Torrance and the car. When we were out of earshot, Parrish took out her cell phone, punched in a number, said to whomever answered it, "It's over. She was made."

I couldn't help myself. "Yeah, who would've guessed they watch TV?"

She raised a brow, the dark humor flying right by, as she returned to her conversation, walking off a few feet, saying, "Contact the PD . . ." The rest of her conversation was subdued, undoubtedly to keep Paolini from overhearing.

Paolini nodded toward several men standing just inside the doors of Etienne Reynard's, their focus clearly on us. "Perhaps a little damage control," he said, turning his back on the group in the doorway, his gaze on mine, assessing. "We came as a date," he said. "It stands to reason that I would not kiss the enemy."

It took me a moment to ensure I'd heard correctly. "Negative. It's *not* in my job description."

He put his hands on my shoulders. "Look behind me at

those men. Your job description is precisely the problem. Especially when it comes to the Fiona Winchester murder."

I wanted to tell him it had nothing to do with the Winchester case, but suddenly I was no longer sure. "What do you know about that?"

"Enough to know that if someone in that room felt threatened, and you are perceived to be the threat . . ." He drew me close, until our faces were mere inches apart.

I couldn't let this happen, I told myself, and said the first thing that came to mind. "You're the enemy—"

His gaze narrowed slightly, and he lowered his mouth to mine, cutting off my words. I felt my heart speed up from the unexpectedness of it, felt the fluttering in my stomach from the knowledge that he *was* the enemy. I ignored it all and told myself that this was an undercover assignment. I was *not* attracted to him.

All thoughts fled at the rev of an engine, the sound of tires screeching.

We looked up at the same time. Saw the dark sedan speeding our way. I had the crazy thought it was Torrance. That he'd seen us kissing. But the sedan came straight at us.

Paolini pushed me to the ground. Dropped beside me. I heard a shot. Heard it hit the lightpost.

The car sped off.

A second car followed, tires skidding as it stopped beside us. Torrance. "Kate?" he called out.

"I'm fine," I said. "Go, go!"

He sped after the suspect's car. I glanced over at Parrish, saw her rooted to the spot, the phone to her ear, her mouth open, her gaze locked on mine. Then, as if she came out of a trance, she said into the phone, "Jesus Christ. Get over here. Shots fired."

8

I took my first solid breath, looked across the street, saw the men in the doorway, Adriana and a glimpse of Kyla beside her. No one moved. No one ran to call 911.

It was as if they knew someone had placed a hit.

Knew and were watching.

Waiting to see who would rise.

It was several seconds before my pulse slowed, before the adrenaline started to recede. Paolini loosened his hold on me. "Are you okay?" he asked.

"A few scrapes. You?"

"Fine." It came out short, terse. He helped me to my feet.

I stood, looked at the lightpost. Saw the shiny gouge from the round that hit. Eye level. Mine. "Christ."

I leaned against the building, facing the restaurant across the street, at the people in the doorway, everyone still present. A million questions swept through my mind. Did it have something to do with the Fiona Winchester case? Or that of Paolini's missing ex-wife?

Or was it simply that the hit man from the bank saw me, knew I was a cop—knew I recognized him?

I glanced at Paolini, wondered at his involvement in this. Thought about the timing of his kiss. If he'd set up this whole thing. But when he touched a scrape on his cheek, his hand shook, and I knew that he wasn't a man easily ruffled.

Either this had been a surprise to him, too, or it was a bit too close for his comfort . . .

I heard a car approaching and reached for my handgun. But it was Torrance. He pulled to the curb, and Paolini opened the back door. I got in, Paolini followed. "Anyone hurt?" Torrance asked, as Parrish slid into the front seat.

"Just shaken," I said. "You get a plate?"

"No. But it's an older model black Mercedes. I lost it not too far from here."

The area was industrial. There were no cars parked on the streets, no reason for anyone to be in the area this late at night. We made a second pass. I looked to our right.

Saw a car down the street, where none had been before. Saw the streetlight glinting off the hood ornament. A black Mercedes.

"There," I said, pointing at the Mercedes just as its headlights switched on. The vehicle moved toward us.

Torrance hit the gas. We sped off, but the Mercedes was on our tail. Torrance made a right. The Mercedes followed. Another right. The headlights grew closer.

"Hold on," Torrance said. The street loomed ahead, a ribbon of black beneath the streetlamps. Farther up, the road forked. The Mercedes was gaining. At the last second, Torrance whipped the car to the left. Our back end slid, then righted itself as he steered out of the turn. I heard the sound of tires losing traction, looked back, saw the Mercedes. Heard the screech of burning rubber. Then the unmistakable sound of massive metal crashing into metal.

The vehicle had hit a lightpost. I called in our location to dispatch. Torrance made a U-turn, then stopped at the top of the hill, where we could see the Mercedes, keep an eye on it while we waited for backup. Maybe two minutes later, we heard sirens. Soon three black-and-whites drove around the corner, positioned themselves for a high-risk felony stop.

Torrance turned off his headlights, then rolled to the crash site. We got out to assist as one of the officers, his handgun pointed at the Mercedes, was calling for the suspect to exit.

There was no response.

The suspect had fled.

After the scene was contained, the investigating officer took Paolini's statement, while I called Lieutenant Andrews to let him know what had occurred. A CSI, my friend, Ginny Richardson, dusted the outside of the suspect vehicle before they towed it off. I watched as she dipped her brush in a small jar of silver-colored powder, something that would contrast nicely against the black paint of the car. I was just about to ask her if she'd found anything when Paolini walked up.

"I'll be leaving now, Inspector," he said. His driver was parked not too far away, waiting for him.

I moved off a few feet away from the car, not wanting to talk to him within hearing of Parrish or Torrance. "About what happened . . ."

He was quiet a moment, then said, "You realize he saw."

God, that's all I needed. "Saw what?" I asked, hoping we were talking about two different things.

Paolini reached out, brushed a few strands of hair from my face. I stood there, surprised. It was such a simple move, yet even more intimate than our kiss outside the restaurant. I tried to decipher why, told myself the kiss was pretense, designed to fool those watching.

"Good night, Inspector," he said, then started to walk to his car, leaving me standing there on the curb, wondering.

It wasn't until I turned around, and saw Torrance, that I knew without a doubt that Paolini was correct. It was there on Torrance's face as his gaze met mine.

He had seen the kiss.

He had undoubtedly seen the way Paolini touched me just now.

And he didn't look happy.

9

My first instinct was to talk to him, to explain, but before I could, I was distracted by Ginny's, "Bingo. Got a beauty of a print here, Kate." Her comment reminded me that we were in the middle of a crime scene and any personal business would have to wait.

I leaned closer to look as Ginny lightly plied the soft brush over a print that was located on the driver's door frame next to the window. The silver powder adhered to the smooth black surface of the car, and she aimed her flashlight just below it to avoid a glare. I could see the print taking shape with each pass of the brush, the powder glistening like fine diamond dust as it adhered to the ridge pattern.

"Do me a favor," she asked. "Can you get me one of the black print cards from my kit?"

"Sure," I said. Her print kit was on the curb in front of the car, and I looked inside. I grabbed the tape and a few of the black cards and brought them over to her, watching as she finished dusting.

When she was satisfied with her work, she had me hold her flashlight, while she took the roll of tape, pulled out several inches, then smoothed it across the latent prints, taking her time to avoid air bubbles or wrinkles in the tape. She lifted the tape from the car's surface, then smoothed it across the face of the slick black card, and handed it to me.

I took a close look, moving beneath the streetlight and saw there were actually two prints on the card, one only a partial. The better print, however, showed full ridge detail forming what latent print examiners called a tented arch. Both prints had a straight line running horizontally through them, undoubtedly a scar, perhaps from a long-ago cut across both fingers. I'd examined a print or two in my day and this lift was, as Ginny said, a beauty. I only hoped whoever had left the prints had a record so we could run them in ALPS, the automated latent print system. If this person had a criminal history anywhere in the US, we'd get a hit in a matter of hours.

Ginny resumed dusting the rest of the car, and I was no longer needed. I'd hoped to find Torrance alone, to explain that what he'd witnessed was nothing, but it wasn't to be. We were constantly surrounded by investigators and technicians. By the time we made it back to the Hall, it was well after one in the morning, and Parrish's presence made it difficult to have any sort of private conversation.

Torrance parked at the side entrance, and Parrish waited in the car, while he walked me to the door. "About tonight . . ." I said. "It's not what you're thinking."

"You have no idea what I'm thinking."

Suddenly I wasn't sure I wanted to know his thoughts on the matter, and I tried not to decipher why, instead watching a couple of uniformed graveyard officers exit the building on their way to the parking garage.

After several seconds of silence, the smile he gave me was bittersweet, and he reached out, ran his thumb across my cheek. "Goodnight, Kate."

And then he turned around and walked back the way he'd come.

I leaned against the door, watching his departing figure, listening to his echoing footsteps. When he disappeared from view, I went inside, changed clothes, then headed home.

I was back late the next morning, to finish up my report—and to call Torrance. "You at the office?" I asked, hoping he was, but not knowing for sure, since I'd called his cell phone.

"Parrish and I are finishing up our reports from last night."

I wanted to talk to him, but not with his partner around.

"I was wondering if we could meet."

"In an hour?" he said.

"That'll be fine. It'll give me time to type my own report. Starbucks?" I said, picking some place neutral, and well away from the Hall.

"I'll see you there."

The meeting, however, never took place, because forty-five minutes later, Shipley called. "I think we found Lucia Paolini," he said.

"Where?"

"A couple blocks from the restaurant, Etienne Reynard's. And she's definitely dead."

10

Rocky and I arrived at the same time. We were met by Shipley and Zim, who both happened to be on call this weekend, which is why they were first at the scene. "All yours," Zim said, wasting no time in getting out of there.

"What's with him?" Rocky asked Shipley.

"Tickets to an exhibition game. Wasn't real excited to get called out. Nearby business owner found our victim after she came over to investigate the sound of an engine running in the alley."

Since the CSIs were busy snapping photos, I took out my notebook and went to talk to the witness, Shelby White, a short woman, early fifties, dark hair. "What time did you first hear the engine?" I asked her, noting the line of empty trash cans set out along the street. There was one behind the car on the sidewalk, also empty. Trash day.

"Seven, seven-thirty, this morning. I had just come in to finish up some paperwork, and truthfully, I didn't really pay any attention. I thought, you know, that she was just warming up the car."

I looked at my notes. "And you called the PD at ten-thirty?"

"Yes, right after I came out to bring in the trash can. That's when it finally sank in. No one warms up their car that long. I walked up, saw the hose in the car window . . .

She's . . . dead, isn't she?" The woman looked away, and I let her have a moment to compose herself.

After several seconds, I asked, "Do you remember seeing her car parked there before?"

"No," she said, shaking her head. "It definitely wasn't there last night when I locked up—pretty late. We're moving the radiology records to our new office. It might have been midnight when I finally left."

"Thank you, Mrs. White."

I glanced at Rocky, who was talking to the coroner. When he finished, I told him what our witness had reported.

"She sure she didn't hear it last night?"

"Pretty positive," I said. "Besides, the trash was collected this morning. No way would they have emptied the can if the car had been parked there. Why?"

"Coroner says the stages of rigor aren't matching up to someone who's only been dead a few hours."

"So we can rule out suicide, and pretty much determine by the emptied trash can that the death occurred elsewhere."

"That's what it appears. Let's go have a look."

I followed Rocky to the car.

A green Jaguar—the same car the witnesses at the beauty salon had reported. Even from where I stood, I could see the unmistakable cherry-red coloring of someone who has died from carbon monoxide poisoning. Despite that, however, there was no doubt who we were looking at. Same blue scarf, same low-cut blouse, and ample, though now discolored, cleavage.

"You're never gonna believe this," Rocky said, nodding toward the body in the driver's seat, the woman's head tilted to one side as though she had fallen asleep behind the wheel.

"The woman from the parking lot," I said.

"Jesus. Who woulda guessed we were talking to Lucia Paolini the whole time?"

I was pretty certain it wasn't Lucia, based on the photo I'd seen. Still, that didn't help me identify my victim. Her identity remained to be seen. At the moment, what I really wanted to know was what this person had intended to tell me when she met me in the parking lot.

Who killed Fiona Winchester?

Who tried to kill me at the Twin Palms Motel?

I wondered if she ever really knew the answers.

And if that was why she was killed . . .

God only knew, I thought, as I stared at the discolored face, trying to picture the woman who had approached me in the parking lot. She was still wearing the red wig . . . And that reminded me of Kyla Greene—the resemblance. Never mind that I felt as though I'd seen *this* woman before when I'd spotted her at the bank—something that could have been dismissed as coincidence had it not been for the presence of the unknown white male I'd seen walk into the bank moments before the alleged hit, then seeing the same suspect at the restaurant.

"Rear plate's missing," Rocky said. "You got one up front?"

I walked around to the front of the car. "Nothing up here."

"I'm thinking she took them off right before she met us at the bank."

"You run the VIN?" I asked.

"Yeah. Vehicle comes back registered to Lucia Paolini."

I circled the car again, then stopped when I saw a scrape in the green paint on the right rear fender. There was some gray paint transfer, and I made a note, making sure to point it out to the CSI, in case it turned out to be significant and the gray paint could be matched up to anything.

"What the hell is that?" Rocky asked, staring into the driver's window. "Rose petals?"

I moved next to him, looked in. Red petals were scattered across our victim's lap.

Maybe someone was trying to make a dramatic scene

seem more like a suicide . . . Vaguely I wondered if it could be the same rose she'd been carrying in the bank parking lot.

I walked around the car, looking at it from all angles, then peered into the window at the ignition to see what keys might be present on the key chain. Hanging from the single key in the ignition was a rectangular green plastic tab, the sort that usually came free as a sort of advertisement. No other keys. Nothing. I narrowed my gaze at the key fob, read the gold writing: JIM GREENE'S IMPORTS.

"See something?" Rocky asked.

"Yeah. Our next contact."

11

Saturday afternoon found Jim Greene's car lot a bustle of activity, with banners hanging from the windows that read: BIGGEST SALE OF THE SEASON. Several couples strolled around the lot, looking at cars while salesmen, eager for a commission, followed them around, ready to answer any question that might arise.

Rocky and I had no sooner stepped on the property than we were approached by a young man in a crisp white shirt, blue tie, and black slacks. "Can I help you find a car?" he asked, eyeing first me, then Rocky, then our ring hands, perhaps to determine diamond size and thereby potential commission size.

The last time we'd been there, we'd had no luck finding Jim Greene, though I half suspected once his secretary notified him that the cops were present, he made himself scarce—assuming his sister hadn't called to warn him. Now I wondered if we'd gone about it all wrong. I put my hand on Rocky's shoulder and said, "Honey. What was the name of that man who said he'd give us a good deal on a Mercedes?"

Rocky narrowed his gaze, rubbed his chin, and said in a halfway decent Texan accent, "Don't remember, Sugar. Just pick out a car."

"I thought you said we were going to get matching cars."

"And how am I supposed to explain a new car to my wife?"

"Buy her one, too."

He nodded. "There's a thought. What kinda deal can you get me on three cars?"

The salesman cleared his throat. "Three?"

"Three. So if you need to get the owner to make a deal, then go get him now and let's talk."

In the time it took for me to give Rocky my best fawning look, and run my fingers up his arm, the salesman hurried off, disappearing into the building. About thirty seconds later, Jim Greene came strolling out, a perfect smile affixed to his face—until he saw me.

"So it's true," he said. "You are a cop."

"Seems to me, the only ones worried about my being a cop are the ones with something to hide. Or is there some other reason you have a problem with what I do?"

"Only a problem when you lie about it. What were you doing at Reynard's last night?"

Pretty brazen, considering I was supposed to be the one asking the questions. I decided to answer him anyway, since it suited my purpose."Investigating the missing-persons case of Lucia Paolini."

"Lucia missing? I just got done talking to her on the phone."

"When was that?" I asked, keeping my voice casual.

"Hell if I know. She woke me up from a sound sleep."

"You mind if I ask what she wanted?"

He looked around, then said, "Maybe we should talk in my office."

Rocky and I followed him in. Greene stopped to speak to a woman who appeared to be a receptionist, telling her to hold his calls. While he spoke to her, I glanced down the hall, saw a thin, gray-bearded man exit an office. He looked in our direction, his enameled feather earring evident.

Rocky and I both drew our guns. "Call 911," I ordered, as we took off down the hall after him.

We stopped at the end, a blind corner.

Our weapons at the ready, I nodded to Rocky, and we took the corner.

Empty. Only an exit door with a sign that read: SERVICE CENTER.

We approached, stood to either side of the exit. My fingers on the door, I glanced at Rocky. He gave a nod.

I threw open the door. Scared the crap out of the mechanics. The garage echoed with the clattering of dropped tools, as they raised their hands at the sight of our guns.

"You see a guy with a beard?" I asked, holding up my star.

One of them, a kid of maybe eighteen, pointed toward the parking lot. "He just took off in a blue car."

"What kind?"

He shrugged. "Import. Acura?"

Another shook his head. "Lexus . . . I think."

Rocky was looking out. "Blue car speeding off down the street. Probably him."

Great. I took out my cell phone, called in the incident. They'd have radio cars in the area, checking. In the meantime, Rocky and I returned to Greene's office. He was seated behind his desk when we walked in, looking far too calm, considering we'd just run through his building with our guns drawn. Definitely interesting. "Who was your visitor?" I asked.

"I have no idea," Greene said. "But I'd like to know what he was doing in here."

"He was at the restaurant last night," I said.

"Really?" He gave a shrug. "Maybe he's one of Reynard's friends. Always sending them over here to buy cars. Helps having rich acquaintances. What is it you're here for?"

"For starters, any idea who took a couple shots at me last night?"

"Like I told the cops at the restaurant, I was just as surprised as the next guy standing there."

"Forgive me if I say that no one seemed too surprised over the incident."

"Call it shock."

Rocky said, "Shock that someone missed?"

Greene shifted in his seat. "That's not what I meant—"

"What exactly did you mean?" I asked. "Because from my point of view, nobody seemed in a hurry to call the cops."

"Let's just say for someone to attempt a hit on someone like Nick Paolini—and miss—well, it's not the brightest thing to do."

"It probably wouldn't be too bright to make that attempt in a car that could be traced back to the owner, wouldn't you agree?"

"What are you trying to say?"

"The suspect's car happens to be registered to you, Mr. Greene."

There was a slight hesitation, then, "Apparently we had a car stolen off our lot last night."

"Did you?"

He pressed a button on his phone. "Mary, can you get me the case number from the report you made this morning?" he asked into the speaker. He looked up at us. "We came in this morning and discovered one of our cars was missing. A black Mercedes. We called the police, of course."

"Of course," I said. That would be easy enough to verify—the report, that is. Whether there was an actual theft was an entirely different story. I kept that thought to myself, and a moment later, the door opened and a young, petite, brunette came walking in.

She gave Rocky and me a pleasant smile and handed a piece of paper to Greene, then left.

"Would you like the number?" he asked.

"Sure," I said, more to be polite than anything else; since we'd have a record of it. He read it off and I jotted it down. "About the shooting last night," I said, turning the page in my notebook. "You made it sound as though it was a deliberate hit on Paolini."

"Why the hell would someone care about you?"

"Because I'm a cop who is digging around in a certain murder that everyone had thought had been put to bed years ago."

He stared at me, waiting.

"Fiona Winchester ring a bell?"

"God damn," he said, shaking his head.

"Nice way to speak of the dead."

"She was a pain in the ass."

"One you happened to have dated . . .?"

He picked up a pen from his desk and turned it over and over in his fingers. "Fiona had a few problems, an out-of-control cocaine habit being one of them, *courtesy* of Stephen Reynard's late partner."

"So you knew her?"

"Yeah, I knew her. When I met her, she was a waitress in his restaurant . . ." He hesitated, looked from me to Rocky and back, then said, "I know you're not going to believe this, but I only tried to help her."

"Really?" I said, and let that hang until he felt compelled to fill in the silence.

"We went out a few times, but she was going through coke faster than I could afford it. She wanted a way to earn more money . . ." He gave a shrug of his shoulders. "I set her up as an escort."

"How very kind."

"We're not talking sex, just female companionship. It's all legitimate."

"So your sister, Kyla Greene, tells us."

"Kyla? She—" He stopped. Seemed to think about it, then

said, "What my sister does on her own time is her own business. I'm trying to run a car dealership and the last thing I need is to get the rep of some pimp. I stay away from that sort of stuff. I've given up my evil ways."

"Ready for sainthood, are you?"

"I make an honest living."

"Escort service?" I leaned forward, resting my chin on my hand. "You just help set them up in the business?"

"You could say that," Greene said.

"For a small cut?"

"Yeah—I mean, no. You're putting words in my mouth."

"You have any idea who killed her or why?"

"My guess is she was in the wrong place at the wrong time."

"Why's that?"

"She went to buy some coke. Took her to a not-so-nice part of town."

"You know she went there to go buy coke?"

"Everyone knew."

"Everyone?"

"Everyone who knew her. She lost her source when Reynard's partner got caught by the police and killed himself. Didn't take her too long to get herself killed either from what I recall. A few days . . ."

"Reynard's partner?" I asked. Sometimes playing dumb yielded great results.

"Marcel Etienne. The guy who got her hooked. He and Reynard started Etienne Reynard's. Marcel used it as a front to sell coke to some high-priced clientele. They'd come in for a drink, leave with a bindle tucked in a matchbook, or an eightball tucked in their to-go order."

I made a note to pull the case and review it more thoroughly. "Any chance that's still going on? The coke dealing?"

"How would I know?"

"Oh, maybe because you were being investigated for dealing yourself?"

"Like I said, I'm reformed."

"Would you happen to know who it was that shot at me?"

"We're back to that again?"

"Let's say I have a one-track mind."

"Not a clue. I told you, the car was stolen."

"Where do you keep your vehicles' keys?"

"In a lockbox in the sales manager's office."

"And spares?"

"Same place."

"You check to see if the keys were missing?"

He opened his mouth to speak, closed it, then stood. "I honestly can't tell you. I didn't make the report. Mary did. I only found out when I came in this morning."

Jim Greene led us into the sales manager's office, showed us the lockbox, then checked for the keys himself. "There's a set missing," he said. "I'll have to look into how that happened, since this room is kept secured when no one is in it, and the lockbox is supposed to be locked when the room is open."

I didn't mention that we'd be interviewing the rest of his staff anyway as part of our investigation. "I do have one other matter I need to bring up," I said. "Lucia Paolini. You said she called you last night?"

"More like early this morning. I was asleep in bed."

"What'd she want?"

"Good question. She wasn't making sense. Said she hit her head? Hit something. I don't know. I could barely understand her. I think she was in her car. Heard the engine running. Why?"

"And you think that was early this morning?"

"It was still dark out, but well after I went to bed."

I calculated the time in my head. Rocky had said the coroner put our victim's death hours before. I was fairly certain our victim was not Lucia. But since she was found in Lucia's car, perhaps Lucia was the intended target. I made a note to see if we could come up with phone records. "What can you tell me about her?"

He sat on the edge of the desk and crossed his arms. "What do you want to know?"

"Who might want her dead?"

"That's easy. Nick Paolini. Who else?"

12

"Nick Paolini wanted his ex-wife dead?" I asked.

Jim Greene nodded. "Lucia's probably the one person who has the power to put him away for good."

"And you know about this because . . .?"

"Everyone knew. That's why she was afraid of him."

"Lucia was afraid of Paolini?"

"She was going to get a restraining order on him. He'd made death threats on her from what I heard." Greene leaned back slightly and crossed his feet at the ankles. "Some big to-do at the bank. Which is why no one was surprised when they took a shot at Paolini."

I looked up from my notebook. "You're saying the attempted hit last night was in retribution for something that happened at the bank? The robbery perhaps?"

"Robbery . . . ?" he said, his expression almost a smirk. "Someone should give that guy a reward for killing Millhouse. He was an asshole extraordinaire." Apparently compassion ran deep. "This was before the robbery, though. Day before. But don't ask me what. I have no idea."

Before I could dig further, his secretary came into the office. "Sorry to interrupt, but Jonathan's on line three."

"Jonathan?"

"From the auction?" she said, raising her brows, making

me wonder if the phone call was a ploy. "Wants to know if you want to make a bid?"

"Damn. I almost forgot. I have to take this call," he said to me. "Is there anything else?"

"I need to talk to your employees," I said.

He hesitated. "Employees?"

"The people who work for you?"

"Uh, yeah. Sure. Mary can call them in for you." And with that he walked out, leaving us in the presence of his secretary.

She looked at Rocky and me, a nervous smile on her face.

What the hell. I might as well start my interviews with her. I pointed to the lockbox. "Does everyone have access to this?"

"The keys?" she said. "Well, the salesmen do. They each have their own lockbox key. When the officer came out to take the report this morning, we discovered that the spare set to the stolen car was missing. One of the salesmen thought he might have left the office unlocked for a short period late yesterday afternoon, but he can't be sure."

"Before we leave, I'd like a list of anyone who drove that car the last few days." She seemed taken aback by the request, but gave us the list of names, anyway—none on there that I recognized, but I'd run them later. That was about the most information we got—from her or the other employees working there. And, other than the list, it was a fruitless effort, and Rocky and I were both ready for a break when we left two hours later after speaking with the last employee. We grabbed a breakfast burrito from a nearby Taco Bell, then drove back to the Hall.

"You think Greene's dirty?" Rocky asked me, between bites.

"Of something. Whether it's murder or attempted murder, we need a tad more to go on than his almost admission that he runs an escort business and that he dated Fiona Winchester three years ago."

"Obviously, if he killed her, it would be motive to try to take you out last night. Coulda done it at the restaurant. Get on the phone, tell someone to pick up the car, then swing by and pop off a few rounds."

A distinct possibility, I thought, as I pulled onto the freeway. My mind flashed back to the sight of Greene on his cell phone. Had he called in a hit? But there was also that conversation I'd overheard. The one between the two women in the ladies' room. Adriana Reynard, who definitely had issues with my being a cop. She was speaking to Kyla—who I earlier saw talking to our suspected hit man from the bank. Was it possible that it was Kyla Greene who was setting up a second hit?

Suddenly it seemed important that I find out if Kyla had been interviewed last night. Before we got back to the Hall, I called and had Gypsy track down a copy of last night's report—or rather the names listed on the report, since the narrative wouldn't yet be done. The report was waiting for me when I got there.

So was Mike Torrance.

He was standing near my desk, staring out the window when I walked in. He glanced over at me, didn't smile, which is when I remembered I was supposed to have met him at Starbucks.

"Hello, Kate."

"I'm sorry. I got called out to a homicide . . ."

"I know."

Rocky walked in just then and anything else we could have said was lost. Now that Rocky was here, Torrance would not reveal his feelings to me—about our missed appointment, or even the fact he'd probably witnessed the damn kiss last night. But judging from his closed look, I was going to have to bring it up with him and soon, not something I was looking forward to.

"Hey, Torrance," Rocky said. "Heard you guys had a little excitement last night."

"A bit," he said. "I brought in a surveillance photo of our bank robber." He handed it to me.

"Definitely the man I saw at Etienne's last night," I said as Andrews walked in. "And also the same guy Rocky and I saw at Jim Greene's car dealership."

"You sure it was him?" Torrance asked.

"No doubt. He fled the moment he saw us."

I handed the photo to Rocky, who looked at it and nodded. "Greene acted as though he didn't know him," he said. "He also seemed pretty nervous about his presence."

I proceeded to tell them about our conversation with Greene, including his insistence that he'd spoken with Lucia sometime this morning.

"Of course," Rocky added, "he could be lying. The coroner says Lucia's been dead a long time. Definitely before he could have received this call."

"I don't believe it's Lucia," I said, then told them about the photo that Paolino had showed me at the restaurant.

Andrews rubbed his chin. "Anyone check with the morgue to see who she was?"

"No," I said. "The only thing I know for sure is that she was the woman who approached me in the parking lot at the bank."

"Get me an ID," Andrews said.

Rocky picked up the phone, called the morgue. "The WFA that came in this morning? Carbon monoxide poisoning? You get an ID on her yet?"

He waited a second, then said, "They're checking. They put me on hold."

Andrews eyed me and the report I held. "Looking for anyone in particular?"

"Yeah," I said, tossing the report on my desk. "Aside from our alleged bank robber hit man being at the restaurant last night, Jim Greene's sister, Kyla, was there talking to him. The curious thing was that she bore an uncanny resemblance to our CO victim."

"Any chance she was our victim?" Andrews asked.

"No way. The women at the restaurant was smaller in stature, more delicate. Who knows. Maybe they're related. There was definitely a sense of familiarity with both women. Like I'd seen one or the other before, only I can't recall where."

Rocky covered the mouthpiece of the phone and said, "Maybe it's just one of those faces. You know, looks like everyone else's. Remember that time you saw that woman who looked like the movie star from that space flick?"

"It was that movie star."

"No, it wasn't."

"Yes, it was."

"About the report," Andrews said, bringing us back on topic, since Rocky and I were bound to argue forever over that matter. Besides, he was wrong.

"I wanted to see if Kyla is listed here, I said. "If they interviewed her. Her name doesn't appear to be here."

I was sure I'd seen her standing in the doorway right after the shots had been fired. Had she taken off before we could ID her?

Andrews sat on the edge of Rocky's desk, while Rocky waited on the phone. "I think you should go out to the restaurant. See if you can learn anything about who our victim was, maybe about our robbery suspect as well, which reminds me, I'd also like a tail on Jim Greene. Markowski and Shipley can handle that after they attempt to contact Kyla Greene. Gillespie, you take the restaurant. Zim will be here in about five to help out."

"I can go with her," Torrance said, making me grateful that I didn't have to be partnered with Zim, yet apprehensive about being partnered with Torrance. I glanced over at him, and the look he gave told me that we'd be discussing a lot more than homicide.

13

Rocky was still waiting for ID when we left. Me, I was temporarily saved from any discussion of my "undercover" role in kissing Paolini when Torrance's cell phone rang as he pulled out of the Hall of Justice parking garage. His partner on official FBI business. She wanted an update on the case and Torrance was relating it to her as he drove, including the discovery of the body in the green Jaguar, and the fact we were en route to the restaurant. By the time he finished, my cell phone rang.

It was Rocky. "Got an ID on our victim. Name's Louise Smith. Prints on file for prostitution, one arrest about five years ago out at the Twin Palms, of all places. CDL even matches," he said, referring to her driver's license. "But that's not the biggie. Our Louise Smith is not a she at all."

I pressed the phone closer to my ear, wondering if I'd heard right. "She's a he?"

"As in he's got the full hardware below, and different hardware up top. A rack job . . . You think Paolini knew he was married to a dude?"

"I'm pretty sure a detail like that wouldn't escape him, rack job or not, which tells me that unless Paolini is bisexual, something I don't see him being, our victim is definitely *not* Lucia Paolini."

"I'm beginning to wonder if there ever *was* a Lucia Paolini."

"Why is that?" I asked, beginning to wonder if Paolini was telling the truth about that photo at the restaurant.

"Well, that's where it gets interesting. With the exception of the car registered to her, the name doesn't exist. At least not according to the Department of Motor Vehicles. No license. Nothing but the car registration. And nothing here at the Hall, according to our records. No arrest records, no criminal history."

"But we're sure Louise Smith does have a record?"

"Got her—his—whatever, got the photo sitting right in front of me. Definitely the subject in the car. And definitely the subject from the parking lot." He gave a decidedly evil chuckle. "Zim thought she was quite the looker. Wait'll he finds out the she's a he."

The implication of what Rocky had told me suddenly hit. "Oh God!"

"You think Zim might take it wrong?"

"What? Yeah. He might shoot you. He's about as homophobic as a guy can get. Forget that. We need to find Madame Korsakoff."

"Why?"

"Why? Think about it. Korsakoff's also a transsexual. What are the chances—"

"That she's a nut?"

"Nut or not, she's involved, someway, somehow. We need to find her before someone else does," I said. Rocky promised he'd start the search, and I disconnected and told Torrance the news.

A minute later, we were pulling up to Etienne Reynard's. Torrance parked in the passenger loading zone out front of the restaurant, then pulled the radio microphone from the glove box, and hung it over the rearview mirror, a clue for any overzealous parking attendants not to ticket the car.

The restaurant was closed, but we knocked on the door, hoping someone would answer. No one did, and I decided to cross the street to the corner where Paolini and I had stood the night before. Torrance followed, and when he saw the gouge in the lightpost, he reached up and touched the shiny metal, his finger tracing the path of the bullet. "You were damn lucky," he said.

"I know." Nothing like returning to the scene of the crime to bring it back in all its reality. I tried to figure out how everything was connected. The robbery, the hit, our dead transsexual, Madame Korsakoff—nothing made sense, I thought, as I looked up the street to the parking garage. That would have been where Torrance was the moment that Paolini had kissed me. The moment right before someone had shot at us. If Torrance had seen that, he had to have seen the kiss . . . I put that from my mind to concentrate on the shooting and glanced across the street at the restaurant entrance, where Kyla Greene had stood seconds after, only to disappear before the police could ID her. Where had she gone? Out the alley to the back exit? I wondered, then paused when I thought I saw a man looking at us from the front window of the restaurant.

"Someone's there," I said, nodding in that direction.

Torrance glanced over. "Let's try knocking again."

We crossed over and rapped on the door. Whoever was inside, they weren't acknowledging our presence. "The back entrance?" I suggested.

"Worth a try."

We followed a catwalk between the side of that building and the building next door to a narrow street, or rather an alley, which ran behind the restaurant and dead-ended about a hundred yards to our left. Everything was gray and desolate, from the buildings surrounding us, to the grease-stained concrete beneath our feet. Even the sky was overcast and I shivered, though I didn't know why. Just a feeling, perhaps, but maybe something more, and I looked around, thinking again that we were being watched. I didn't see anyone looking out the sole rear window of the restaurant that faced the alley, and tried to remember what room would be back there. Probably the office. The tinting on the window kept me from seeing clearly inside, and I knocked on the back door. Again, no answer.

I turned away and stepped to the center of the alley to get a feel for the area more than anything else, eyeing the building across the way, an old garage, accessed by a large wooden door, the type that slid shut on wheels. At the moment, it was standing wide open, the building vacant. Next to it was the generator I'd heard running last night. It was one of those industrial types, painted bright red, located adjacent to the building. There was a small sign attached to it that read: LIGHTS/EXHAUST FAN.

"Maybe we should come back later," Torrance said, following me into the street. "I wouldn't mind going for coffee."

There was something in his voice that told me he wasn't interested in a caffeine fix, and I knew the direction in which he was heading. I chose to ignore him and instead looked up at the two garage windows, which had accumulated at least a few years' worth of grime, and I recalled seeing the light inside last night while the generator had been running. I wondered what else I might have seen had I not been interrupted by Stephen Reynard, when I made up the flimsy excuse of getting lost on my way to the ladies' room.

Torrance, however, wasn't about to be dissuaded. "I'd like to discuss a couple of things. One, what happened between you and Paolini."

The kiss, undoubtedly.

Which is why I purposely didn't look at him. Staring at the ground seemed far more prudent in that one moment.

"Kate?" He reached out. Put his hand on my shoulder. Took a step closer . . .

I'd like to think that I would have answered him, that I would have faced what happened, analyzed my feelings over it . . . But two things occurred in that moment. I spied what looked like a scrape mark of green paint about twenty inches high on the side post of the garage's doorframe, which coincidentally or not happened to be gray. At the same time, three boys came barreling around the corner, stopping in surprise when they saw us, then taking a stance meant to intimidate, as though sizing us up as potential robbery victims. They looked about thirteen, the same age as my nephew, Kevin.

"What'chu doin' here?" the tallest asked, while his two friends fanned out on either side of him. "This is *our* street." The three took a step toward us, their chests puffing, their chins tilted defiantly. They looked utterly ridiculous. Unfortunately that didn't make them any less dangerous if they suddenly decided to pull a knife or gun and earn their place in the pecking order of their world.

Crime often came about because the opportunity presented itself, even though the suspects had no intention of committing the act when they set out. And since Torrance and I had both been cops long enough to realize this, we came to the same conclusion—not hard to do, considering we were on a dead-end street and they continued advancing. Better to set the little punks straight rather than wait and see what their pea-brains would come up with.

In unison, Torrance and I reached down, pushed our jackets aside, which nicely showed off our badges as we rested our hands in the vicinity of our holstered weapons.

Our actions—though probably more, our badges—had the desired effect, as their cocksure stance deflated and their eyes widened.

"We're here on official police business," I said, then with a patronizing smile, "Did you need assistance?"

"Uh, no," the first boy replied, the other two shaking their heads in agreement. Once they took stock of the situation, they backed up, then, laughing, ran off.

It would be nice to think we'd dissuaded them from a life of crime, but time and opportunity would present themselves on another day. Even so, I'll admit to being grateful for the distraction and, remembering my purpose, as well as choosing to forget Torrance's question, I walked over, glanced inside the open door of the building, then bent down for a closer inspection of the paint transfer.

"Interesting," I said, as though that would explain why I was avoiding his topic of discussion. Call me chicken, but working a homicide case was far preferable to dealing with my personal life.

"You see something?" Torrance asked.

"Green paint on gray."

"Significance?"

"Our victim was driving a green Jaguar—Lucia's car. She—or he, as the case may be—was still in it when we found her this morning. Not to mention the gray paint transfer I found in it."

Torrance eyed the mark, then the inside of the building. "This deserves a closer look."

"That generator was on last night when I walked back here."

"Anyone in here?"

"No, the door was shut at the time. But the light was on," I said, looking up at the ceiling. I saw one fixture hanging from the exposed trusses, but no switch. Someone had been in here last night, or rather someone had gone to the trouble of turning on the generator and light, and I wanted to know why. Maybe it was nothing. Maybe the green paint transfer belonged to another car. Judging from the paint overspray on the cement floor, a rainbow of colors in the shape of a rectangle, this place had been used to paint a number of cars—something that would explain the generator, since there appeared to be no other power source. Yet I saw no paint equipment or tools or anything else that indicated it had been used recently, so again why would someone have been in here last night? There was little inside the building but a workbench on the far wall with a settling of white dust upon it, and a coil of rope in one corner.

But as I scanned the area, something caught my eye beneath the workbench—something long and slender, about the thickness of a rose stem. I walked in, used my foot to drag it out from beneath the workbench, and saw that indeed, that's just what it was.

Except that every petal had been plucked off.

"What is it?" Torrance asked, following me in.

"A long-stemmed rose, minus the petals. If I had to guess, they're the petals scattered on the body we found this morning," I said, pulling out my radio to call for a CSI, at the same time wondering if we could get out without contaminating the crime scene further.

The transmission was broken, and the dispatcher asked me to repeat several times. Finally she said, "Confirm . . . CSI . . . Etienne Reynard's?"

"Behind Etienne Reynard's," I radioed back, then stopped when I heard something outside the door. A scraping. "What was that?" I asked Torrance, my hand automatically going for my weapon.

But before we could move, the door rolled shut.

14

Torrance and I ran over, tried to slide the door open. No use. And though I pictured the three juvenile punks outside, laughing, I heard nothing.

"Hey!" I called out. "Open up!"

Whoever it was ignored me, and I wondered if the same thing had happened to our victim, and if said victim had died here.

I keyed the radio, tried to call for help, but got static. Torrance leaned into the door, bracing his shoulder against it. "Something's holding it shut."

I clipped the radio on my belt, and pulled out my cell phone, then heard the sputtering of an engine. The overhead light in its wire cage flickered at first, then burned steadily as the generator caught, and I suddenly pictured a scene from an old movie I'd recently watched, when a switch is thrown, opening the current to the electric chair, death imminent. I didn't like that my thoughts were going in that direction, but I couldn't help but think about my transsexual victim's lifeless body in Lucia's Jaguar.

I was fairly certain the victim hadn't died there—she'd been killed elsewhere . . .

The rose stem was here. In this garage.

Where we were trapped.

"Why the hell would someone start that thing?" I asked, my voice coming out harsher than I intended.

Torrance eyed the wall that separated us from the generator and the outside world. About a foot off the ground was a vent and he bent down, put his hand in front of it. "Feels like something coming in."

"The sign outside read LIGHTS/EXHAUST."

"Exhaust is supposed to go out, not in."

"Cheery thought, considering my victim was killed by carbon monoxide poisoning," I said, glancing at the display on my cell phone. There was no signal, and I walked around the floor, hoping to find the one place that seemed to register a line, showing that there was the tiniest chance that the call would go through. Perhaps it was the cinderblock walls, or maybe just one of the dead spots that plagued us in the city. Either way I was not about to give up, especially when Torrance had no luck with his cell phone. I tried my radio again, walking over every inch of the building, finally registering a slight signal—right in front of the exhaust vent. Trying not to breathe deeply, I made my call to dispatch. About every other word seemed to cut out, because of the poor signal. I gave them our location, told them to send us backup Code Three, and prayed they heard me, more important, understood over the drone of the generator.

At the same time I wondered how long it would take for the structure to completely fill with carbon monoxide, if in fact that's what was blowing in, and if the responding units would get there before we suffered any ill effects.

"Well, they're on their way . . . I think."

Torrance again tried to force the door. We needed a way out or some heavy-duty ventilation, and I looked up to the ceiling, the trusses and crossbeams casting eerie shadows at the top. The windows were ten feet up from the floor and

there was nothing loose that we could use to break
them . . .

But hell if the rope couldn't be thrown over one of the
crossbeams, I thought, my gaze following one beam to the
window on our right.

While Torrance pushed on the door, I grabbed the rope.
There was maybe twenty feet of corded nylon about the
thickness of my index finger. A ladder would have been better, but in a pinch and with lots of knots tied for gripping . . .
"You any good at rope climbing?"

"I've done it a time or two," he said, looking at me as he
braced his foot on the door.

"Keep working on that," I said, "and I'll tie some knots.
Our best chance might be the window. Don't know how
much carbon monoxide is in here . . ." Or how long we'd
have before we'd pass out, was my unspoken thought. I
knew carbon monoxide and some other poisonous gasses
rose in a fire, but that had to do with the heat. I had no idea
what it would do if it was being blown in at the base of a
building. I only hoped it stayed at the bottom—if that's indeed what it was—and I eyed the beam, then tried to toss the
rope over, only to have it fall short.

Torrance stopped what he was doing, walked over, gathered the rope and tossed it up like a regular cowboy. It flew
over the top, arced, and came down the other side.

Our shoulders touched as he threaded the rope through
the loop, and I felt his warmth against mine. Nothing like a
good life-endangering bit of carbon monoxide to bring on
closeness, I thought, wondering if my headache were psy-
chosomatic.

"Kate?"

I shook myself, realizing that he was holding out his suit
coat, waiting for me to take it.

"Time to get out of here," he said. I threw his jacket over
my shoulder as he grabbed the rope, jumped, and started up.

He didn't get far, maybe about five feet when the light and the generator went off.

We heard the sound of metal scraping against metal. Torrance dropped to the ground. We reached for our weapons as the door slid open, filling the garage with the afternoon light.

15

"**A**nybody here?"

It was Stephen Reynard, holding a tire iron. I unsnapped my holster with my thumb. He stepped into the garage, set the tire iron against the wall, then turned in our direction, his gaze catching on the rope, then us. "What the hell are you two doing here?"

"Wondering who locked us in," I said, noting both his hands were empty. He wasn't wearing a coat and didn't appear to be armed. "You wouldn't happen to know?"

"Didn't realize anyone was in here. Heard the generator on, looked out my office window, and saw that tire iron shoved through the hasp. We've been having street-gang problems. Figured they were up to something, especially after that drive-by shooting last night . . ." He looked from me to Torrance, his gaze dropping to Torrance's badge and gun. "Guess you're a cop, too?"

"FBI," Torrance said, and I thought how strange it was to hear that.

I said, "You mind if we step outside? I've got some backup units that'll be screaming into this alley, guns drawn if I don't call them off."

"Uh, yeah," he said, then led the way.

We followed and I took out my radio, my hope being that

it worked better in the open air. It was still static-filled, but I managed to get out, "Slow it down to Code Two."

"Ten-four."

I turned my attention back to Mr. Reynard. "Who owns this building?"

He furrowed his brow as if the question was something he'd never considered before. "I guess I do, now."

"You guess?"

"It belonged to my partner, Marcel Etienne. That's where he died," he said, nodding into the garage. "Suicide. Cocaine. Couldn't stay away from it . . ." He was quiet for several seconds, then looked at me. "I'm sorry. You were asking about the building?"

"What is it used for?"

"Storage at one time, until the street gang problem started. They discovered an easy source of free canned goods and restaurant supplies. After that, I simply kept it locked until Jim Greene asked to borrow it about a year ago. His shop was being renovated, and he needed a place to paint some cars. Been empty ever since," he said, as two patrol vehicles slid around the corner, tires screeching as they drove into the alley.

The officer in the first vehicle got out, looked us over. "You okay, Inspector?"

"Fine," I said. "We need a CSI team out here. I have a couple of questions I still need to ask Mr. Reynard, then I'll brief you."

Torrance said, "I'll brief the officers."

"Thanks," I replied, then turned my attention back to Reynard. "I'd also like permission for the CSIs to search the restaurant."

"What?" He looked over at the officers, then back at me. "Because some kids locked you in?"

"Because we found something that may be related to a homicide in your storage building."

"Jesus . . ."

"We can get a warrant if you'd rather."

"No, it's not that. Look around all you want. I'm more worried about how my cooks are going to work in the kitchen if there's a bunch of cops tearing it apart."

"We can search that first."

"I'd appreciate it."

"There's a couple things you might answer for me before we get started . . ."

"What's that?"

"Do you know why the generator was running last night?"

"I have no idea. That's what I was on my way to check when I ran into you at the back door. I thought I heard it running, but from up front, well, I can't even be sure when I was aware of it."

"Did you look inside the building?"

"No. I came out, turned it off, then came in for the toast. Figured it was those damn kids playing around. The door was shut, but I didn't look to see if the padlock was on it. Come to think of it, I don't even know where the hell the padlock is."

"CSIs are on their way, Inspector," the officer told me.

"Thanks." To Mr. Reynard, I said, "There was a man and a woman at the restaurant last night. The man was thin, gray hair and beard . . . wore an unusual earring . . . Might have been an enameled feather . . ." He didn't react, and so I added, "The woman was an attractive blonde. She wore a burgundy dress."

"Doesn't ring any bells."

"Are you familiar with Kyla Greene?"

"Jim's sister? She used to be friends with my wife." He gave a shrug. "I heard she was out of state. On a trip."

"You're saying she *wasn't* here last night?"

"Frankly, I have no idea, Inspector. I was too busy seeing to the banquet to recall who was here and who was not."

Interesting. Either he was blatantly lying, or the woman we thought was Kyla Greene happened to be someone else . . . I pretended interest in Kyla Greene, however, and asked him for permission to borrow the photo of her from his wall. He agreed. "One last thing. Exactly *how* did your partner die?"

He shoved his hands in his pockets, glanced inside the building, his gaze fixed at something unknown. "He was drunk. Coked up. Shut himself inside, sat in his car, turned on the engine . . ."

"Maybe it's coincidence," Rocky said, hours later after Torrance and I'd returned to the Hall, finding nothing more of interest in the restaurant or the storage building. "The little street punks lock you two in with the tire iron, turn on the generator, not realizing it's hooked up wrong and blowing CO in instead of out . . . It could happen."

"Not likely," Torrance said.

I shook my head at Rocky. "As a devil's advocate, you suck."

"What? You don't like my theory?"

"Your theory is seriously flawed. And I'll hazard a bet that the suicide investigation of Reynard's partner is flawed as well."

Zim leaned back in his chair. "I remember reading the report. Didn't see anything wrong with it at the time. It was a pretty thorough investigation, primarily because of the coinciding drug case."

Andrews walked in just then. "You have any luck finding Kyla Greene?" he asked.

"Not home," Rocky said. "Strange thing is that her neighbors say she's out of state. Went on some trip or something."

I didn't like the sound of that, since it was the second time I'd heard that Kyla was out of state. "Then who was it we were talking to at the apartment?"

"Not sure," Rocky said. "One of the neighbors said she's

there a lot. Figured she was one of Kyla's roommates. According to him, Kyla seems to have a revolving door of beautiful roommates. He said he suspected she and the others were high-priced hookers. They keep to themselves and are pretty quiet, so none of the neighbors seemed to care."

"What are your thoughts on this?" Andrews asked me.

"Personally, I am beginning to have a bad feeling about it," I said. "She was all too eager to let us believe she was Kyla Greene, not to mention that she seemed to have some intimate knowledge of the case, and a genuine reluctance to divulge it. Her likeness was definitely in that photo that Paolini showed me."

"But didn't he tell you it was Kyla Greene?"

"No. What he said was that Kyla, Fiona, and Lucia appeared in the photo. If he was telling the truth, then the woman we thought was Kyla Greene is actually Lucia Paolini."

"Which would make the other woman in the photo, the one you didn't recognize, Kyla?"

"That would be the logical assumption. So she could very well be out of state."

"Great," Rocky said. "We were that close to Lucia . . ."

"Can't be helped," Andrews said. "Let's work on getting a positive ID on this woman. Find out if she really is Lucia. In the meantime, see if we can't get an ID on Kyla Greene and eliminate her as a possibility. How about the search for Korsakoff?"

Rocky shook his head. "She seems to be laying low for some reason. Could be because of a recent warrant for soliciting for sex, but she's never cared before."

Andrews said, "If she's friends with this person found in Lucia's car, maybe she thinks someone's after her. If that's the case, we bring her in on the warrant and hold her in protective custody. We have anyone sitting on her place?"

"Yeah," Rocky said. "Got a couple cars doing a Code five

on her apartment and the place where she works. Soon as she shows up, they'll call us."

I glanced at the packet of photos from the carbon monoxide death of Louise Smith. "Let's hope it's soon. I have a few questions I'd like to ask Korsakoff about her so-called predictions. Either she has suddenly gained psychic powers she's never had, or it's pure coincidence that she could come up with so many factors."

"Well, we know she ain't psychic," Rocky said. "But why can't it be coincidence? Why can't we have two carbon monoxide deaths that coincidentally take place in the same building without having them both be murder? For that matter, maybe Korsakoff's got nothing to do with the dead transsexual we found in Lucia's car."

I figured Rocky was being his typical cynical self, but I answered anyway. "One, because someone tried to kill me and Torrance in that same place in which we *coincidentally* happened to find the stem to a rose, probably belonging to the petals scattered over a victim who died by carbon monoxide. Two, because I think it might be a little too convenient that Marcel Etienne, a guy under investigation for one of the biggest cocaine trafficking cases, which could implicate some pretty big players, just decides to get drunk and suck up some CO fumes. And three, because someone decided to take a pot shot at me last night just a few short minutes after I happened to walk back there and see that damn generator running."

"She's right," Lieutenant Andrews said. "There's too much coincidence for my comfort. Zim, dig up that suicide on Reynard's partner, and get a copy to Gillespie. It seemed cut and dried at the time, but now . . . Reinterview the witnesses if necessary. See if there's something that comes to light."

Zim gave him a pseudo salute and left the office to get a copy of the case. As soon as the door closed behind him,

Andrews looked right at me. "I have the results from IBIS," he said, referring to our image analysis database system. It was used to identify weapons and rounds fired from them by mapping the fingerprint-like striations left on the bullets. He opened up a manila envelope and pulled out a sheet of paper, then looked at us. "This is regarding the weapon that your suspect used in the Bay Town Mutual robbery . . . They recovered the round that killed Earl Millhouse. It happens to be the same weapon used to kill Fiona Winchester. I'd like to say it ends there, but it doesn't." He handed the report to me. "You might want to read that last line."

I took the report and read. "Jesus Christ," I said, handing the report back to Andrews. I rubbed my arm, feeling an ache that wasn't there a moment before. I wasn't sure what to say, and as Torrance watched me, his dark gaze holding mine, I realized that he knew.

"What the hell was in the report?" Rocky asked.

I ignored him, my gaze fixed on Torrance. "When did you find out?" I asked him.

"This morning. Right after Andrews received the report and called me."

"Knew what?" Rocky asked.

I don't know why, but it ticked me off that he'd known and hadn't said a thing. "And you were going to tell me, when?"

Torrance crossed his arms. "When you asked me to meet you at Starbucks . . . and later when I asked you to go for coffee."

"You said you wanted to talk about . . . something else."

He was quiet a moment, then said, "That, too."

"I need a serious caffeine fix," I said.

Rocky stood. "Enough with the cryptic bullshit. What the hell was in the report?"

I looked at Rocky, then took a cleansing breath, not sure

how I felt about this latest revelation, or where I stood with Torrance, or . . . anything. "The gun that was used in the robbery and in Fiona Winchester's murder happens to be the same gun someone used to shoot me at the Twin Palms."

And with that I walked out the door.

16

I started down the hallway toward the elevator, when I heard Torrance say, "Kate."

I stopped, turned, and he caught up with me. "Why didn't you tell me?" I asked. "Is this some top secret FBI thing I couldn't be told about?"

"We were interrupted if you recall."

"There were plenty of opportunities—" I stopped at the look he gave me, the slight raise of his brows that told me he thought otherwise. "What?" I said.

He drew me into the stairwell, out of immediate view. "Once again, you're running away."

"I'm . . .?" Hell, I thought, crossing my arms. I hated it when he turned the tables on me. "You're saying it's my fault?"

"No. I'm saying had you not been so busy avoiding me and any conversation I attempted, I could have told you there in the car, and again in the alley."

I looked away, not wanting to face the truth of his words, and he crooked his finger beneath my chin so that I had no choice but to face him.

"You know damn well the hit in IBIS has nothing to do with why you're upset. The real issue," he said, his gaze penetrating mine, "is why what happened last night, this kiss, bothers *you* so much."

"Me? I—"

He put his finger across my lips, silencing me, as he said, "What are you running from?"

I didn't respond.

He held my gaze for the longest moment. "When you can answer that," he said, "call me."

But I couldn't speak, and then he walked down the stairs, and I stood there, not moving, listening to his footsteps growing fainter.

Was I running?

Surely not from Mike Torrance? Hadn't I spent the last year of my life trying to get my act together just to be with him?

Or had I?

Was there more to this kiss with Paolini than I had imagined? Had I been partly responsible because I was afraid of any commitment with Torrance? Setting myself up to take a fall, just to avoid a relationship?

If that was true, what the hell was I thinking?

Torrance was every woman's dream—well, this woman's dream. Paolini was a goddamned crime boss.

A crime boss who had questions to answer in the disappearance of his ex-wife, as well as the discovery of a victim in his ex-wife's car.

I returned to my office and called Paolini. "I need to meet with you."

He told me he was at the park and gave me the location.

I didn't stop to ask what he was doing there. "I'll see you in about ten minutes."

Not about to rendezvous with Paolini alone, I got Rocky to go with me, and we left. When I drove in the opposite direction, Rocky said, "That park's the other way."

"First things first," I said. "I need coffee." I hit Starbucks en route, got my coffee, then tossed the keys to Rocky. "I have a lot on my mind. You okay driving?"

"Sure," he said, then turned on the AM radio to an ultra-

conservative talk show, whose host was discussing the latest
blunders in San Francisco's political arena.

I tuned it out, sipped my mocha, and thought about Torrance and what he'd said. Then I thought about Paolini and
my reaction to his kiss. I thought about a lot of things, until
Rocky said, "We're here."

"I knew that." Not. Damn good thing I had him drive.

The park seemed an odd place to meet, but it was acces-
sible and public, two pluses in my opinion. Paolini was sitting on a bench, watching some kids swinging. He seemed
out of place, overdressed in comparison to the others present, everyone from teenagers babysitting, to grandparents.
No one, however, seemed to give him a second glance, as
though men in several-thousand-dollar business suits with
limos waiting nearby were the norm. And who the hell
knew? Maybe they were.

Rocky waited by the car about ten feet from where Nick
Paolini sat. Paolini glanced at him as I approached, then
said, "So you are here for official reasons."

As if I'd contact him for other reasons? I kept silent, however, and he indicated I should take a seat on the bench near
him. "You have word on Lucia?" he asked.

"Did she ever go by the name Louise Smith?"

He hesitated, his gaze penetrating. "She used that name
among others . . . Did you find her? Lucia?"

Interesting, I thought, that he'd ask about Lucia specifically, especially if that was a name Lucia had used. Who
then, was Louise Smith? And how did she, or he, know
Lucia? The resemblance made me wonder if they were not
related. But I wasn't comfortable asking Paolini, since I
didn't want to tip him off to what we knew. I decided to keep
things vague, as though we still had not yet identified our
victim—or discovered that she was transsexual. I was curious about this aka that Lucia Paolini had used. One more in
what seemed to be a growing list of names. "We found

someone in a car registered to Lucia. Cause of death was carbon monoxide poisoning—a suicide or something made to look like one. Our victim was wearing a red wig. The ID comes back to a Louise Smith . . ."

He looked away, stared out at the children, focusing it seemed, on a towheaded boy of about seven, who was balancing on a swing on his belly, his arms outstretched, while he made zooming noises. Hard to imagine Paolini getting caught up in the innocence of youth, yet here he was seeming to be genuinely interested in the antics of the boy. After what seemed an eternity, Paolini looked back at me. "You're sure it was her?"

"Her prints came back to a Louise Smith. She was found in a green Jaguar . . ."

He leaned forward, resting his elbows on his knees as he watched the children play. "Lucia's green Jaguar. I gave that to her . . ." He sat up straight, his voice hard, unyielding. "What happened?"

"Other than the cause of death, I can't say."

"Can't or won't?"

"Both. I don't yet know. The autopsy is not complete."

"Lucia would never have killed herself, and she was too careful for it to be an accident," he said, looking out at the child once more.

"There are those who say you wanted her dead."

His narrowed gaze met mine, held it. "Whoever told you that, Inspector, is wrong," he said in a voice tinged with anger, an anger that seemed barely in check.

"Who is not important. The question is did you have reason to kill her?"

He didn't answer right away. He looked down at his hand, the fist he made, his knuckles white. And then, as though coming to terms with something in his own mind, he relaxed, opened his hand, and brushed some invisible speck from the knee of his suit. "No," he said, as though I had simply asked him if he thought it might rain.

"Even though she knew things about you? Could ruin you?"

He faced me, his voice quiet, so that I had to strain to hear over the noise of the children laughing, shouting . . . playing airplane. "If you mean did she have it in her power to inform the police of things they might have an interest in, then, yes. She had that power. Would she have used it? Not in the way you think, so, yes, that possibility still exists. Knowing that she may still try to do me harm, would I have harmed her? The answer to that rests with the child," he said, nodding to the boy on the swing, who, still on his belly, was now twisting the seat around and around, letting go, then spinning.

"Who is he?" I asked out of curiosity, since I wasn't aware Paolini had any children.

"Lucia's son, Adam, who, for the first two years of his life, I thought was mine. Lucia had an affair, and Adam is the result." His expression softened as he watched the boy. "Have you ever loved someone so much it hurt?"

I didn't answer and he continued.

"Even after the paternity test proved that Adam was not my son, I still felt that love. You don't nurture a child, and then just lose that feeling, because a piece of paper and your ex-wife's attorney tells you that child is not yours. But then, that's a battle we'll be fighting in court . . ." He took a breath, sighed. "What is it you need of me, Inspector?"

"Keeping in mind we have not made a positive identification, why would someone want to kill Lucia?"

"Many reasons. Perhaps her current lover, the late Earl Millhouse, felt she was a threat. And there's his wife, who I'm sure wasn't too pleased to know the woman she thought was her friend was sleeping with her husband. And that doesn't even count the extracurricular banking activities Millhouse allegedly dealt in at the bank that she might have knowledge of."

"Anything you were involved in?"

"Not anymore. I withdrew my business from that bank years ago."

Curious, I thought, since the FBI was specifically interested in Paolini. "You have no accounts there?"

"One or two. Nothing current."

"What do you know of the Fiona Winchester murder?"

"She was killed presumably after buying some cocaine at the Twin Palms."

"And when I was shot . . . ?"

"I believe I have been questioned about that ad nauseam."

"Suffice it to say I still have my doubts as to the veracity of your statement."

"I expect there are some things we will never see in the same light," he said, looking at his watch. "I have but a few minutes, Inspector. If we are dredging up old history, I must assume you believe these events are related?"

"They are."

"Interesting. In what way?"

"Ballistics."

He stared out at the playground, didn't respond.

"A woman wearing a disguise and using the name Jane Smith met me at the bank just before it was robbed. She was killed in your ex-wife's car."

"What did she want?"

"She said she knew who killed Fiona . . . and who shot me at the Twin Palms."

"And did she tell you?"

I thought about lying, just to see his reaction, but decided that the truth might serve me better. "No."

"I can tell you this much, Inspector. If it was Lucia who contacted you, I would be suspicious of anything she told you."

"Why is that?"

"In the three years we were married, her lies became so tangled, I had to hire a PI to follow her."

I noticed he didn't deny that Lucia might have direct

knowledge of the Twin Palms incidents. No, what he was saying, what he seemed to be saying, was that if she did have knowledge of it, her information was suspect. Well, I had news for him. Everyone who was involved was suspect. "Why have her followed by a PI at all?" I asked.

"One, I was trying to find out who Adam's father was. A fruitless effort. Two, because I found out that I didn't really know Lucia at all. Or rather her alleged occupation."

"Meaning what?"

"Meaning I was concerned when I saw her at the restaurant last night."

"You saw her?"

"More of a glimpse, actually."

"Considering that's why we were—" I stopped myself. This was not the time to voice my displeasure, and so I finished with a calmer, "I'd think you would have mentioned it."

"You seemed intent on getting out of there."

"And this alleged occupation . . .?"

"Lucia Paolini had a peculiar hobby that rivaled even the late Antonio Foust," he said, then stood and looked at his watch. "My time is up, Inspector. Enjoy the remainder of your afternoon."

I sat there, stunned by his revelation. Pulling myself together, I caught up with him, followed him to his limo. "But Antonio Foust was a hit man," I said.

"Exactly."

17

"What's this about a hit man?" Rocky asked, after Paolini's limo drove off, and I'd told him what Paolini had said.

"He alluded that Lucia was one."

"Lucia a hit man? Hit woman?"

The implications of it struck me. "Paolini said he saw her at the restaurant last night. That comes close to satisfying my belief that our 'Kyla' is definitely Lucia."

"You see who it was who took a shot at you from the car?"

I thought about it, tried to imagine if it could have been a woman. "I have no idea. It was too dark . . ."

"Jesus," he said. "Think what it means to the Twin Palms cases. What if she's the one who took a shot at you? Maybe it wasn't Antonio Foust at all."

"It's worth looking at. What I'd like to know is why it all resurfaced now. The robbery, the gun from the Twin Palms shooting . . ."

"Easy. Your TV spot on the cold case."

"It wasn't like the Fiona Winchester case disappeared."

"It wasn't like it got attention, either. You said that Reynard's wife brought up Fiona's name at the restaurant?"

"Yeah, a few minutes before someone took a shot at us."

"The question is whether it was an attempt on your life, or Paolini's."

"Or merely some sort of scare tactic," I said, recalling the overheard conversation in the ladies' room about diamonds and competition. "Before we head in that direction, though, I want to talk to Sophie Millhouse, the wife of our murdered bank CFO. Paolini implicated her among others as having a possible motive in wanting Lucia killed."

"Didn't Shipley and the FBI go out there initially?"

"Yes, but that was before we knew the robbery was anything more. There wasn't a lot of usable info—which is not to say we'll be any more successful."

"Worth a shot," he said, then pulled out his cell phone. "I'll call it in, and check to see if there's any word on Korsakoff."

"Good idea. I'm beginning to get worried about her." As far as we knew, Korsakoff had never been involved with organized crime, and there was no reason to believe that had changed. Which meant if she had stumbled into this somehow, she was probably in way over her head.

I waited for Rocky to finish the call. When he disconnected, he said, "Might as well cruise out to Mrs. Millhouse's place. No sign of Korsakoff yet. They'll call us the moment she surfaces."

Mrs. Millhouse lived in a modest home located in North Beach. I found a parking spot about two blocks down the hill. It was a good hike up, but the breeze was nice, the sun was warm, and we couldn't complain.

There was a For Sale sign out in front, and I wondered how long the home had been on the market—specifically before or after Millhouse's murder? It was something worth looking into, I decided, as I knocked on the door.

It was answered by a petite redheaded woman, midthirties, wearing sweats and holding a glass filled with an amber liquid over ice. This early in the day, I hoped it was ice tea. Judging from her bloodshot eyes, I doubted it, and I reminded myself that she had recently lost her husband and was entitled.

I showed her my star, told her who we were, and asked if she was Mrs. Millhouse.

"Yeah, I'm her," she said, her voice thick, and definitely smelling as though she'd been drinking. "Are you here because of that son of a bitch I married?" As she moved into the light, I saw an overabundance of makeup on her left eye, and beneath it, the telltale bruising of a shiner.

"We would like to talk to you," I said, trying to remain neutral. It was hard to say if she was angry due to the stages of grief, or if she had a valid reason to be angry—judging from the black eye, highly possible. "May we come in?"

"Sure," she said, stepping aside and waving her hand with a bit too much flourish. "Why not? You want a drink, too?"

"No, thanks," I said. She led us into a lavishly furnished living room, indicating we should take a seat. Rocky chose a wingback chair, while I sat at one end of a French Provincial sofa, opposite Mrs. Millhouse. "I apologize for stopping by unannounced," I said, "but some things have come up in our investigation of the bank robbery, and we were hoping that perhaps you might be able to answer some questions for us."

She took a sip of her drink, smiled weakly, and said, "What the hell? My life has become an open book since this all happened. You think you know someone . . ."

"What do you mean by that?" I asked, wondering if she was talking about her husband's affair, the black eye, or both.

"Do you realize that my husband let his insurance policy lapse? Never mind the piddly one the bank gives all their employees. Ten thousand dollars," she said, then took a good long sip. "The damn funeral took most of that."

"Is that why the house is for sale?"

"Actually we were going to move to a bigger place. I wanted to start a family. We were going to a fertility clinic . . ." She stared out the window, seemingly at nothing, as she brushed her fingers through her short red hair.

And here I was delving into whether or not he'd had an affair. Hi, we're here to investigate your loved one's death, and by the way, we've been told he was having an affair. Then again, if she didn't love him, the question might not matter. Unfortunately I didn't have a crystal ball, and had no way of knowing beforehand what sort of reaction my question might provoke. "I hate to ask this, but did you and your husband have any problems in your marriage? Any indication that all was not right?"

"What does this have to do with the bank robbery?"

"We're covering all angles. Routine."

"I honestly have no idea. I mean, he was a tyrant, a goddamned anal tyrant, did everything by the book, everything on time, and heaven forbid if I was late. But as long as things went smoothly, we were happy."

"And was there a time when things weren't smooth?"

"Every marriage has that, doesn't it? Of course."

"Was your husband seeing anyone?"

I caught her midsip, and she nearly choked on her drink. "If he was, he didn't tell me, but isn't that usually the way of things?"

"And there was no hint that anything was amiss?"

"None."

"You mind if I ask how you got the black eye?"

"Black eye?" She reached up, lightly touched the area above her left cheek, then shrugged. "Drank too much. Hit the damn door."

"Do you know Lucia Paolini?"

Her gaze widened as though this question surprised her even more than that of her husband's alleged affair. Interesting, considering that Lucia was the one having the affair with him. "Yeah," she finally said. "I know her."

"Could you describe her?"

She swirled the drink in her glass. "Short? Pretty?"

"What color hair?"

"Depends on her mood. Last I saw her, she was blond. She likes to wear wigs. Expensive wigs."

"Did your husband know her?"

"You mean intimately?" I didn't respond, let her draw her own conclusions, and a moment later, she said, "If it's true, my husband never admitted it."

"What do you mean if it's true?"

"I mean I don't know. I heard it from someone, and now that my husband is dead, I suppose it's a moot point."

"Who did you hear it from?"

"Adriana Reynard."

"When was that?"

"A few weeks ago."

"Did you talk to your husband about it?"

"No. Now if you'll excuse me, I would prefer to get thoroughly drunk on my own, while I try to figure out how I'm going to survive on nothing."

She stood, her expression telling us the interview was over, and Rocky and I thanked her for her time, then left.

As we started down the hill to the car, Rocky said, "That's one bitter woman. She definitely knows her husband was screwing around."

"You think she's bitter enough to hire someone to kill him?"

"Hard to say. I've definitely worked cases where scorned women have done worse for less. Battered women, too. Of course, if she did kill him, then found out he didn't have any insurance, it'd take an awful lotta glasses of bourbon to swallow that pill."

"It definitely would."

"Where to next?" he asked as we got into the car.

"To see Mrs. Adriana Reynard."

To say that Adriana Reynard was not pleased to see us at her door might have been an understatement. "Do you have to come in?" she asked, looking terribly annoyed. "I'm sort of in a hurry."

"That's the beauty of homicide," I said. "The dead stay dead forever, which gives us all the time in the world. Would you like to talk here or at the station?" I smiled.

She did not smile in return. She did, however, open the door for us to enter. "What is it you want?" she asked, leading us into the living room, though not asking us to take a seat.

"We're here about the Fiona Winchester case. You seemed to know something about it the other night at the restaurant."

"Of course I know something about it. She was a waitress in my husband's restaurant. At least she was before Jim Greene got a hold of her."

"And what happened then?"

"He wooed her, tempted her with the high life, then set her to work in his little side business. Escorting."

"Prostitution?"

She shrugged. "Truthfully, I have no idea. I've never heard anyone say anything like that, but it doesn't mean it isn't so." She looked at her watch. "Is this going to take long? I have an appointment."

"Murder is always so inconvenient. I do apologize."

She gave an annoyed little smile, crossing her arms. "What is it you want?"

"Do you know someone named Louise Smith?"

"I'm guessing you must mean Lucia Paolini. I'm pretty sure she uses that name. For what, I don't know, but I saw her ID once, and it had that name on it."

"Was she at the restaurant last night and if so can you describe her?"

"I don't remember seeing her, but there were so many people. As to what she looks like, she's one of those disgusting blondes who is gorgeous and this big around," she said, holding up her little finger, which, had there been any question, ruled out my homicide victim, Louise Smith, as being Lucia. "I've heard she's into cocaine . . . You aren't going to tell her I said anything . . . ?"

"Not a word," I said. "Right now I'm more interested about your little outburst at the restaurant last night."

"Outburst?"

"Pointing out to Paolini that I was a cop."

The look she gave me had the word "duh" written all over it. "You do *realize* he doesn't like cops?"

"And you think it was your business to interfere? Or was there something else?"

"What else would there be?"

"I overheard a conversation in the ladies' room, something about a necklace I was wearing and not liking the competition. Never mind that when I first walked into the restaurant, you didn't seem too happy about my accompanying Paolini—even before you found out I was a cop."

"Necklace?" she asked, looking confused. She gave a shrug. "Whatever. The point is that I like Nicky. I've liked him for a long time, even *before* he married Lucia. You think he'd even notice me? I'm Stephen's wife to him, nothing more. I tried to tell him Lucia was a piece of shit, that she was *using* him—even I knew the kid wasn't Nicky's—but he wouldn't listen. He thought I was jealous . . ." She gave a self-deprecating laugh. "Okay, maybe I was. I mean if you had your choice between *me* and someone who worked on cars, who would you pick?"

"Lucia worked on cars?"

"Trust me, I was surprised, too. All these years I've known her, who would have guessed? I mean, I practically *dragged* Lucia to this facial spa party. The whole time, she's saying, 'How quaint. A facial party.' I thought she was just being funny. If I'd known she was going to embarrass me in front of everyone when the hostess asked us to introduce ourselves, I *never* would have brought her."

"What happened?"

"We were supposed to say our names and what we did for a living, which was a laugh in itself, since we're *all* married to rich men, and my jaw just about *dropped* when she told everyone she was a mechanic."

Rocky perked up when he heard her mention the slang term for an assassin. "A mechanic?" he asked.

"Yeah. Not that I believed her. She was laughing, and I mean, she *hardly* looks like she works on cars. She has a very warped sense of humor. She pulls fly wings from their little bodies."

"When was this?" I asked.

"The fly thing?"

"No, the mechanic thing."

"Oh, God, I don't know. Right after she started screwing Earl Millhouse. A year ago? Now *that* was an affair I never thought would happen, considering that right after she left Nicky, she hooked up with her first ex-husband, Jim Greene. Well, not publicly, but almost everyone knew that they were meeting on the sly all the time."

"I take it Mr. Millhouse had a problem with Mr. Greene?"

"A problem? He hated him. Blamed him for all the troubles they were having at the bank. I don't know the particulars, but I did overhear them fighting a week or two ago, when they were at the restaurant."

"Did you hear what the fight was about?"

"No. But I heard what Jim Greene said to him right before he stormed out. It was something like, 'I'll kill you, you goddamned bastard. Try it and see if I don't.' That was pretty much it," she said, then looked at her watch again. "Hope you don't mind, but I *do* have a hair appointment. It takes *months* to get in to this guy."

"Just one more thing," I said. "When's the last time you saw Lucia?"

"About five minutes before someone took a shot at you last night. I mean, she was there one second, and the next . . . gone."

*   *   *

"What do you think?" I asked Rocky, once we got back in the car.

"You mean, besides she's a snobby airhead?"

"Never mind she forgot her own lie. First she tells us Lucia wasn't there, next she tells us she was."

"I'm still trying to get it all straight in my head. Lucia Paolini dumps her mob boss husband for her first husband, Jim Greene, then hooks up with Earl Millhouse, the bank CFO. Unbeknownst to everyone, she's a killer for the mob. Then her lover, Millhouse, ends up dead from a supposed bank robbery that's actually a hit, then some transsexual with an uncanny resemblance to Kyla Greene uses the same name that Lucia uses, and ends up dead in Lucia's car. Aren't you seeing a problem with this?"

"You mean that somebody should have known how she earned her pocket change?"

"At the very least. Would Paolini be so in the dark that he had to hire a PI to find out what she did? Why is it no one can find her and everyone is lying about seeing her? And who the hell is this dead transsexual who looks like Kyla Greene—or is it Lucia?"

"I don't know."

"What I'd really like to know is if she's the person who killed Fiona. That would wrap up some nice loose ends."

Was she the person who shot me? I wanted to ask. I didn't, though. It seemed selfish. A woman was dead, and I was still here. This wasn't about me, I thought, as Rocky's cell phone rang.

"It's Shipley," he said, after answering it. "Madame Korsakoff just walked into the Purple Moon."

18

The Purple Moon was a touristy nightspot known for its singing and dancing shows. The actors, however, were transsexuals and cross-dressers—definitely talented in their sometimes over-the-top performances, as the Purple Moon managed to get decent reviews each time it headlined a new show.

A sign out front listed business hours as starting at five P.M., and the front door was locked. I knocked anyway, and a moment later a burly man, probably the bouncer, opened the door. "Can I help you?"

I showed him my star. "SFPD, Homicide Detail. We're looking for someone who calls herself Madame Korsakoff."

He opened the door wider, allowed us in, then nodded to the stage. "That'd be the dude in the red dress," he said. There were several "women" on stage, dressed in 1920s flapper costumes, practicing a song-and-dance number reminiscent of that time. "Hey, Korsakoff! Ya got visitors."

Korsakoff looked up, saw us, then jumped from the stage. Rocky and I ran after her. She reached the back door.

I grabbed her arm, pulled her back. Rocky slammed the door shut, blocking her escape.

"I didn't do it!" she said. "I didn't do it!"

"Do what?" I asked.

"Nothing. I—I thought you were someone else."

"Who?"

"No one."

"Interesting," I said. "There a place we can talk?"

Her gaze darted from me to Rocky to the door, as though assessing her chances. I didn't bother telling her we had officers posted just outside. Nor did I mention our intent to arrest her, then hold her in protective custody. "Um, the dressing room?" She nodded toward the stage.

"Let's go," I said.

"And don't try anything stupid," Rocky added, taking her other arm.

"I'm not some common criminal that has to be *man*handled," she told him, as we led her down the hall.

"Ain't you the witty one," Rocky said. He opened the door, looking inside before we entered to make sure there were no surprise escape routes. The room was long and narrow, and ran the length of the stage, and we could hear muted singing through the walls. Costumes hung on a rack, their bright colors reflecting in the mirror opposite. Korsakoff pulled out a chair from beneath a counter littered with makeup and wigs, sat, then pushed a wig stand out of the way to get to a pack of cigarettes. I studied her as she tapped one from the pack, lifted it to her mouth, her hand shaking, and I realized that, had I not known, I would never have guessed that she was not born a woman. Now that I know, however, I could see the subtle differences, the larger-boned hands, the Adam's apple.

"Mind if I smoke?" she asked, lighting up, inhaling so hard, I thought she might suck the filter right into her lungs.

She blew a stream of smoke to one side, then said, "If you're here about that phone call I made the other day, I don't really remember the details."

No feigned accent this time. "Not even something about being careful near money? A man from the past?"

"You know those visions . . . Come and go."

"A little too conveniently. What can you tell us about Louise Smith?"

"Nothing," she said, her voice cracking. She cleared her throat. "She works here, like me."

"When's the last time you saw her?"

She shrugged. "Couldn't say."

I looked at Rocky. He knew Korsakoff from past cases, knew what made her tick, so when he rubbed his thumb against his fingers, signifying money, I said, "Too bad. There's a reward just waiting, and you were the only caller who was even close. If we just had the right info . . ."

She hesitated. "It's anonymous, right?"

"Actually we were thinking, you know, TV cameras, public awareness. Imagine the attention it would bring to your business. You'd have people lined up outside your door for psychic readings."

"No!"

"No?"

"No cameras. No TV."

"Why not?"

"They'll know I—" She clamped her mouth shut.

"Who will know what?"

She took a quick drag from her cigarette, looked at her reflection as she exhaled, then closed her eyes. "God. It seemed like such an easy way to make a buck, you know?"

"What did?"

Korsakoff opened her eyes, looked at me in the glass. "I overheard Louise talking to someone that day I called you. They were in the office right next door, and I was in here, putting on my makeup for a dress rehearsal. The walls are thin, and when no one's singing on stage, you can hear just about every word. What can I say? I put my ear up to the wall and listened. That's when I heard this woman trying to talk Louise into calling the cops, because they'd never believe her if she did it herself. It was right after you were on TV offering a reward. She insisted Louise do it her way, but said that Louise could keep the reward money and she'd double the reward if Louise called and got you to meet her at the bank so Louise could give you the name of the murderer. All the woman wanted was this person to be caught, now that she knew who he was."

"You mean she told Louise who the murderer was?"

"That's exactly what I mean."

"And did she give a name?"

"Trust me. If I'd heard it, or Louise would have told me, I would've collected the damn reward myself that first day. As it was, I had enough trouble convincing Louise to meet with you so she could get the money."

"You convinced her?"

"She changed her mind. Didn't want to go. I mean, it was a thousand dollars. How was I supposed to know the bank was going to be robbed? I'm not getting in trouble for that, am I?" she asked, looking from me to Rocky.

"Not that," Rocky said. "It just depends on what else you did."

"I told you. I didn't do anything."

"Then why'd you run?" he asked.

"I couldn't see because of the stage lights. I thought you were that guy."

"What guy?"

"Ever since the bank robbery, Louise thought she was being followed. We get the occasional gawker, you know, someone who comes in, wants to see the show, see what it's like. But it's usually a one-time thing, unless they're . . . you know, into it. Trust me, this man is definitely not the type."

I took notes as she spoke, and flipping the page, asked, "When's the last time you saw him?"

"Last night. He came in, supposedly to see the show, then left right after Louise did, but not before he gave me a look that sent a chill down my spine."

I waited and she crossed her arms as though suddenly cold. "It was like he knew that I knew. And he'd come after me next."

I looked up from my notebook. "What do you mean come after you next?"

"I don't know. Maybe it's just a feeling I got. Louise gets a phone call and leaves, and then the guy leaves right after. I saw him hanging out front this morning when I came in for work. He was standing a few doors down and started walking toward me when I came in, but then Rick, the bartender, walked up and he left." I made a note to check with the officers, see if they recalled seeing anyone.

"What'd he look like?"

"Thin, gray hair, beard . . . And he wore an earring, something dangling, like a dagger."

Rocky's gaze met mine for an instant, undoubtedly thinking the same thing I was, that he was the guy we saw in Jim Greene's office. Our hit man from the bank.

"Any idea where Louise took off to, when she got the call?" I asked.

"To get her reward money from her sister would be my guess. She was pretty pissed off when she didn't get paid."

"Her *sister?*"

"Well, yeah. I'm pretty sure that's who set her up to call you and get you to the bank."

"How do you know?"

"Two reasons. No one's called her Louis in at least ten years."

"Louis?"

"Yeah. That's her—his real name. But once he started taking the hormones, he changed it to Louise. And the few times Louise's sister did call, Louise *always* complained."

"About what?"

She gave a shrug. "That the woman was crazy. A real nut case."

"And the other reason you thought it was Louise's sister?"

"It's just a guess, mind you. I only saw her for a second—but there was a definite resemblance."

I thought of the woman we'd believed was Kyla Greene, but now suspected was Lucia Paolini. Louise's sister? It made sense. Definitely a resemblance. And since Louise was in Lucia's car, it added credence to this theory. More importantly, if, as Paolini had suggested, Lucia was some sort of assassin, then she could very well have set up the drive-by shooting in front of the restaurant. The question of course, was who was the target? Me? Or Paolini?

Or both?

19

"So," Rocky said. "You're thinking Lucia is *not* dead, and Louise is really her brother?"

"Think about it, Rocky. Paolini wouldn't let something like that slip by him. Paolini with a transsexual wife? Don't think so."

"Maybe he's bi?"

"I can assure you he isn't," I said, though I wasn't about to go into detail as to how I knew. "There's too much of a physical resemblance between Louise and the woman we thought was Kyla Greene for her not to be related. And everything points to her being Lucia." I said, as we walked into Homicide. "Regardless, I'd feel better if we could come up with a solid ID. At least a license check on Kyla Greene to verify they are two different people."

We spent the next several minutes gathering the reports related to the Fiona Winchester homicide and the suicide of Reynard's partner, Marcel Etienne, as well as my shooting from the Twin Palms. I wanted to look them over, see if I couldn't make a connection. I placed the binders in a handled carton with the labeled spines facing out, and Rocky was working on getting a solid ID on Kyla Greene when Lieutenant Andrews walked in.

He eyed me, and then the case files. "You look tired."

"Nothing a good nap and a week's vacation couldn't fix," I

said, trying to smile. "In the meantime, we've had some interesting developments." I informed him of what we'd learned after visiting Sophie Millhouse, Adriana Reynard, and finally Korsakoff, whom we'd taken into protective custody.

When I finished, Andrews said, "You're thinking this woman at the restaurant was Lucia and *not* Kyla Greene?"

"I'd say the possibility is pretty high."

"I don't like that Paolini didn't mention it to you when you were at the restaurant. I have to wonder at his motive."

"Yeah," Rocky said. "Especially considering what Paolini told Gillespie about Lucia's hobby—playing hit woman. Why was he so fired up to get her to that fundraiser at the restaurant? Since when does he help the cops?"

I put the last case file in the box. "His alleged cooperation definitely makes me suspicious. His reasoning for it was that he wanted her found to clear his name of any suspicion in her disappearance. And, according to him, she has something that belongs to him."

Andrews said nothing at first, then, "If she is a contract killer, she could certainly have been the one to take a shot at you last night."

"I'd say it was more likely that she set it up, since I saw her talking to our suspected hit man at the restaurant," I said. "But what if the alleged hit attempt last night was a bluff to draw attention away from the Winchester investigation? It can't have escaped notice that my timing on TV, dredging up the case from the past, happened to coincide with the fundraiser at Etienne's. Makes you wonder if someone wasn't worried about something . . . Maybe we should tail Paolini. See what he's up to."

Andrews nodded. "Him and a couple of other people. I'd like to know what they're all up to. I want Lucia picked up. I want backgrounds done on Jim Greene, Stephen Reynard, and both their businesses."

"We did a permissive search on Reynard's restaurant," I

said. "Right after Torrance and I were locked in that garage behind his place. We didn't find a thing. Well, except the photograph that allegedly contains Kyla Greene, Fiona Winchester, and Lucia Paolini."

"We go further," Andrews replied. "Bank records, bookkeeping. Either of you have a chance to look into the old Narcotics investigation involving Reynard's partner?"

"Just got it," I said, patting the box of files.

"While you're at it, let's look into Bay Trust Mutual. Gillespie, follow up on the bank leads. Contact the FBI, find out what they've done. We don't want to duplicate any work."

"Yes, sir," I said, though I wasn't thrilled about the contacting the FBI part, since what that really meant was contacting Torrance. We hadn't exactly left on the most comfortable of terms.

"Markowski," he continued, "you look into Jim Greene's car dealership. I'll have Shipley coordinate the surveillance. I want every one of these guys followed, including Paolini."

Markowski nodded. "You want us to start that now?"

"No," Andrews said. "You two need to get some rest. Take your stuff, go home. Read. Sleep. We'll reconvene in the morning. I'll call in Zim to help Shipley get a team together for the surveillance. Right now they're helping the Robbery Detail on a lead from the diamond heist. We're going to have to pull them off to work this. They can start while you two catch a couple of hours."

I stood. "Sounds like a plan," I said, glad to be going home. I picked up the box to leave.

"You're going to call Torrance?" Andrews asked.

I hesitated. That was not a call I wanted to make when others were listening.

"Yeah," I said. "As soon as I get a bite to eat. I'm starved."

I left before Andrews could respond. Where Torrance was concerned, I had other issues besides the present cases to deal with, and I had no idea what I was going to tell him. He wanted answers, and I wasn't sure I had them. But the case gave me the excuse to call. And the drive gave me the time to think.

Traffic was light crossing the Bay Bridge, and by the time I turned onto University Avenue in Berkeley, I was no closer to coming up with what I was going to tell him. I needed some intelligent way of explaining this thing, this kiss from Paolini, and my reaction to it, to him . . . Damn, I couldn't figure it out myself. How the hell was I going to make Torrance understand?

What I needed was a bite to eat, I told myself, ignoring that this was probably another great stalling tactic on my part. Instead of making a left up the hill to my apartment, I made a quick right, heading to the bagel shop. I was in luck, found a space in front, parked, checked my mirror, let a dark blue Lexus drive past, then opened my door and got out. Five minutes later, jalapeño bagel in hand, I was back in the car.

No more stalls.

Time to go home, make the call. I signaled, pulled out into traffic.

Hi, Mike. It's me, Kate. That thing you said about Paolini's kiss and me running away . . .?

I tried to ignore that I couldn't get past that part of the conversation, even in my head.

It was just a kiss, nothing more.

I was not attracted to a crime boss.

It was Torrance I wanted, needed, desired.

What then was that butterfly-like feeling in the pit of my stomach when Paolini kissed me? Nerves from kissing a crook undoubtedly. Anyone would feel that, under the circumstance.

Hell . . . maybe I should have picked up a six-pack instead of a bagel.

With a sigh, I looked into my rearview mirror as I signaled for a lane change, and saw a dark blue sedan about two car-lengths back. Surely it wasn't the same Lexus that had passed me when I stopped for food?

Some poor guy looking for a parking space? But I'd just pulled out of one. Why not take it?

I slowed. The vehicle slowed.

I sped up. The same.

Not good.

He was either following me or this was one anal driver, keeping the exact distance between vehicles.

Somehow I doubted it.

I made a quick right, then a left, turning into a residential area, figuring I could lose whoever it was by taking the backstreets home.

Watching my rearview mirror, I didn't see the car make the last turn. Maybe it was nothing after all.

I turned onto the next street, and hell if the blue Lexus wasn't parked up ahead, facing my way.

I was either terribly paranoid and that was the driver's destination the entire time, or he had anticipated my direction— which meant he knew where I lived, where I was going.

Definitely not good.

If this was the same guy who had taken a shot at me and Paolini the other night, I was not about to take a chance and drive past him.

I made a U-turn, checked my rearview mirror, and saw his vehicle closing the distance between us.

"Son of a bitch."

I sped up, unsnapped my holster, then switched over to the Berkeley PD channel. "SFPD officer needs assistance," I said into the radio.

"Go ahead."

"I need Code Three backup. I'm being pursued by an un-known subject in a dark blue Lexus." I gave the street name and direction, then my vehicle description.

"Ten-four. Can you copy the license?"

I looked in my mirror. The vehicle was closer. "Negative." I stepped on the gas.

Officers confirmed they were en route. I didn't have time to listen from that point on. I was in multitask overload. It was one thing during the pursuit of a suspect to call in your location and try not to hit any pedestrians or vehicles, all while driving at a high rate of speed. It was quite another to *be* pursued, and still have to do the same. Either way, the bad guys didn't worry about the stuff I was worrying about. They didn't think about intersections or red lights. Why would they care if they killed a pedestrian or two in the course of trying to kill me?

The blue vehicle was on my tail. A four-way intersection was ahead. I could blow through it and hope, pray there was no cross traffic. I turned on my lights and siren, then slowed. Looked both ways. Clear. Glanced in my rearview mirror. Saw the Lexus. I wasn't sure, but it looked as if there might be someone else, a passenger in the car. Someone trying to lie low. Could just be something on the seat. But that's not what made me hesitate. I saw the driver's face.

I wasn't close enough to see if there was a feather earring. But hell if it didn't look like the same bearded guy I saw walking out of Jim Greene's office. And hell if that didn't look like a gun in his hand.

I needed to lose him. I made a succession of turns, trying to call in my location as I drove. I worried about coming out in a busy area, driving on the main streets. I didn't want him shooting at me and missing, hitting someone else—hell, I didn't want him shooting at me, period. Then again, if he was going to the trouble to kill me, having a witness or two might not be a bad idea.

Having a lot of witnesses would be better.

Turning onto a dead-end street, however, really sucked.

The city of Berkeley closed off certain streets with giant

cement blockades in order to allow pedestrian traffic through, but no vehicles. Good for the homeowners who didn't have to deal with commuter thoroughfares. Not good for cops being chased by killers.

I needed a plan of action. The end of the street was coming up fast. I looked in my rearview mirror, just as the suspect's vehicle turned down the street. I didn't have time to think. I hit the gas, drove to the dead end. Slammed the brakes. The front end shook as I came to a stop. I pulled the keys, grabbed my purse, then got the hell out. I didn't bother shutting the door. I didn't look back. Just ran between the cement blockades to the street beyond.

20

I heard the screech of tires on pavement.

I dared a glance back. Saw the blue car skid to a stop behind mine.

No time to think. Just run.

I turned the corner, out of sight. Darted toward the house on my left. Ran down the driveway into the backyard. An older home, brick. The garage was separate and I ran toward the far side of it.

Another dead end.

Don't know what I expected, but I was stuck. I drew my gun, hunkered down. Tried to catch my breath.

My heart pounded. Even more so when I heard the heavy footfall of someone running. Then silence as they stopped. Probably trying to decide what direction I'd taken.

Dare I pull out my cell phone? Call Berkeley PD? I decided against it. Even if the dispatcher could hear me over my labored breathing, so could the suspect.

"Kate Gillespie?" the man shouted. He was definitely in front of the house. "I'm here to help!"

Yeah, right. I wasn't about to give up my position unless I saw a Berkeley PD patrol car behind a uniformed officer. I glanced around, hoping for an escape route. The yard was neat, tidy, an orange tree in the center of the lawn. No cover or concealment.

I looked toward the house, the lace curtains in the window. Now was a good time for a miracle, I thought, hearing the sirens in the distance, growing louder.

A comforting sound, but useless. They'd find my car and have no idea which way I went.

A movement in the window caught my attention. The lace curtains moving. A moment later, a panel cut into the back door opened, and a large black lab bounded out. It ran straight toward me.

My heart rate doubled. Please don't let it start barking. Please don't let it attack . . .

It did neither. It stuck its snout near my face, sniffed, then licked my cheek. With my free hand, I reached up, tried to push it back so I could see around it. That was when I saw the gray-haired woman, possibly seventy or so, staring at me through the window. It seemed to me that her gaze dropped to my gun, but only for a moment. She seemed intent on watching what the black lab was doing. Again I tried to push the dog's face away, whispering for it to move. Suddenly it raised its head, then spun around and ran to the edge of the garage. It stopped, gave a low growl, then started barking as the sirens grew louder.

I glanced at the window, at the lady, who was now watching the dog, not me, her hand covering her mouth. She moved away from the window, and a moment later, opened the door a crack and peeked out. "Can I help you, Mister?" she said, over the dog's barking. She was looking toward the end of the garage, at someone out of my view.

Jesus. I gripped my gun tighter, aimed in that direction.

"I'm looking for a lady," I heard the man say.

"Oh. Are you the police?" she asked him, then, "Shadow, hush." The dog's bark turned to a low growl. "That dog has been going crazy. I called your dispatcher and told her I saw a woman. I figured she was a burglar."

"Where?" he asked, and I could hear my heart beating as I waited for her answer.

"Your other officers should be here any second. I gave them this address."

"Where?" he demanded.

"Why, she's hiding across the street in the back yard. The gray house with white trim."

There was a long moment of silence. I couldn't believe it. I wondered if he would . . .

Finally I heard him say, "Uh, thanks. I'll go check it out before they get here. Your . . . dog ain't going after me . . . ?"

"Shadow, stay," she said, firmly.

I heard the man, his footsteps, rather, as he ran down her drive. She remained where she was, then a few seconds later, opened her door wide and motioned for me to come in.

I hesitated. If he came back, she'd be in danger. But when I saw the black lab run up the steps toward her, I was convinced he'd left. The dog seemed protective.

I stood, my limbs feeling shaky. I edged my way to the garage, took a quick look down the drive. All clear, I ran to the back steps. "Thanks," I said, holstering my gun as I entered a small laundry room. "How did you know I wasn't some escaped convict?"

"Shadow was my first clue," she said, patting her thigh. The lab moved to her side, then sat, as she picked up the phone to call 911. "He's got a sixth sense about those things. If he liked you, then I liked you. Of course, it helped when I saw the badge on your belt," she added with a wink. "If you were hiding, I figured you needed help—Yes," she said, into the phone, undoubtedly to the 911 operator. "My name is Nancy. Nancy Rodich-Hodges, and I want to report an officer that needs help."

She confirmed her addresss, then disconnected. "They're the next block over," she said. "Should be right here."

I wanted to laugh. I wanted to cry. I wanted my nausea to pass, now that the adrenaline rush had left my body weak and unwieldy. But there was no time, especially when I heard the sirens wailing outside the front of the house, then shut off as the officers arrived.

Our momentary peace was over as the officers took first my statement, then that of Nancy Rodich-Hodges. The suspect, still unidentified, had fled, not taking a chance that the cops were truly en route, as my savior had somewhat falsely reported. Apparently he'd found it more prudent to hightail it back to his car, which they were now in pursuit of.

I gave Shadow a last pat on the head, then bid my good-bye to Nancy, promising myself that I'd thank her for her brave kindness sometime in the not-so-distant future—when it was safe to do so. An officer gave me a ride back to my car, pulling up beside it, and only then did it occur to me that the driver's door was closed.

"Maybe someone from the neighborhood shut it," he suggested, after I'd told him I'd left it open.

"You mind coming up to the car with me? Just to be sure?"

"Not a problem," he said, exiting.

We walked up together, and I half expected to see our suspect hiding in the backseat. The car was empty.

Almost.

There on the driver's seat was a single, long-stemmed rose.

21

A rose was the last thing I expected to see, and now a definite link to the homicide of Louise Smith—or whatever her real name happened to be. I did not like the implication. That someone had singled me out. Was sending me a message.

As if being chased by a deranged killer wasn't clear enough.

I turned to the Berkeley PD officer. "I don't suppose your Watch Commander would mind if we had a CSI come out, process the car for prints?"

"I take it the rose has significance?"

"Yeah. I just haven't figured out what, yet."

It was another half hour before a CSI came out, snapped a couple photos, then threw some dust on the car. She lifted a nice set of prints from the door frame, where someone might have touched it to close the door.

"Could be yours," she said. "It's a common place to touch a door."

She handed me the card and the moment I saw them, I knew she was wrong. One of the prints had a tented arch, and a line going through it, as though from a scar.

"I'm not a print expert," I said, "but we lifted another set pretty similar. Tented arch, scar."

"Any match?"

"I haven't heard yet."

"If nothing else, we can compare them to these. I'll contact your department as soon as I get to the station."

"I'm not sure, but there might have been a second subject in the car."

"I'll keep that in mind when I'm processing the prints. In the meantime, I think I'll take the rose. See if I can't lift some prints from the stem. Never know."

It was worth a try, I thought, following the officer to Berkeley PD. I definitely felt safer, having a black-and-white escort. Even so, I found myself looking at every blue car, wondering if he was out there, watching, which was the primary reason I didn't head home like I wanted.

By the time we hit the parking lot of the PD, I was feeling slightly better, less shaky. I took out my cell phone to call Lieutenant Andrews, let him know what happened. At the last second I pressed the speed dial for Torrance's cell phone. I wasn't sure why I called him instead. Perhaps it was because I'd told Andrews I would, but I doubted it.

It rang twice before he answered, saying, "Torrance."

"Mike? It's Kate."

"What's wrong?"

I closed my eyes, realizing right then why I'd called him. I didn't have to say a thing. Whether he heard it in my voice, or guessed, it didn't matter. He knew.

I told him what happened and finished with, "I'm at Berkeley PD now."

"Don't leave there. I'll come get you."

"Where are you?"

"Just leaving my office. I'll be there in half an hour."

I didn't argue with him. I didn't have the energy. Instead, I walked into the PD with the officers, waited in the Watch Commander's office, which was empty. I took a moment to call the lieutenant.

That done, I had nothing to do but wait, and I figured I'd

just close my eyes for a minute. The next thing I knew, Torrance was standing over me, his hand on my shoulder. "You okay?" he asked.

I nodded.

His gaze held mine, his look skeptical.

"I'm fine, trust me," I said, rising from my chair. "I'm not even sure why I called you."

"That I do believe," he said. "I'll follow you home."

I was going to say something smart, but the look in his eye stopped me. I grabbed my purse. "I'm parked out back. I don't suppose they caught the guy?"

"No. They found his car. He wasn't in it."

"Great." I started toward the door, feeling very tired and very cranky. "All I want to do is go home, take a shower, and go to bed. Or are you going to tell me that's out, now?"

"Until we know who is after you and he's caught . . ."

I stopped in my tracks, wanting to tell Torrance exactly what I thought about the unfairness of being uprooted from my life, all because some crook with a penchant for roses had it in for me—let alone who the hell was Torrance, thinking he could come in and dictate my life? Anything I was about to say, however, died at his expression. Two things occurred to me in that one moment he held my gaze. First, I was the one who called him. Second, I wasn't the only one whose life was being disrupted.

I took a breath, gave a sigh, and offered, "I'm sorry."

He said nothing. Just gave me one of those half smiles that told me he, too, was sorry, though I had a feeling it was for something entirely different—something I really didn't want to examine right now . . .

He held out his hand, indicating I should precede him out the door.

"Can we at least stop by my place so I can grab a few essentials?"

He glanced at me and I saw the spark of the man he could be when the weight of an investigation wasn't on his shoulders. But any witty remark he was about to make was lost when the Watch Commander called out to me as we neared the lobby.

"We had a car stolen in the vicinity of where our suspect abandoned the blue Lexus," he said, handing me a computer printout of the theft report. "Not sure if it's related, but too much of a coincidence not to think so."

"Thanks," I said, taking the report.

I scanned it and had a feeling he was right.

The stolen car was a black Lexus.

Torrance followed me to my place, where a Berkeley PD officer was standing by on the off chance that our suspect might decide to show up there before I'd gotten the hell out.

As Torrance and I walked up the steps, I heard a loud meow. Dinky, the landlord's oversized orange tabby, scurried past us, waiting for me at the top of the porch. I leaned down, scooped her up with one hand, and then unlocked the door with the other.

"Anything I can help you with?" Torrance asked when we were inside.

"You can get Dinky some milk, while I pack a few things," I said, handing him the cat.

I left him in the kitchen and went to my bedroom, pulling a suitcase out of my closet and putting it on the bed. I kept the basics in my car, toothbrush, toothpaste, underwear, for the unexpected overnighters that came about as a result of some investigation, and would grab that bag on the way out.

I figured on two days' worth of clothes, and pajamas, and threw in some jeans, wondering if I should pack a turtleneck. Since my bedroom overlooked the street below, I glanced out, trying to get a feel for the weather. The police cruiser, I noticed, was parked about two houses down, the officer writing a report, his clipboard balanced against the steering wheel. In some ways I missed those days, patrol, the constant calls, the endless reports . . .

My gaze drifted with the memories of untold graveyards. That was when I saw a black Lexus cruising slowly up the hill, five car lengths separating him from the parked police car, the officer seemingly unaware.

Maybe it wasn't the suspect's car. Maybe he would drive right past. But if he was willing to come after me in broad daylight—hell, he'd already killed the banker in broad daylight—what chance did the officer have, just sitting there?

"Torrance!" I unlocked the window, pulled it open to warn the officer. Before I could say a word, the Lexus stopped suddenly, pulled into a driveway, backed out, then sped off in the opposite direction.

"What happened?" Torrance said, running into the room.

"I saw a black Lexus driving up the street. He may have spotted the officer. Taken off. Assuming it was him."

Torrance looked out the window, then closed and locked it. "All the more reason to get you out of here, and soon. I'll call Berkeley PD and let them know."

"I'm almost done," I said, throwing a few extra things in the suitcase, then zipping it up, weather be damned. I didn't know how long this was going to take, and if worse came to worst, I could buy something.

While Torrance notified the PD of what had just occurred, I took one last look around, grabbed a coat, and waited for him to finish. When he hung up, I said, "I'm ready. All we need is the case files and my overnight bag out of my car."

Torrance picked up the suitcase. "Let's go."

"Any place in particular?"

There was a slight hesitation as he looked me in the eye. "My place," he said, and I wondered what I was getting myself into.

22

Of course, I tried to act normal. I'd never been to Torrance's home. I knew he lived somewhere in Marin County, a condominium, I believed, and we were halfway there when I started to rethink the contents of my suitcase. Suddenly everything I packed seemed wrong—maybe because I wasn't expecting to be spending the night with the man I wanted to sleep with.

"You sure you wouldn't rather drop me off at Scolari's?" I asked, despite the fact that we were crossing the Richmond-San Rafael Bridge and it would be miles out of the way.

"What are you worried about, Kate?"

"Nothing," I said a little too quickly.

He gave me a sidelong glance before returning his attention to the road. After a few agonizing seconds of silence, he said, "We have several cases to read, my partner will be meeting us there later tonight, and Scolari smokes." This last was added as if that settled the matter.

I supposed it did. It effectively stopped any argument I had about where we were going, and it certainly clarified that our time together was purely business. Even the kiss with Paolini was business. Come to think of it, every relationship I had, whether real or perceived, was business, and I wondered how the hell my life had become so screwed up.

The remainder of our drive was quiet. It tends to get that way when you're waching the mirrors, wondering if you're being followed, and I was glad when we reached Marin County. I was curious to see where Torrance lived, how he spent his time away from work. I was not anxious, however, to be alone with him. Despite being a man of few words, he had this uncanny way of probing into the depths of my soul, making me learn things about myself that I didn't want to face . . .

And several minutes after he left the freeway, then pulled into the garage of his hillside condo, I wondered if that was not the gist of what he'd meant by asking me what I was running away from . . .

He opened his door, exited, and started to get the things from the trunk.

Me, I just sat there. I couldn't believe that it had finally hit me. Was I running away from Torrance because he made me face things about myself?

I didn't have time to answer, since Torrance already had my suitcase in hand and was unlocking the condo's door.

I got out, grabbed my overnight bag, as he turned on the lights, deactivated the alarm, then held the door for me. "The code is my old badge number," he said. "In case you need it."

We walked past a guest bath, as well as a bedroom, and on through a short hallway that opened into the main living area, consisting of the kitchen and what I would call a family room, except that Torrance didn't have any family that I knew of. I vaguely remember hearing that he'd left home as a teen, had lived with a foster family, but couldn't remember where I'd heard it. There was definitely that bachelor feel. A soft distressed leather sofa and two matching arm chairs facing a fireplace. A sliding glass door led out to a small balcony, shaded by eucalyptus trees. A set of wind chimes, tiny bits of stained glass, hung on the eaves outside the patio door—I loved wind chimes, wished I had a place to hang them myself, and was pleased that Torrance had given in to this small flight of fancy. It was an unusually still day for the north bay, however, and they were silent. I resisted the temptation to walk out, run my fingers through them myself. Inside, there were pictures of horses on the walls, and over the mantel a winter painting of a cowboy on horseback, watching over a herd of cattle as evening fell. A single star hung in the deepening sky and there was a light dusting of snow on the ground.

I was drawn to the painting, but before I could figure out why, Torrance said, "I'll put your suitcase in your room and let you get settled."

"I can get it," I said, but he had already started up the stairs, and so I followed. There were two bedrooms at the top, one accessed by double doors. Torrance opened the single door, entered the room and put the suitcase on the double-sized bed. "There are towels in the hall cabinet. I'll put some in the guest bath for you."

"Thanks," I said, as the phone rang.

I stood aside, and he moved past me into his bedroom to answer the phone. I tried not to listen, but clearly heard him say, "Something came up . . . I'm sorry . . . I had to leave the city before—Yes, Chloe, it's work, again . . ."

Not wanting to intrude—for more reasons than I cared to think about—I decided to unpack a few of my things and use the bathroom to freshen up. When I'd finished, he was already downstairs in the kitchen, breaking open some eggs in a bowl. "Are you hungry?" he asked.

"Starved."

He smiled. "You have your choice of cheese omelet or scrambled eggs. Not exactly the most inspiring choices . . ."

"The omelet sounds great. Can I help you with something?"

"Grating cheese."

"Deal."

Fifteen minutes later, we were sitting down to breakfast at dinner, and we talked about the case and my recent witness interviews.

When I finished, Torrance said, "We seem to have a lot of hearsay about a woman we can't verify an identity for."

"Reynard's wife mentioned that Lucia had even called herself a 'mechanic.' "

"Maybe she was more of a broker."

"A broker?"

"Someone who set up things, but didn't actually get her own hands dirty."

"That's certainly a possibility," I said, getting up to clear my plate. "Especially when you consider the trouble she went to in order to get Louise into that parking lot," I said, rinsing the dish, and putting it in the dishwasher. That done, I picked up the binder containing all the reports from my shooting at the Twin Palms. I wanted to find some link between that case and the others—independent of the fact that the same gun had been used there and at the bank robbery.

Torrance took another binder and started reading through that. It was quiet and comfortable, the two of us sitting there, across the table from each other . . .

I put that fantasy out of my head—far too domestic—and I concentrated on the case, stifling a yawn.

"Coffee?"

"Definitely. Case review makes for some dry reading."

I got up with Torrance and cleared the remaining dishes, putting them in the dishwasher, while he set about making coffee.

Since there were a couple of minutes of downtime before the coffee was finished, I wandered into the living room and took a better look at the painting over the hearth. "I love this," I said. "Where'd you get it?"

"It was a gift."

"Really?"

"It's supposed to be me."

I could certainly see a resemblance and took a closer look at the signature. Chloe Demetrias. The name I remembered well. It belonged to someone I called the Greek Goddess. She was an amazingly beautiful young woman I'd seen Torrance with on occasion, which made me think about the phone call I'd overheard upstairs while I was unpacking. I assumed she was the one who had called, who Torrance had apologized to, because work got in the way—work being me.

Torrance and I had never said anything about an exclusive, date-only-each-other thing. It never occurred to me that I needed to say anything. But after hearing that call upstairs, I began to wonder what the extent of Torrance's relationship with this woman was. Looking at the painting, I wasn't sure I wanted to know. She had captured what he was about, which, in my opinion, meant she knew him quite well. A solitary man, doing his duty, no matter the time, no matter the place, and I realized that was why I liked the painting when I saw it. What I didn't like was the feeling that someone else knew this about him, had discovered it, perhaps, before I had.

I was jealous.

I was jealous of this woman I'd seen twice and met once.

I was jealous of her beauty and her talent, and that Torrance had seen fit to hang this painting in so prominent a place in his life. I hated that I admired it, that it was good, that she had painted it . . .

"Half and half okay?" Torrance asked from the kitchen.

"That's fine," I said, not taking my eyes off the cowboy, thinking that what I hated most of all was that I was being so ridiculously juvenile about the whole thing.

"The painting's not all that fascinating, Kate."

If he only knew . . . I turned and looked at him, saw him watching me from the kitchen. "What is she to you?"

He looked at me for a very long time, before he finally crossed the room. Then, his voice quiet, he asked, "Why do you want to know?"

"Why?" I wanted to tell him to just answer the question, damn it, but what came out of my mouth was, "I—I felt something in my stomach when Paolini kissed me. This— this flutter thing . . ."

My voice died as I realized what I'd said and I counted several heartbeats in the ensuing silence.

What had I done?

"A flutter?"

I nodded.

"Do you think you were attracted to him?" His voice seemed cold, hard.

I knew right then the answer was no—I'd always known it was no—but I couldn't speak, and he closed the distance between us, took me into his arms, and before I could say another word, kissed me.

23

The kiss started slow, as Torrance threaded his fingers through my hair with one hand, traced my spine with the other.

My breath caught, my heart raced, and he deepened the kiss, brought my hips against his. The touch of him against me, the heat, sent a shiver through me. My knees went weak and I put my arms around him.

And then he moved his mouth from mine, brought his lips to my ear, whispered against them. "Do you feel a flutter?"

My brain refused to work. "A what?"

He took his hand from my hair, trailed it down my neck, across my breast, kissed me again as he splayed his hand against my stomach, sending every nerve rippling. And then he said, "You told me you felt a flutter when Paolini kissed you. Did my kiss make your stomach flutter?"

"No," I said.

He raised his brows.

I sighed, leaned my head against his chest, soaking up the warmth. I felt like a cat in a window, purely content. "It was more like an earthquake."

He just held me for several seconds. Finally, he pulled slightly away, lifting my chin so that I was looking right at him.

Whatever he'd been about to say or do was lost. The doorbell rang at that precise moment, and he smiled, somewhat satisfied if I had to interpret it.

"Aren't you going to get the door?"

He stroked my cheek with his thumb, before letting go. "It's undoubtedly my partner."

And as I watched him walk into the entryway, it occurred to me that he had yet to answer my original question. I looked up at the painting, the cowboy staring out at the single star in the sky, and I wondered about the woman who had painted it. Who was Chloe Demetrias, and what was or had been her relationship with Torrance?

I decided I had to know the answer. Unfortunately, with the arrival of Torrance's partner, it was going to be a while, and I walked over to the door pretending to act very pleased to see Jackie Parrish standing there, a notebook in her hand. Torrance shut the door and set the alarm, and she moved past him, into the foyer.

"We were making coffee," he said, when he showed her into the kitchen.

She gave a nod. "I could use a cup."

As Torrance got out a third mug and poured her a fresh cup, it occurred to me that she reminded me of some sort of alien species on *Star Trek*. It wasn't that she had no emotions—more that she didn't know how to use them, I thought, as he poured the half and half in, and handed the cup to her.

"Thanks." Her cup in hand, she walked into the family room. I was just taking a sip from my mug when she stopped in front of the painting over the mantel, looked up at it and said, "This is the picture your foster sister painted for you?"

I somehow managed to swallow the coffee without choking, and I glanced at Torrance, who, I might add, would not look at me. "That's the one," he said, his voice entirely too quiet.

I wasn't sure what to make of it. He had let me believe

something entirely untrue about someone, and I felt like an idiot. Not only that, but here was his new partner, a woman he couldn't have known for more than a week or two at best, and she knew about Chloe Demetrias. She knew that Torrance had a foster sister who painted. She knew that there was an oil painting of a cowboy on his wall that was supposed to be him, and I pictured the two of them sitting around, talking about the parts of Torrance's life I had always wondered about—his past, his present, his dreams . . .

Pretty much everything, I realized, not sure if what I felt was anger or sadness, or maybe both. Right now, though, I had to get past it. We had work to do and I moved to the table and the open file of my Twin Palms shooting. I'd studied it for weeks while recuperating, trying to find out who it was who'd shot me. I'd taken it out again after reading about the fundraiser being held at Etienne Reynard's, in preparation for my appearance on *San Francisco's Most Wanted*. But as I looked at it here in Torrance's kitchen, there was one name that had been lost in the long list of witnesses present at the motel the night I was shot. One name that had seemed as insignificant as all the others.

Until now.

The name of Louise Smith—my transsexual witness from the parking lot. My murder victim found in Lucia Paolini's green Jaguar.

"Look at this," I said to Torrance. I turned the binder around for him to see as I put my finger next to Louise Smith's name.

"Wasn't that the aka that Lucia also used?" he asked.

"Yes. Which gives us two possibilities. Either Lucia or our transsexual victim, Louise Smith, could have been present at that shooting."

Parrish joined us, and we discussed the ramifications of this knowledge, after which I scanned the other cases, trying to see if either name popped up there. Parrish and Torrance each took a case and started reading. I was going through Fiona Winchester's murder case, and every now and then, I felt Torrance's gaze resting on me. I told myself to concentrate and when I finally managed to do that, I found out a few interesting things.

There was an envelope, manila, in the back of the binder, that wasn't there before, and I assumed Rocky had stuck it there, when he was gathering the case files together. I opened it, pulled out one burglary report, and one suspicious circumstances report, both related to the Winchester case. The burglary was at the Winchester home about two days before Fiona had been killed—a stereo was taken. The suspicious circumstance took place at Fiona and Kyla Greene's apartment the day before, this one reported by a neighbor, who thought she saw someone coming out when the two women weren't home, though both Fiona and the real Kyla Greene had been questioned by the cops, and reported that nothing had been taken.

I handed the reports to Torrance. He read through them, before passing them on to Parrish. "Someone looking for something?" he asked.

"Seems that way," I said, moving on to the Marcel Etienne suicide, where I found out a few more interesting facts.

One, when Etienne had allegedly committed suicide, he had left a handwritten note to his partner, apologizing for bringing the drugs into the restaurant. The note had been checked, determined to have been written by him and to contain only his fingerprints—something that in my experience didn't mean squat. I knew better than to take that at face value.

Two, he was in a car leased from Jim Greene's car lot, and Greene was being looked at as an accomplice in the cocaine dealing—though that was certainly no revelation.

Three, Lucia and Nick Paolini were eating dinner at the restaurant that night and were listed as witnesses. Lucia was

definitely one of the common threads and I went back to
Fiona's statement to see if there was anything that might
stand out, since Fiona was the person who found Etienne's
body. She gave an initial statement—and was murdered just
a few days later.

It was pretty cut and dried. Fiona had come to the restaurant to pick up her paycheck. Marcel Etienne had called her
a couple hours before. When she got there, a cook had told
her he saw Etienne walk into the storage building behind the
restaurant. She went out there, opened the door, found him
passed out in his car, the engine running.

The entire scenario bothered me, but I couldn't place why.
Parrish got up to rinse out her coffee cup, then refill it with
water, and I glanced at Torrance, saw him watching me. I
looked away, still not sure about my feelings yet, and a moment later, Parrish was sitting at the table and it was back to
business.

"I'm done with the bank robbery," she said, pushing the
binder to the middle of the table. "Frankly, I don't think I
can read much more. Not without falling asleep."

"You sure you want to drive back to the city tonight?"
Torrance asked her.

She yawned. "Cup of coffee will get me back. I think."

"There's a spare room down the hall. You're welcome to it."

"Might not be a bad idea. I'll get my bag from the car."

She left to get her things, and it turned exceedingly quiet.

"Kate—"

"You know," I said, holding up my hand, "I really don't
think I can talk about this right now."

He stood, held my gaze for several seconds, then finally
said, "Good night, then," and left me sitting there at the
table, completely alone.

I pretended great interest in my cases when Parrish returned from the car and he showed her to her room, then left
for his own.

Another fine chapter in Kate Gillespie's book of failed relationships, I thought, looking over at the painting, knowing full well I should have given Torrance a chance to explain. But I had a feeling that what he was about to say was not what I wanted to hear right then—that, as usual, I was the one who had jumped to the wrong conclusion. I had created Chloe as the competition in my own mind, and there was no one to blame but myself.

Of course, had he *mentioned* that she was merely his foster sister, not a date, that night I saw him with her at Murphy's Law, or even later at her parents' restaurant, I might not be sitting here alone right now.

The thought did little to comfort me. Torrance had a whole past I knew nothing about. I didn't realize he had a foster sister. I didn't realize a lot about him, and I was frankly a little perturbed that his new partner was better informed. I ignored the fact that she probably helped to do his background investigation when he had applied to the FBI. That, I decided, was besides the point.

I stood. I was going to tell him exactly what I thought, and walked upstairs to do just that. I might have succeeded had it not hit me what had been bothering me about the Marcel Etienne suicide.

24

I stopped midway, turned on my heel, headed back down the stairs, and opened the binder.

Fiona Winchester had started off her career as a waitress at Etienne Reynard's, before Jim Greene allegedly recruited her to work for his escort service. I had no verification that she was running drugs for Marcel Etienne while she was a waitress, but if so, would she leave the one for the other? Perhaps in her mind, escorting was less of an evil than drug running?

Why then did she need to go to Etienne Reynard's to pick up a paycheck? I had to imagine that two weeks of waitress pay was not about to come close to what she made as an escort in a single night, or even what she must surely have been paid to run drugs for Marcel Etienne. And if she was running drugs, no way would he be paying her on the books—which made it seem odd that she'd make a special trip just to pick up a measly check for waitressing. And why have her pick it up on that particular day? Unless it was an excuse to get her there to use her for an alibi? Or perhaps she was lying and there never was a check?

Which meant she knew or suspected that Etienne was murdered . . . ?

Which would certainly be motive enough to have her killed.

And that, of course, set me to thinking about other things. Such as Torrance's suggestion—if what Paolini said about Lucia was true—that Lucia was more a broker of hits than the one who actually pulled the trigger. Which then made me wonder about the bank robbery, and the death of her lover. If she had brokered the hit, it explained why she had pretended to be Kyla Greene, when we'd showed up at Greene's apartment. The FBI suspected from the beginning that it wasn't a robbery at all. That the whole thing was a set-up to have Millhouse killed. A hit. The question remained: What was the motive for the hit?

I thought about the call I received to get me to the bank, the fact the caller knew about Scolari dragging me from the hallway. The caller, assuming it was Louise Smith, either knew the exact words, or someone told her what was needed to get me to that bank parking lot at that very place and time to witness the robbery, the killing of Millhouse, and the suspect fleeing the bank.

The same weapon had been used in that shooting, the murder of Fiona Winchester, and the slug fired at me at the Twin Palms. But if those were all hits, or attempted hits, mine being the one that failed, why then was I set up to meet this Louise Smith in the bank parking lot?

Someone, Lucia perhaps, had a purpose for my presence.

A witness to prove Lucia hadn't pulled the trigger, should someone try to point the finger at her?

Or was it something else?

A chilling thought entered my mind, sickened me.

I prayed I was wrong . . .

But we had been set up. We were brought to the scene at the exact time of the robbery. We were told to be in an exact place at an exact time. Korsakoff had said that the woman who met with Louise had insisted they do it her way . . . The suspect had entered the bank from one direction, and left by another—by the route *we* had been set up to watch . . . We'd had a clear shot, up until the moment that bystander had gotten in the way—stepped into our line of fire. Our suspect had made his escape by taking her hostage . . .

I don't know how long I sat there, several minutes at least. I told myself it was ridiculous. The logistics to set up something like that . . .

But if true, it was pretty apparent. We were supposed to have killed him . . .

True or not, because of a stroke of fate—an innocent passerby—the suspect got away . . . Only to come after me on a different day. Because someone sent him? Or because he knew I could ID him?

Tired, and unable to come up with a clear answer, I rose, turned out the lights, and stared out the sliding glass door into the dark. We were above the freeway and I watched the cars, the tiny red and white trails of light, speeding by on the 101.

I stood there for I don't know how long, when something caught my eye down on the hill. A movement.

I stilled.

Something—or someone—was down there.

I watched. Waited.

Perhaps a deer or a dog, I decided, when I saw nothing further. Even so, I checked the slider. Locked.

And just to be safe, I checked the garage door and then the front door before I went up, used the bathroom, changed into pajamas and climbed into bed.

When I finally closed my eyes, felt sleep overtake me, I found myself at the top of the stairs at the Twin Palms, Scolari in front of me. I knew I was dreaming, knew this had happened before, but I couldn't force myself to wake . . . "Don't step on the condom," Scolari said, pushing me to the side, his voice sounding a million miles away.

I must have tripped, hit my shoulder, because I felt it burning. Then I saw the man duck into the apartment door—

•

but it was above me now, as though the world had tilted. There was pain and screaming. Loud voices, people running. And I saw the chair, the chair I hadn't wanted to remember, and the woman just sitting there, staring.

So calm, amid the chaos.

"Officer down! Officer down!" Scolari yelling in my ear. Dragging me back, his gun out, pointing it. We slammed into the wall, fell, and I saw her again, just a glimpse . . . Suddenly her face changed. Different, yet not so different . . .

And she was holding something, something I knew I needed to see.

I woke. Sat up, my heart beating hard in my chest.

I didn't move, just sat there in the dark, told myself it was the same dream I'd had before . . . but when I closed my eyes, I saw what it was I had blocked from my mind.

My God, I thought. No wonder Louise had seemed so familiar to me when I'd first seen her in the parking lot. Though I vaguely remembered that someone had been sitting there in that chair the night I was shot, never before had I actually placed a face to that image. And when I finally had, I couldn't be sure of who it was I had seen. Lucia Paolini or Louise Smith?

I sat there for quite some time, wondering. Maybe my dream had merit, and maybe it was just that. A dream . . .

What I needed right now was some sleep.

No such luck. All I did was toss and turn with the knowledge, and finally decided to get a glass of water.

I got up, opened my door, stepped out onto the landing. It was dark and took me a moment to get my bearings. I glanced over, saw the double doors to Torrance's room, closed.

How tempting . . .

25

Just knock. Reach out. Open his door . . .

But I couldn't do it. Yes, I wanted to sleep with him. And, though I was pretty certain that he felt the same way, the knowledge that Parrish was downstairs tempered my desire. That and the fact that I was the biggest sort of chicken, afraid to tell him what I really wanted. Besides, I couldn't get the current case out of my head. This was not the time to start an affair.

With a sigh, I turned in the other direction, started down the stairs, then paused at the bottom, at the little green light flashing on the alarm panel.

It should have been solid red. Which meant two things, the first being that someone had deactivated the alarm.

The second being that somewhere in the house there was a door or window . . . open.

I froze on the landing. Had Torrance forgotten to set the alarm? I doubted it. He was too careful to allow a slip like that. And he certainly would not have gone to bed, when the panel clearly showed an open door or window.

My gaze lit on the front door, saw it was slightly ajar.

Jesus.

Before I had a chance to move, it swung open.

Jackie Parrish stood there, her hand on the knob. "What are you doing up?" she asked.

"Thirsty," I said, relieved to see who it was, ticked she had scared the crap out of me, and surprised she couldn't hear the pounding of my heart. "Why were you outside?"

"I was checking my car. I thought I forgot to lock it," she said, closing the door and turning the deadbolt. She held a paper, eyed it, then entered the alarm code that Torrance had given her.

Other than that her hands were empty.

"No car keys?"

She punched in the last number, then looked over at me. Her expression never wavered. "Aren't you being just a bit paranoid?"

"Maybe because someone's tried to kill me twice in as many days."

"Trust me. I'm not your threat," she said, then started off toward her room. She stopped about midway, her gaze direct, unemotional. "Is there something going on between you and Torrance?"

I said nothing at first, trying to figure out why she wanted to know—making me glad I hadn't knocked on his door, in case she could hear it . . . Then again, maybe it was just plain curiosity on her part, and I decided to go with that route, so I laughed as though the thought of me and Torrance together was no big deal. "Nothing at all," I said.

"Interesting." That was it, and I watched her walk off, trying to interpret exactly what she meant. Was she going to make a move if I didn't? Or was it her belief that Torrance would set his sights elsewhere?

Hell, I thought as I walked into the kitchen. I got my water, stood there and drank it, eyeing the painting, the lone cowboy. Could he go for someone like Parrish? They were similar in many ways—coolly professional, though I knew from experience that Torrance warmed up, and quite nicely. Why then could I not get my act together?

It was a question I didn't need to ask. I knew the answer. The only thing standing between me and Torrance was . . . me.

Every stumbling block, every stalling tactic, every perceived threat, I had put it there. I couldn't even throw myself at him in a proper manner.

I turned off the light, telling myself that Torrance wasn't likely to wait around forever. Hell, I was surprised he'd stood by me this long . . .

I put the glass down, determined to take care of things, talk to Torrance right then—except that I heard the soft tinkling of the wind chimes just outside the sliding glass door.

Only one problem.

There didn't seem to be any wind.

26

Any other time I might have admired the view, the lights sparkling from the houses on the hills around us and from the freeway below. All I could see, though, was the silhouette of the eucalyptus trees, their leaves hanging like twisted, gnarled daggers, not one of them moving. The air was still, as it had been earlier, but I had definitely heard the wind chimes ringing.

Something had caused them to move.

Let it be a raccoon, I thought, grateful I had turned off the lights after I'd gotten the water. But I was literally trapped in the kitchen, unable to move without being seen from the patio—if in fact someone was out there. Please let it be my imagination. But I had not imagined it. And a raccoon would have one hell of a time reaching down from the second story to bat at a set of wind chimes on a balcony below.

I looked around for the phone, wondered if I could get to it, call 911. I saw it on the coffee table, right in front of the patio door. No way was I walking out there. Exposing myself to view. I'd already been shot at once. Had no idea if whoever was out there wouldn't take a shot at me right through the glass door. I couldn't get to my gun upstairs, not without moving, exposing my position. At least the alarm was set. I'd seen Parrish do that.

Unless they knew how to bypass an alarm . . .

I glanced at the kitchen window. There was nothing beneath it, just a drop to the hillside . . .

I stilled. Listened. Heard what sounded like a movement on the balcony . . . Heard my own heart beating faster . . .

They were after me—but there were two other people in this house who needed to be warned. Two other people who could be harmed . . .

I heard a scrape. Like the sound of a foot on the patio. Only one thing to do, I realized. I reached over to the kitchen window. I pressed the latch. Slid it open.

Set off the alarm.

The screech of it pierced my eardrums.

I closed and locked the window, covered my ears. A moment later, Parrish tore out of her room, her gun drawn.

"What happened?" she yelled over the alarm.

I pointed to the balcony. "I think someone is—Someone was out there," I shouted as Torrance ran down the stairs, gun in hand.

He moved beside me, said loudly in my ear. "Go shut off the alarm."

He and Parrish, their guns at the ready, approached the balcony, Parrish looking calm, as though this were routine. Torrance switched on the outside light. The balcony was empty. I left. What the hell was the code? Badge number. I shut off the alarm, glanced at the front door, worried, saw it was still locked, then hurried back through to the kitchen.

Torrance opened the slider, and he and Parrish stepped out, checking over the side the six-foot drop to the ground. They came back in, and he locked the door. "What's going on?" he asked, his voice quiet, his relief evident that we were all standing in one piece, though he had yet to assess what the danger might be.

He was dressed in pajama bottoms, and I took a breath, put aside the fact that I'd already made a fool out of myself once in front of him tonight over that damn painting. My ears were still ringing from the alarm and I felt myself start to shake from the loss of adrenaline. I leaned against the counter, trying to opt for calm. "I heard the wind chimes."

Parrish gave me a quizzical look. "Wind chimes?"

"You see any wind out there?"

They both looked. So did I, certain that with the way my luck was running, a breeze would pick up right then. But the eucalyptus trees, with their dagger-shaped leaves, were still.

Torrance reached down, picked up the portable phone from the coffee table, and called the sheriff's office.

That done, all we could do was wait. We were not exactly dressed to go searching the premises, but Torrance went up, put on some sweats anyway. Five minutes later, two deputies were at the door. Torrance spoke briefly with them. One of them walked over to the patio, stepped out, looked at the wind chimes. "Someone could definitely have bumped them," he said.

His partner, older by a few years, with five hash marks up his uniform sleeve, said, "If he jumped off, he's going to have a hard time getting back to the street. Property's blocked off by a wrought iron fence on either side of the condos." And then, as partners who have worked together for a long time often do, they looked at each other, both said, "Dog," and the senior officer called for a canine unit.

Sometime later, there was a knock at the door.

Torrance looked out the window, saw it was one of the deputies, the one with all the hash marks on his sleeve. He turned off the alarm, then opened the door. Parrish and I both walked up just as the deputy said, "The dog alerted on our suspect. Looks like he was trying to make his way to a black Lexus parked down at the end of the street. Comes back stolen out of Berkeley."

"So he's in custody?" Torrance asked.

"En route to the hospital now. Dog took a good chunk out of his thigh—he'll be walking with a limp for quite some time. But then, that's what he gets for pulling a gun, wouldn't you say?"

Worked for me. "Did you get a name?" I asked.

"David Cole. Short, thin guy, gray hair, beard . . ."

"Earring?" I asked, though I was pretty certain it was the same guy.

"Yeah. Some little spike thing hanging from his ear. We'll run his prints, even if we have to ink them in the hospital. My guess is they'll stitch him up real quick like, give him a couple aspirin, and release him for jail posthaste. Our ER folks don't take too kindly to guys pulling guns on cops, you know what I mean?"

Pretty much the consensus with most emergency rooms, I thought, as he got the contact information from the three of us for his report. It was close to two after he left, and if truth be told, I was feeling rather smug when Parrish said, "Good call, Gillespie."

"Thanks."

Torrance glanced at the clock on the kitchen wall. "We should all try to get some rest. Early day tomorrow."

"Good night," I said, and I went to bed, eventually drifting off into a restless sleep, bothered by something I couldn't name.

Torrance was in the kitchen making toast when I walked in, and I wondered what he thought about that little episode last night—not the arrest of the suspect, but the thing about the painting. As usual, I was unable to gauge his thoughts. He did, however, look well rested, unlike me. I tossed and turned all night, and if I wasn't reliving the nightmare I'd had of the Twin Palms shooting, I was thinking about him—wondering what he was thinking about me jealous of his foster sister.

Definitely not one of my brighter moves, but then, I wasn't exactly known for my finesse when it came to relationships with the opposite sex.

He handed me a cup of coffee and some buttered toast. "Gourmet breakfast."

"Compared to what I usually get, it is," I said, as Parrish walked in.

"Morning," she said.

"Coffee?" Torrance asked her.

"Definitely. I kept thinking I heard something outside all night after the deputies finally left. I hope you two slept better than I did."

I know I didn't, and I glanced at Torrance wondering if he at least had the grace to lose a little sleep.

There were no circles under his eyes, though, and he avoided the question completely, saying, "Smart move, setting off the alarm."

"Thanks."

Parrish stirred her coffee. "I was thinking about it last night. It'd make a good scenario for Hogan's Alley," she said, referring to the town set up at the FBI Academy, used for training purposes. She glanced at Torrance, her expression so clinical. "Somewhat like that exercise on communication?"

"Which one?"

She raised a brow and I almost laughed. The woman was pure Vulcan—straight off the set of *Star Trek*—and I wondered if she even knew how to smile. "Yeah. Sometimes they get creative. The one I'm talking about is the bank robbery, where you're taken hostage, and you have to communicate who the suspects are without letting the suspects know."

"We did a few of those," he said. "I was killed once or twice."

"Better there than for real on the street." She looked right at me, then. "Good job. Scared the crap out of me when the alarm went off, but well worth the result."

"Thanks," I said, surprised, not only by her praise, but that she'd been scared. I *never* would have guessed.

Torrance eyed the clock. "We should leave now if we hope to get through the traffic."

Five minutes later, we were ready to go, standing in the garage while Torrance set the alarm, then pressed the opener for the garage door. It rolled up slowly, the motor grinding overhead.

I yawned. "We are going to stop for coffee en route? One cup didn't quite do it for me," I said, as Parrish walked toward the opening.

She stopped suddenly and said, "What the hell?"

I looked out, stared, not believing.

There were rose petals.

Everywhere.

27

Any thought that the rose petals had been overlooked the night before, perhaps missed by the deputies after they had arrested the suspected hit man, ended when we also found rose petals on Torrance's porch. Those had definitely not been there when the deputies had driven off last night. Which meant someone came after. Whether this latest suspect had been watching remained to be seen. There were no signs of forced entry, nothing to indicate that whoever had left the rose petals had tried to get in, however. Even so, we weren't taking any chances that the suspect wasn't lurking around the area, and we called the sheriff's office once again.

Parrish eyed the deputies out front, as one bent down, picked up some rose petals and put them into a paper bag. "Obviously," she said, "the first suspect followed you two when you were in Berkeley. I'd like to know who the second person is. And what the significance of the rose petals could be."

"They may have something to do with the rose petals we found on the body of Louise Smith, the transsexual."

"Some sort of sick message," she said. "And what looks like a warning."

"Whatever the reason," Torrance said, "I'll feel more comfortable when we get back to the Hall."

We left shortly after the deputies finished taking their report, Torrance and I in his car, and Parrish in hers.

Torrance looked over at me as we drove south on 101. "What's on your mind, Kate?"

Wondering what was on his, I thought. Too chicken to ask, I said, "I need more coffee."

"I meant about last night."

Obviously he had more guts than I.

Figured. I thought about it for a moment, closing my eyes from sheer exhaustion. I knew what it was he really wanted to discuss. My reaction to Chloe and the painting. "Why'd you let me believe Chloe meant something different to you?"

"Besides my initial amusement that you figured I might be attracted to someone that young?"

I gave a little laugh, my eyes still closed, and I shifted in my seat, feeling comfortable, warm, and tired, a combination that lent itself to one thing only. Sleep. "Yeah," I said, trying my damnedest to stay awake. "Besides that."

"The truth," I heard him say, his voice sounding very far off, "is that sometimes, Kate, you jump into things without looking, and I want nothing more than to shake some sense in you. Make you see . . ."

I don't know if he stopped talking or if I fell asleep, or both. And then I heard him say, "Other times all I want to do is catch you in my arms . . . keep you from falling . . ."

Maybe I *was* dreaming, I don't know, but I felt a smile on my lips. Somehow in this mess that was my life, I had stumbled across a very good thing . . .

When I awoke, it was to the realization that we were no longer moving and the world was lit by fluorescent lights, not the sun. My neck was stiff from having fallen asleep in the car, and I rubbed it, while trying to place the familiarity of our surroundings. "Where are we?"

"Coffee run," Torrance said.

I sat up, finally recognizing the parking garage adjacent to Starbucks. A moment later, I saw Parrish walking toward us, a cardboard carrier in her hands with three coffee cups.

Torrance opened the window. She handed him some money and then the carrier. "Your change and your coffee," she said, removing one of the cups for herself.

"Thanks."

"See you at the Hall in a couple."

She walked to her car and Torrance handed one of the cups to me. "Figured you might need this," he said.

"Figured right. I'd swear we left Marin only five minutes ago."

He looked down at my coffee cup, a definite sparkle in his eye as he started the car. "Aren't you going to drink?"

"Why?" I asked, immediately suspicious.

"You're the one who told me mochas were better than sex. I want to know if it's still true."

"It is if you aren't getting any."

He laughed, put the car in reverse and backed out of the space.

Parrish was waiting for us in the conference room when we got there, an empty seat beside her and one across the table from her between Zim and Rocky. There were twelve people present. The entire Homicide Detail, and a few inspectors from Robbery. A dry erase board on one wall had a timeline of the homicides drawn upon it, and there were a few charts pinned up on the bulletin board as well.

Lieutenant Andrews eyed me as I took the seat next to Rocky. "You look tired, Gillespie. I thought I sent you home to get some rest?"

"Had a couple unplanned interruptions along the way," I said. "I take it you heard about our suspect running around Marin last night, and the rose petals we found this morning?"

"Parrish told us. One threat out of the way, another still out there. Which means, you step out of this building, even off this floor, you have backup with you, twenty-four seven."

"I get overtime?"

"Don't push it. You come up with anything after reviewing the cases?"

"With the suicide of Reynard's partner, Marcel Etienne. Fiona Winchester allegedly went there to pick up her last paycheck, because Etienne called her, told her it was there. I have a hard time believing, one, that she'd care about a puny paycheck sitting there for weeks on end—so much so, that she'd come down immediately for it. Not when she's getting money from more lucrative sources. Two, if Etienne's so busy getting drunk and snorting coke, could he possibly have taken a moment to realize that Fiona had a check sitting there?"

Andrews nodded. "Logical assumptions. Markowski?"

"Yeah. I finally got a confirmation on Kyla Greene's identity. The woman me and Gillespie talked to at the apartment is definitely not her. The license she showed us was legit, but the thumb print didn't match up to Kyla's old licenses on file. Neither did the photos for that matter. I'd have to say it's looking more and more like our fake Kyla Greene is actually Lucia Paolini." He passed around copies of the licenses, then continued. "I also got the wonderful task of looking into the finances of the restaurant. Once we got the records, it was easy to see they were in a financial bind right around that same time. If Etienne was dealing coke, he wasn't funneling the money into his restaurant, that's for damn sure. Reynard isn't doing much better. Bay Trust coincidentally is holding the note."

"Shipley?"

"Jim Greene's lean mean machines aren't turning much of a profit, either. Haven't been for quite some time. He owes Bay Trust Mutual big bucks and they're getting ready to foreclose."

Andrews looked at Torrance and Parrish. "Your agency have a chance to dig into Bay Trust Mutual?"

"Some," Parrish said, opening her notebook. "It'll take weeks to sort through most of it. Right now we're concentrating on the more obvious accounts, but it's possible that any illegal funds are spread over a number of smaller accounts, perhaps even different financial institutions. It'd be nice to find something a little more definitive, something to make our work easier." She turned a page, then said, "As already mentioned, Bay Trust has the distinction of holding the notes on a number of businesses on the brink of bankruptcy, including the two previously mentioned, as well as an import company owned by Paolini. It seems that right before Millhouse was killed during the alleged robbery, he had contacted each of the business owners, letting them know he was calling in the note. Greene and Reynard were both overheard threatening Millhouse if he did."

"What about Paolini?" Andrews asked.

"A bank employee heard him tell Millhouse that if Lucia didn't give him what he wanted, then he was going to see them both rot in hell . . ." Parrish looked down at her notes and read, " 'just like the corpses she thinks she put there.' "

Rocky leaned back in his chair. "Thinks? What's that supposed to mean?"

"That's unknown," Parrish said. "Is she an assassin, or is this a false lead? We still haven't been able to verify that Lucia was actually at Etienne's, since we don't have a positive ID of her. I tend to think that Gillespie is correct, that the woman posing as Kyla Greene is actually Lucia. If so, it appears she was in the doorway of the restaurant when someone took a shot at Paolini and Gillespie—"

Zim gave a laugh. "You mean when Gillespie was locking lips with Paolini?"

The room went quiet. I don't know if I imagined the slight narrowing of Torrance's gaze, but I tried not to look at him, even as I tried not to point fingers at Parrish, who must certainly have told Zim about this kiss. It was hard enough seeing the gamut of expressions on the faces of everyone else in the room who hadn't known—everything from horrified disgust to prurient delight, this last from Zim, as he added, "Taking your undercover role a bit too far?"

"Maybe," Torrance said, his voice deathly quiet, as he looked directly at Zim, "she had a reason."

"I was only joking," Zim said, shifting in his seat.

Andrews cleared his throat. "And as usual in poor taste. Why don't you explain, Gillespie?"

I told them how Reynard's wife had openly accused me of being a cop, and about our sudden decision to leave immediately because of my spotting our suspected hit man. "Paolini suggested the kiss as a way of giving weight to my role as his date, regardless of my occupation."

"Or," Andrews said, "as a way to keep you in one place for the shooter?"

I didn't answer, primarily because I didn't want to think that of Paolini, despite the fact that he was a criminal. At one time he'd told me he respected me because I played by the rules. Perhaps I was foolish but I'd believed him, just as I now believed that if he did respect me, he wouldn't hold me so someone else could kill me. I had to remember, though, that he was a con, could play the game, and he might have had some other reason for kissing me at that moment . . .

I shook myself, tried to concentrate on what Andrews was saying.

"We aren't ruling anyone out yet. But there have been some matters that have come to light since then that may or may not change your views. One, we received a hit on the prints sent to ALPS. Shipley?"

"The hit," Shipley said, "is of the shooter at Etienne's,

prints lifted off the stolen car from Jim Greene's lot. We matched those to the prints on Gillespie's car in the Berkeley incident. I'm waiting for confirmation from Marin to see if it comes back to the guy they arrested last night at Torrance's place. My guess is yes. The Marin cops said he has a similar scar on his fingers. We should hear back in a few minutes. Our prints belong to a David Cole. The guy's got a rap sheet a mile long," he said, holding up a thick sheaf of teletype paper. "And that doesn't include his sealed juvenile record. I've been in touch with some of the agencies back east, where he's from. They suspect he's done a number of hits, but as of yet, haven't been able to pin any on him. Thought we might have him on ours, but it turns out he test drove the vehicle from Greene's lot the day before it was stolen."

"You get a photo?" I asked.

"Yeah. Markowski identified him as being the guy you two saw in Greene's office the day you went to talk to him. They had a photocopy of his license for the test drive. Apparently he went back to buy the car, was told it was stolen, and left in a huff, which is when you saw him. Markowski went back to question the salesman, who said he didn't mention it before, because you guys didn't ask."

"Convenient," I said.

"If his prints were on your car," Shipley said, "he'll have an excuse and it'll check out—that excuse being exactly what he set it up to be, just like at Greene's lot. He was going to buy the car. My contact in Chicago says this David Cole's a pro and he covers all his bases. When I talked to the detective in Marin, I was told Cole invoked. Won't say a word to anyone. More importantly is that he's strictly a gun for hire. Which means he's working for someone else. The most they've ever been able to do back east is put him away for petty stuff."

"Which," Andrews said, "is the real question. Because if

he's after Gillespie, then someone hired him. I want to know who and why."

I said, "Since this all started with the Fiona Winchester case, I have to believe there's something there we're not seeing—something the original players in all this may have overlooked until now." I told them about my dream last night, and seeing someone, possibly Louise Smith, sitting in that chair.

"A dream?" Zim said. "That'll hold up in court."

"That's not the point," I said. "The two look so much alike, at least when Louise is in drag, that it may be an important lead if it is one over the other."

Parrish eyed me. "How can we prove who it was?"

"We have the police sketch of Louise Smith and we have the photo from the restaurant. We show both to my old partner," I said. "Sam Scolari was there with me. If anyone will remember who was sitting in that chair in that apartment when I got shot, he will."

Andrews said, "Someone else can do that. I think you can better utilize your time working intel."

"You're taking me off the street?"

"Someone's trying to kill you, Gillespie."

Parrish said, "Actually that might be a good reason to leave her out there."

As much as I wanted to work the case, her comment made me wonder just whose side she was on, and I waited for her to explain.

"If someone is after Gillespie, we must assume they are watching her, hence the rose petals on the porch this morning."

"Your point?" Andrews said, eyeing her.

She met his gaze. "My point is that we do a little counter-surveillance. We follow Gillespie to see who is following her."

28

"I can't believe she told Zim about the kiss," I said, after we'd left the meeting.

"Miss Prim-and-Proper Parrish?" Rocky said. "I'd ask how you knew it was her, but I know damn well Torrance would never have mentioned it. Really, though, she didn't mean anything by it. She was just explaining what happened."

"But to Zim?"

"Face it, he's weird," Rocky said as we walked down the hall. "Parrish is another story. Just when I thought I got her figured out, pow!"

"She reminds me of a Vulcan. All she needs is the pointy ears."

"And the tight body suit. That's what all the good-looking aliens wear on *Star Trek*."

"Well, don't go hitting on her. She's Torrance's partner. I'd like to have somewhat of a good working relationship with her if they're going to be together all the time."

"She's not exactly the huggy, kissy type," he said as we walked into our office.

At my desk, I picked up the phone, and called my old partner, Sam Scolari.

"Hey, Kate."

"I have an interesting case—"

"Did I mention I retired a few months back?"

"Without me, you'd turn old and gray and die of boredom."

"I'm already old and gray, and boredom ain't such a bad thing when there's a baseball game coming on in a couple of hours and a six-pack chilling in the fridge. What's up?"

"You heard about the bank robbery at Bay Trust?"

"Read it in the paper, yeah."

"Well, I think it's related to the Fiona Winchester case—"

"Which reminds me. Saw you on TV the other night when you were talking about it. That thing about adding an extra ten pounds when you're on camera? Didn't look near that much."

"All that guilt I was feeling about interrupting your game? Gone. But I'll let you redeem yourself if you let me pick your brain on the Twin Palms cases. Any chance we could meet for a few?"

"If we can do it at my office. I've got a few things I need to do while I'm there. We can go downstairs for lunch if you have time."

Rocky and I left a few minutes later in his car, taking the photo and a copy of the sketch artist's rendering of Louise Smith with us. And as Rocky pulled out of the parking garage, so did two other cars, both assigned to follow us. Torrance and Parrish were in one. A couple guys from Robbery in another.

Scolari's office was situated over a Chinese restaurant. A dark stairwell led up to the office door with a simple plaque that read: SCOLARI, PI. I knocked, then turned the handle and entered the office, two rooms if you counted the small water closet. His desk, what you could see of it beneath the mountains of papers, photos, and empty Chinese food cartons, faced the door. He was seated behind it, looking much the same as he always did, gray hair, face lined with worries normal people didn't have to think about. He was looking at some photographs of a man lifting weights, but put them down when we entered. "You happen to call your aunt, Kate?"

"About what?"

"About Kevin," he said, referring to my thirteen-year-old nephew. Scolari had become Kevin's surrogate uncle ever since the murder of his wife. Scolari needed interaction with the living, and Kevin needed interaction with a father-figure. "I got some literature on this COPS camp. It's like a grief-counseling thing for kids who had parents killed in the line of duty. I figured I could take him . . ."

"You?"

"Yeah. Barton took her kids there after her husband was killed a couple of years ago in that SWAT operation. She swears by it. Made a big difference for her kids."

Actually I was thrilled he wanted to do it. I'd heard great things about the COPS camp. But I figured it was worth a jab or two. "Hmmm . . . You? In a sleeping bag? No TV? No beer? Lots of mosquitoes?"

"Funny. Just remember when Kev grows up to be the president, you'll have me to thank."

"I'll call her when I can."

Rocky picked up one of the pictures of the weight lifter. "Let me guess," he said. "Your subject's entering the Mr Universe contest and they think he's taking steroids?"

"Yeah, right. Worker's comp case," he said. "Guy's supposed to have a bad back. Not sure how much longer I can do this stuff, but it pays the bills and then some. Whatcha got, Kate?"

"How about a little murder for a change of pace? I was wondering what you could tell me about the night I was shot at the Twin Palms. What you remembered."

"I'm guessing you have a specific reason for this?"

"Yeah. Maybe some solid leads if I can put them together. Only problem is I don't remember much except going up the steps, then getting shot at the top. Everything else is pretty much a blur."

He leaned back in his chair, crossing his arms. "That's about it. You were right behind me. A shot was fired. You went down, I dragged you out of the hallway. End of story."

"But what did you see?" I didn't want to ask specifically. I wanted to know what he recalled, not something I suggested.

"Jesus. That was a few years ago. I don't remember much else. We walked up the goddamned steps—"

"And you swore that a used condom saved my life . . ."

"Yeah," he said. "How'd I forget that? Let's see . . . We went up the steps. I almost stepped on it. Swore, pushed you back so you wouldn't. Heard the shot. Looked up, saw a woman sitting in a chair, watching us from that second door on the left. Saw a guy with a gun run in the same door when he saw us."

"You wrote in your report that the woman said he broke into her apartment, pointed the gun at her right before we came up the steps. He fired at me, then jumped out the window."

"Pretty much how I remember it, except there was no sign of forced entry. He's the one we think was Antonio Foust," he said, referring to the man who had long been suspected of shooting me.

"Is it possible this woman could have pulled the trigger?"

He shook his head. "No way. I saw her sitting there in this ragged armchair the whole time. Why?"

"You ever met Paolini's ex-wife?"

"Never."

"Her name of somewhat dubious record may be Lucia Paolini. She was married to the car dealer, Jim Greene. Divorced him, married and divorced Paolini a few years ago, and had an affair with Earl Millhouse, CFO of Bay Trust Mutual. Paolini suggested that she was a contract killer—"

"There's a match made in heaven."

"According to Paolini, he wasn't aware of it until afterward. Apparently she had a child she at first claimed was his, then recanted when they separated. Paternity showed it was someone else's—whose, he says he doesn't know. But he hired a PI to follow her, hoping to find out. That's how he allegedly found out what she did on the side."

"Ya gotta love the irony of it all."

"And if it's true, it could change a number of things on some of the cases we thought were cut and dried."

"You got a picture of her?"

"I do have this," I said, pulling out the artist's sketch. I wanted to see his reaciton to it before I showed him the photo from the restaurant. I handed it to him.

He took it from me, looked at it a few moments, nodded. "Been a while . . . Don't remember her having a mole on her mouth, or being that heavy, but definitely a resemblance."

"To whom?"

He handed me the sketch. "To the lady sitting in that armchair at the Twin Palms."

I showed him the photograph of the three women. I said nothing.

He eyed it, pointed to the likeness of the woman we believed was Lucia. "That's her," he said. "That's the woman I saw sitting there. She was either a very cool cucumber or a goddamned nut."

"What makes you say that?" I asked.

"Because she never moved from that armchair the whole time. Guns are going off, people are getting shot at. She just sat there, holding some goddamned rose."

29

"**G**uess that narrows it down," I said, as we left Scolari's office, thinking about my dream, wondering if it held any remnants from the past—and any significance for the future.

"Yeah, but is it really Lucia?" Rocky asked. "The woman's got a gazillion akas. Lotta good it does us if we don't get some ID on her. And what's with all the roses?"

"Who the hell knows," I said, wishing we could have had a solid ID. At least we could positively place her at the Twin Palms. A step in the right direction. The roses I wasn't sure about. "Whatever the damn roses mean, I've seen more than my fair share."

"Guessing if Torrance brought you a dozen right now—" I stopped at his words.

"What?" he asked.

"How could I have forgotten it?"

"Forgotten what?"

"Someone sent a rose the day after I appeared on *San Francisco's Most Wanted*. I thought it was one of you guys, playing a joke."

"A joke that cost money? That should have been your first clue."

"True," I said, continuing on to the car. I thought of the cellophane, the opportunity for prints, lost . . . "We need to gct back to the Hall. Check with the florists. See if anyone delivered a single rose."

"Assuming the suspect was that stupid. Hell, for all you know, it could have been bought at one of those curbside bucket things."

"Somebody had to have delivered it to my desk. If we're lucky, we'll find out who."

"Can't hurt."

We drove back to the Hall, undoubtedly shadowed by our entourage, though where they were, we couldn't tell—a good thing, considering we didn't want anyone to know we were being watched.

Rocky parked in the garage, and about two minutes later, Torrance and Parrish pulled in. Torrance was talking to somebody on the phone as he got out of the car and walked toward us, Parrish at his side.

"That was Evans," he said, when he finished the call. "He thinks he saw a car following mine, but it turned off before he could get close enough to get a plate or a visual."

"Following your car?" I said, glancing at Parrish, and noting that, like me, she wore her shoulder-length hair back in a ponytail. "You think they thought Parrish was me?"

"Possibly. The rear windows are tinted. They might not have gotten close enough to tell," he said as we walked into the building. "How'd your interview with Scolari go?"

I told him what Scolari had said, that it was Lucia there—holding a rose. I also mentioned the rose sent to me.

"Where is it?" Parrish asked. "The rose?"

"I tossed it. The card was blank. My desk was filled with practical jokes from everyone because of my TV appearance. I figured it was another joke."

Her expression was so steadfast that I wondered if anyone had ever played a joke on her. I decided they hadn't. Parrish wasn't the type to accept it, or rather laugh at it, though whether it was because of some personality flaw or because someone had played a joke that had gone awry, I had no idea.

I think she was still trying to come to terms with the whole joke aspect when we arrived at Homicide. Andrews was waiting for us when we got there. "How'd it go?"

Torrance informed him of what Evans had seen, and I filled him in on my conversation with Scolari—all roses included.

He listened intently, was quiet for a moment when we'd finished, then said, "We need to come up with plan B for sleeping arrangements. Gillespie's apartment is out. Obviously after last night's and this morning's incidents, Torrance's condo in Marin is out."

"Parrish and I were discussing that while we were waiting for Gillespie at Scolari's office. She suggested we use one of the hotels the FBI has used in the past for dignitaries. They're already set up with security cameras and alarms. No one gets in or out without us knowing."

I was beginning to feel like a cop in a gilded cage, but knew better than to ask if it was necessary. I'd been shot at and chased one too many times to worry about not sleeping in my own bed tonight.

"Which hotel?" Andrews asked.

"The Fairmont."

Not bad for a working girl.

Andrews wrote down the hotel name, looked right at me and said, "That doesn't mean carte blanche on the room service, Gillespie."

"Darn, I guess that means caviar is out?"

"I'd be worried if I thought you liked the stuff," he said, looking at his watch. "Food aside, what's next on your agenda?"

"Personally," I said, "I think we need to revisit Fiona Winchester's family."

"Why is that?"

"They were less than cooperative the first time they were interviewed three years ago right after Fiona was killed, never mind the burglary of their house. And then when Rocky and I showed up at their door the other day, we were met with a shotgun, all because I'd reopened the case. Personally I'd like to know what they're afraid of."

"You think it's a good idea if you're being followed?" Andrews asked.

"Good question. If there is something going on, something they're afraid of, I'm not sure I want whoever is watching me to know we're going back there again."

"What do you suggest?" Andrews asked Torrance.

"Parrish and I can go out again as a decoy, while Evans and his partner follow."

Andrews nodded. "I'll have a second team following Gillespie just in case." He looked at me. "You okay with that, Gillespie?"

"With a plan like that, what could go wrong?"

30

The first thing to go wrong was that Parrish and I ended up in the elevator together. Alone.

She pressed the Down button, stared straight ahead at the door, and said, "You seemed upset at the meeting. At me."

Great. Just what I needed. A heart-to-heart in the elevator. I decided to be blunt. "Do the words 'locking lips with Paolini' sound familiar?"

She looked over at me, clearly surprised. And then, to my utter dismay, she reached out and hit the Stop button, and the elevator came to a halt. "I made a mistake. I wasn't aware he'd bring it up publicly. I apologize."

But she didn't move, and it was clear there was more she wanted to say, so, being somewhat of a captive audience, I stood there, waiting.

Finally, she gave a small smile, the first real friendliness I'd seen her exhibit, and then she said, "You might not like me, but the truth is, I admire you. I admire the way you take things in stride. The way you make everything seem so easy. The way you joke. The way others joke with you . . . Unlike me, you're good with relationships—"

"*Some* relationships," I corrected.

She reached out, hit the Run button, and as the elevator started its descent once more, she said, "Simple logistics.

See what happens when you put two people in an enclosed space?"

The elevator stopped, the door opened, and she stepped out. I followed, not even pretending to know what she was talking about when it came to logistics and relationships. I supposed that it didn't matter. She'd offered the olive branch and I was willing to take it.

Torrance and Rocky were waiting for us downstairs in the parking garage, as were Evans and Bob Waugh, who was part of the team now assigned to follow Rocky and me. The other was John Bell, also from Robbery. "You guys aren't working the diamond heist?" I asked.

Bell shook his head. "It's on hold. Every lead fizzled." He put his arm around my shoulder as we walked. "How've you been?"

"Not bad. You?"

"Busy, but good," he said, as we reached the car. We'd been rookies together, closed down Murphy's Law, one of the local cop bars, on more than one occasion.

Torrance, Parrish, and their team took off first. My team took off about five minutes later, driving the circuitous route just in case someone was trying to follow me.

When we got the all clear from Bell and his partner, Waugh, we hopped on the freeway, then took the exit to the Winchester place.

About a block from the house, we stopped and I called to let them know we were coming in hopes of avoiding the whole shotgun thing. Winchester's daughter answered. "Dad! It's the police."

"Where?" I heard in the background.

"On the phone."

"Hell." Then a few seconds later, he picked up, his voice brusque, gravelly, like someone who had spent his entire life smoking.

When I told him what we wanted, he was less than

pleased. "You didn't get it right the first and second time you guys came here. What makes you think I want you here again?"

"It's important," I said.

"Everybody's stuff is always more important than someone else's, ain't it?"

I didn't answer. In a way he was right.

Finally he said, "Yeah, come over. I'll let you in. But just you."

"Gotta have my partner."

"Same guy you were with last time?"

"Same."

"Him, too. No one else."

"We're just up the street. We'll be there in about two minutes."

I briefed Bell and Waugh, who agreed they would stay out of sight, since Winchester seemed far too eager to pull out his shotgun—loaded or not.

Rocky and I parked in front of the neighbor's house. Winchester was waiting on his porch when we arrived. We sat in the car a moment, watching, making sure there were no surprises. The place hadn't changed much, with the exception of the screen door, which by now had completely fallen off and was propped up on the side of the house. The broken window was still taped, and paint was still peeling.

"Watch yer step," Winchester said as we started up the walkway to the front porch. We skipped the broken stair and he held the front door open for us, taking a quick look up and down the street before we entered. Interesting, I thought.

The inside of his house was dark, but clean, not what I expected, considering the dilapidated state of the outside. He led us into the kitchen, turning on an overhead light, indicating we should take a seat at the olive-green Formica table. "What is it yer looking for this time?" he asked me.

"Let's just say I had some questions that I don't think were properly addressed the first time around."

"Second, you mean?"

"I've only been here once before," I said, not wanting to get in an argument with him. "You'll have to forgive me if I've missed something that you told the other investigators."

"Didn't tell them nothing. Didn't want to end up dead like Fiona."

"Why would that happen?"

"You ever heard of dirty cops?"

"Unfortunately, yes."

"There you go. Now what is it you needed to know?"

"I was hoping to talk to your daughter again."

He looked at me, his head cocked to one side, his gaze narrowed as though considering his options right then. Finally he called out, "Lizzie!"

A moment later, his youngest daughter walked into the kitchen, dressed much the same as she had been the first time we'd seen her, baggy T-shirt, blue jeans, bad short haircut. She didn't look at her father, kept her gaze on the floor.

"Hi," I said.

It was several seconds before she would look at us, and then not until I said, "How are you, Lizzie?"

She shrugged.

"Do you remember what we talked about the last time we were here?"

Lizzie's gaze flicked to her father, as though fearing what he might think. Surprisingly, he gave a nod, and she looked at me and said, "Yes."

"You told us about your sister bringing over some things the last time you saw her?"

"I remember."

"Any chance there were any papers or anything in that stuff she brought?"

She shook her head.

"Maybe some jewelry or something expensive?"

"No. Just some clothes and things."

"What sort of things?"

"A couple of boxes. Little boxes that had some cards and things in them."

"Can we look?"

She glanced at her father, who again nodded and she said, "They're in our room."

Lizzie led us to the back of the house, across the clean but scarred hardwood floor. There were only two bedrooms, her father's and one she had apparently shared with her sister. There were two twin beds, neatly made, the white chenille coverlets threadbare.

As Lizzie kneeled beside one of the beds and pulled out a cardboard box, I asked, "A couple days before your sister was killed, there was a break-in here. Do you know what was taken?"

"Just my stereo. I think it was someone from my school."

"Why is that?"

"Because they didn't take anything else," she replied, as she opened the box. Just as she had said, it was filled with clothes and a small shoebox containing cards that apparently Lizzie had mailed to Fiona after she had moved out. Rocky and I were going through each one, just in case something was slipped inside, maybe overlooked, worried that whatever we were looking for had been taken in the burglary, and the Winchesters weren't even aware of what it was.

"Is there anything else she brought you? Anything she mentioned?" I asked, hoping for some sort of a clue or lead.

"She talked about insurance, but I guess it wasn't any good, since her boyfriend paid for the coffin."

Rocky and I both looked up from the cards we were reading. "Insurance?" I asked.

"Yeah. When my dad was yelling at her that she was gonna get herself killed, she told him she had insurance."

"Did she say anything else about it? What it was, or where it was . . . ?"

Lizzie shook her head.

Her statement reaffirmed my belief it was no ordinary burglary, and I wondered if they'd found whatever it was they were after. Rocky and I continued our search through the box, and just as we put the last card away, finding nothing, her father appeared in the doorway.

"This what yer looking for?" he asked, holding a business-sized envelope, stuffed with several sheets of paper, judging from the thickness.

"What is it?" I asked, as he handed it to me. It bore his name and address on the front, but no return address. The postmark showed it was mailed three years before.

"Fiona's so-called insurance. Didn't do us a lot of good when she died. Looks like a bunch of nothing to me."

I pulled out the papers, several sheets with nothing but numbers on them. Long numbers.

The sort that might belong to bank accounts.

31

"**W**here did these come from?" I asked Mr. Winchester.

"Fiona sent them. She said it was her insurance that nothing was gonna happen to her. Told me if anything did, I was supposed to get them to the cops."

"She was killed three years ago. Why on earth did you hold on to them so long?"

"Cause right after she sent it, someone broke into our house, looking for the thing. Least, that's what it looked like to me. I was going to call the cops, but Fiona changed her mind after her boss killed himself. She told me there was some bad sorts running around, and 'til she knew who it was, I should just play dumb or they might do something to me or—" He didn't say it, but his glance strayed toward Lizzie.

"Did she give you any indication what this was about or what she meant?"

"She told me a name. Some cop with a long name that started with an *A*. Abercrombie or something."

"Abernathy?" I said.

"Yeah. She told me he was looking for this here list."

"He's dead. Killed a few months ago in a hit-and-run," I said. Abernathy was suspected of a long list of crimes, including murder and money laundering.

"Yeah, well he's the one she said was looking for this here

list of numbers. All I know is I don't hear from her in weeks and weeks, then I get this packet of papers I'm supposed to give to the cops, and then she calls me frantic to hide them and don't tell the cops, because of this Abernathy guy. Stuck them under a floorboard. Good thing, too, or they mighta been found."

I looked over the papers once more, not really sure what we held, but knowing it was something significant. "Why now?" I asked. "Why give them to me?"

He took a breath, looked at his daughter, and said, "I don't want Lizzie living like this no more." And then his gaze met mine. "We both watched you on TV. At first I was mad, but after I called you, Lizzie, she said you looked nice. Like you didn't believe it was right that Fiona was killed no matter what she did. That's how I felt, too. I'm still mad at her, but she didn't deserve to die."

I glanced at Lizzie, tried to offer an encouraging smile, and was pleased to see that she smiled back. It transformed her entire face, and if truth be told, made me glad I'd taken the time to bring up Fiona's case on TV.

Rocky and I left shortly thereafter, both feeling better with the knowledge that the Winchesters intended to call SFPD if necessary, instead of relying on their own survival technique of pulling a shotgun every time someone came to the door—not that I blamed them. I could well understand their distrust after Fiona's report of Abernathy searching for this list. Hell if that wasn't motive enough to take Fiona out. If Abernathy suspected her of taking it, and it could lead to him somehow, her days were numbered from that moment on.

In retrospect, it all made sense. Abernathy, a narcotics officer at the time, was working with Foust. Foust was suspected of shooting at me at the Twin Palms. I had gone there to investigate the shooting death of Fiona Winchester.

But with both Abernathy and Foust being dead, and

someone very clearly trying to take me out, all because I had reopened the case, well, even a rookie officer could figure out that whoever had orchestrated Fiona's murder and my attempted murder at the Twin Palms was still out there. And there was one man I knew who had been involved one way or another in this entire case from the very beginning.

"Where to?" Rocky asked as we pulled away from the curb.

"I think we need another talk with Nick Paolini."

I called the lieutenant to let him know what we'd learned. He was quiet a moment when I suggested a recontact with Paolini.

"I don't want you alone with him."

"You know he doesn't talk in front of anyone else."

"Then he doesn't talk," was all he said.

I called Paolini's cell phone and got his usual response: "Inspector. To what do I owe the pleasure?"

"I need a few minutes of your time."

There was a slight hesitation, then, "Where?"

"Starbucks, near the parking garage, in . . . half an hour?"

"As you wish."

That would give me time to get back to the Hall, pick up the dress and necklace he had sent, then make sure I had enough backup should there be any errant gunmen, or women, floating around. It would also give Rocky a place to stand nearby, without sitting at the actual table with us, since I knew full well Paolini would refuse to talk otherwise.

He arrived about ten minutes after we did, his driver letting him off out front. He walked in, eyed Rocky, who stood watch near the back door, before approaching my table against the wall.

"What is it you want?" he asked, dispensing with the usual pleasantries. Interesting. Paolini under pressure?

"I have some things that belong to you," I said, nodding

at the gold box propped against the window, and then patting an envelope containing the Tiffany necklace.

As though neither item were of importance to him, he said, "Would you like a fresh cup of coffee?"

"No, thank you," I said, taking a sip of my mocha, if for no other reason than to show I needed nothing.

Paolini put in his order, coffee, black, then gave the cashier a ten. When she handed him his change, he put it in the tip jar, then thanked the girl, who looked as though she would melt right there. He took his coffee, turned away, thereby missing the be-still-my-heart sign she gave to the other girl behind the counter. I was tempted to tell her that he'd probably been killing people before she was even born. The reality was that despite knowing what he did for a living, he still cut an imposing figure. And perhaps knowing what he did added to his mystique. He was dangerous, but he also happened to be handsome, rich, impeccably mannered.

I glanced over at Rocky, who was still positioned by the parking garage door, the better to see both directions. Bell and Waugh were outside, though I couldn't see them. I didn't try too hard, however, as Paolini walked up with his coffee, then sat across from me.

I pushed the envelope toward him.

"The necklace?" he said.

"Yes."

"You should keep it."

"As tempting as it sounds, I like my job better."

He reached across the table, brushed his finger across my hand, my wrist. It was everything I could do not to draw back. I didn't want him to think I was affected. "Who would know?"

"Me," I said, trying to sound casual. It didn't matter that I did not trust him, or even that I knew what he was capable of. Sometimes dealing with Paolini was like dealing with the devil and fighting the temptation to hand him your soul at the mere suggested promise of delights unknown. Frankly, I was glad that I was in a very public place surrounded by cops who, while not making their presence known, were definitely out there watching, especially when Paolini leaned closer, his gaze locked on mine as he said, "Tell me you haven't wondered . . . just once what it would be like . . ."

I knew what he meant, and it had nothing to do with the necklace. "We're here to talk about murder."

"A woman like you should wake up every morning, your lips swollen from kissing."

"You're right. And if I could figure out how to get the man I want to do that, I'd be one hell of a happy woman. But right now I have more pressing matters . . ."

He leaned back in his chair, a flash of anger replaced by amusement. My guess was that Paolini was not often spurned, and I was somewhat relieved to hear him say, "If I didn't like you so much, I might take offense. Why have you asked me here?"

"I have some questions about the unsolved Bay Trust Mutual robbery."

He gave a slight tilt of his head as though to indicate he might answer—but would reserve his right to silence.

"Who killed Earl Millhouse?"

"A street punk."

"His name was David Cole. We have him in custody, though he has yet to confess."

"As I said . . ."

"Where do you know him from?"

"I don't recall."

I hated that any information I got from him had to be extracted, and even then it was suspect. What he chose to divulge, and the reason behind his choice had little to do with altruism, I was sure. It was as though to him it was all a game. In a way, I suppose it was, a game I intended to win.

"Did you have any problems with Earl Millhouse?" I asked.

"Let's say the thoughts I've entertained about Mr. Millhouse have not been pleasant."

"What had he done?"

He gave a grim smile. "To answer that without my attorney would not be prudent, Inspector."

It didn't take a legal expert to determine that ill-gotten money was a factor. Even so, I was getting nowhere, though what did I expect? For him to confess all and land in jail? I knew full well that he was involved in some way, but no matter how much he wanted to sleep with me—assuming it wasn't just another ploy—I seriously doubted he was willing to serve time in order for me to solve my case.

Which meant I'd have to hope for the best and read between the lines. I thought about the account numbers Fiona had sent to her father. Marcel Etienne's suicide notwithstanding, Fiona's was the first homicide that seemed to start all this . . . "Do you know who killed Fiona Winchester?"

He took a sip of his coffee, set the cup down. "We have gone into this before."

"Humor me."

"I believe, as do you, that it was Antonio Foust."

Easy for him to say, since Foust was dead. "Do you know who he was working for?"

"I'd heard Abernathy." This was the second time today that Abernathy's name was mentioned, which certainly lent it more weight. Abernathy had worked Narcotics before he was killed. He'd worked on the drug smuggling investigation into Marcel Etienne's restaurant and subsequent suicide. That the smuggling case had somehow gone by the wayside since then was enough to make me think we needed a closer look at Etienne's business partner, Stephen Reynard.

I asked, "Was Antonio Foust working with Abernathy or *for* Abernathy?"

"I have no idea."

"Any idea how or why the gun used in Fiona's murder and my subsequent shooting at the Twin Palms ended up in this David Cole's hands when both Foust and Abernathy are dead?"

He stared at his cup, tracing his finger around the edge of the lid. Finally he met my gaze. "Perhaps, Inspector, someone *wanted* you to find it."

Now, that was an intriguing prospect. To think that someone had purposely placed that gun out there, in this suspect's hands to commit this so-called robbery, knowing we'd be there, shoot him, find the gun . . . In my mind, that would have been done for one reason only, to throw us off the track, not help us. "What makes you think someone wanted us to find it?"

"You are asking that which I cannot answer."

"Tell me about your ex-wife. How is she involved?"

He hesitated, then said, "I have my suspicions."

"Which are . . .?"

He didn't answer.

"You mentioned the other day that she had something you wanted."

"Again, without an attorney . . ." He gave an apologetic shrug.

"Does any of this have to do with her kid?"

"None whatsoever," he said, in a tone that brooked no argument.

"I take it you knew Lucia wasn't killed? That it was her brother?"

"I suspected it when you first told me."

"Why didn't you mention it then?"

"Your coroner would have found out by the time of the autopsy if not sooner. There were certain anatomical differences that were bound to be noticed, despite their similar appearances . . . and his mode of dress."

"Why would she send her brother to the bank?"

"I don't know."

"Did she ever talk to you about her presence at the Twin Palms the night I was shot?"

"No."

"Any reason to think she might be involved in my shooting?"

"You mean besides the fact that she might be jealous?"

"Jealous?" I said, surprised.

"Of us."

"There is no *us*."

"Ah, but she does not know that."

"Meaning what?"

"That three years ago, after she and I separated, she saw us together when you and your undercover *brother* were searching for trumped-up evidence against me for money laundering. Let me put it this way, Inspector. She was not happy. I expect she had a similar reaction when she saw us in the restaurant the other night."

"You didn't tell her back then it was a setup? That I was only passing as his sister, so he could introduce me to you? Gather evidence on you?"

"It suited my purposes at the time not to."

I wondered if this could get any more twisted. "Is that why you kissed me outside the restaurant?" I asked. "Because it suited your purpose to incite her jealousy?"

He took a deep breath as though trying to maintain his composure. "The answer to that, Inspector, is no." He slid back his chair, rose. "I find I am at the end of my patience. What is it you want from me?" he asked, his voice low, tinged with annoyance.

"I want to find Lucia."

"She will not have the answers you are looking for."

"Regardless . . ."

I waited. Finally he said, "On one condition." His gaze penetrated mine, and it was everything I could do not to shift beneath its intensity. "Tell me the thought of you and me together has never crossed your mind."

"Not once," I said.

And then he laughed. "You are not the best of liars," he replied, picking up the envelope with the necklace in it. He ripped it open, and the diamond necklace slid out, sparkling beneath the fluorescent light. He dropped the necklace into his coat pocket as though it were nothing but some change, and then pulling out a pen, he wrote something on the envelope, folded it in half, dropped it on the table, and walked out, leaving the dress behind.

32

I had to wonder at Paolini's motive for giving us Lucia's address. Regardless, I wasn't going to ignore it.

Nor was I going to ignore Lucia's uncertain past, never mind her current involvement in this case, which is why we called out the SWAT team and hostage negotiators. We were taking no chances.

After they had geared up, we assembled in the meeting room and went over the details. "Someone doing a Code five on the place?" the SWAT commander asked.

"Yes sir," I said, reporting on what we'd learned so far. "We have two unmarked units at each end of the street. A woman matching Lucia's description entered the structure about fifteen minutes ago. No other movement noon. She has a son, who has been staying with his nanny these past few days. That's been verified and we have units watching that place as well."

He noted the time on a pad of paper, then listened while Rocky gave him the description of the premises and the surrounding area.

Twenty minutes later, they were setting up their command post about two blocks from the scene in a church parking lot, and I watched the SWAT officers climb into the back of their armored panel truck, dressed in black fatigues, black masks over their faces. After the panel truck drove off, we waited, listening to our police radios on the tactical channel. It seemed it took them forever to set up, but once they did, the entry and subsequent warrant arrest of Lucia Paolini took less than three minutes. Rocky was heading up the team to search her place, while Torrance, Parrish, and I returned to question her at the jail, where she'd been transported by a marked radio car.

I walked in, wondering just who it was we'd arrested. The real Lucia Paolini? Lucia had so many AKAs, I was beginning to think of her as a chameleon, able to change her appearance and identity as she saw fit. Add a dash of Lorelei, the siren who lured the sailors to their death, and I realized that was undoubtedly how she'd survived. A first-rate con.

I wondered how she'd fare being interrogated by a female.

We watched her from our darkened room through the one-way glass. Her smile reminded me of the Mona Lisa, as though she knew some great secret, and it occurred to me that she was very much aware of our presence.

Torrance put his hand on my shoulder. "You ready?"

"Ready," I said, notebook and pen in hand. I opened the door, entered, then closed it behind me. There were two chairs and a table. Lucia sat at one end, and I pulled my chair around so that there was nothing between us. It was one of those body language things they taught us at interview and interrogation school. No barriers between you and the suspect.

Judging from her expression, I don't know that it would have made much difference what I did. There was something about her, something that told me she truly believed she had the upper hand.

"Lucia Paolini?" I said.

She gave a slight nod.

"Before I get started, I would like to read you your rights." I held out my Miranda card, more for the hidden camera's benefit than hers. If there was any question, her attorney wouldn't be able to dispute the fact. I read Lucia her rights verbatim, then asked if she understood them.

"Yes."

"Okay. We seem to be having some problems with your identity, since we find no record of your driver's license or anything else."

"I don't have a license."

"Lucia Paolini is your true name?"

"Yes."

"And why did you identify yourself as Kyla Greene?"

"What would you do if two cops showed up at your door, asking about a murder victim?

"Since we hadn't yet mentioned Fiona Winchester's name . . ."

"I saw you on TV. I knew that's why you were there."

"And where is Kyla?"

"On a trip with a client of hers. She's in the escort business, too. I watch her apartment when she's gone."

"Before you were married to Paolini, what names did you go by?"

"Lucia Smith, then Greene."

"As in Jim Greene?"

"As in his ex-wife."

"When was this?"

"Seven, eight years ago. It was a short-lived marriage."

"Did Paolini know?"

"Of course he knew."

"Is he the father of your son?"

"Earl Millhouse is."

"Does Paolini know that?"

"Yes."

"You're sure?"

"I told him myself a couple of weeks ago."

"And what was his reaction?"

"Nick said he'd kill Earl if he so much as looked at the boy. I'm afraid he has never accepted the idea that my son is not his."

"Did Earl Millhouse know?"

"He did when Nick confronted him."

"When was this?" I asked, though I shouldn't have been surprised that Paolini had lied about not knowing who the father was. I'm sure he'd lied about a lot of things. Trying to sift through the truths of any of his statements was difficult at best.

"At the bank a couple of weeks ago. There was a rather big argument over the matter. I'd heard that Sophie, Earl's wife, was there at the time. I think she might have been more upset than Nick."

"Hard to imagine."

"Isn't it?" She smiled as though the thought were completely beyond her.

Mrs. Millhouse never mentioned anything about this at all, and once again, I hid my surprise over a fact that, if true, had completely blind-sided me. It seemed there was more truth to Paolini's suggestion that someone might need to take a number when it came to a motive in Earl Millhouse's murder.

"Nick seems to think you have something that he wants."

"My son."

"He says that's not what it is at all."

"That's all I have that belongs to him."

Interesting choice of words, considering the boy was her son and allegedly not Nick's at all. "Perhaps there is something that doesn't necessarily *belong* to him, but that you have possession of?"

"I can't imagine what that would be."

"Money?"

She merely smiled at the suggestion, but said nothing.

"What do you know of Fiona Winchester?"

"She was the waitress at Etienne's who was killed a few days after Marcel Etienne committed suicide."

"Do you really believe he killed himself?"

"I have no reason not to."

"Did you know a cop named Abernathy?"

"Yes. He was a frequent visitor at the restaurant."

"Do you know who he associated with there?"

"Everyone."

"Do you know who killed Fiona?"

"I'd heard it was a guy named Tony," she said, undoubtedly referring to Antonio Foust. "Someone my husband knew."

"Which husband?"

"Nick, I guess. But come to think of it, Jim knew him, too."

"Were you aware of Fiona's relationship to Jim Greene?"

Lucia hesitated, glanced toward the one-way glass, at our reflections, as though stalling, gathering something to say, then, "There was nothing between them. He . . . used her."

"For what?"

"For his business, hobby, whatever you want to call it. He has an escort service. It's all legit, in the phone book. One of his girls quit. He needed someone to fill in and so he . . . sort of courted her to get her to do it."

"Did you work for him?"

"Occasionally," she said, looking at the mirrored window again, then running both her hands upward between her thighs, lifting her skirt slightly. She was most definitely aware of the others outside the window—was playing to them, just as she'd done to Rocky that first day we'd met her. Her next words confirmed it, because she said it not to me, but to the window, the reflection. "I enjoyed the excitement. The thought that this man I was with wanted . . . what I had to give."

"It was a prostitution service?"

Her eyes flashed with anger as she looked at me. "Hardly. I am *not* a whore."

"Anyone in particular you dated?"

"Nick for one."

"I have a hard time believing he would marry someone from a dating service."

"Defending him?"

"No. Stating a fact of character."

"He didn't know. It was a favor to Jim."

"Dating him or marrying him?"

"Dating. Nick fell hard. I enjoyed the attention, and I was pregnant. I needed to settle down."

"Pregnant with Earl Millhouse's child?"

"I wanted an abortion, but Jim talked me out of it."

"Why?"

"Blackmail, trump card, who knows? Jim was sure it would come in handy down the road, since Earl's wife didn't know and he stood to lose a lot if she divorced him. By the time I came to my senses, it was too late for an abortion." She gave an annoyed laugh. "Do you realize how long it took me to get my stomach flat again?"

"I can't imagine," I said, wondering why some people were allowed to reproduce. She made a face, and I thought of the child I'd seen at the park, playing with abandon, wondering who hugged him, tucked him in bed at night as he was growing up. Probably the nanny he was staying with. Surely not this woman. "I take it Paolini was upset when he found out the child wasn't his?"

"That *is* why we're divorced. One of the reasons, at least."

"The other?"

"He sort of found out what I did for a living."

"Which is . . .?"

She stared at me as though I'd lost my mind. "We just went *over* that. I date men."

"Who else?"

"You mean who did I sleep with or who did I date? They're two separate things. I was selective about who I slept with, but I couldn't tell you who all I went out with."

"Who you slept with, then."

"Stephen Reynard and Marcel Etienne—oh, and Earl Millhouse, of course."

"Jim set you up with all these men?"

"The escort part. *I'm* the one who decided *who* I would sleep with," she said, glancing toward the window, with what could only be described as a suggestive gesture.

I was tempted to tell her that she was wasting her time, since Torrance was beyond her wiles, and Parrish didn't look her type.

"There's some speculation that you've had your hand in the business of murder."

She laughed. "Please. That is so ridiculous I can't imagine where the idea came from."

"I saw someone who looked like you at the Twin Palms the night I was shot."

"I was visiting my brother, Louis. He'd left to get Chinese food."

"You lied to the police and gave them the name he used?"

"It seemed the prudent thing to do under the circumstances. Giving them the last name of Paolini seemed like an automatic ticket to hours of interrogation."

She was right about that.

"And you were in contact with your brother at his club, recently?"

"Who told you that?" she asked, looking surprised.

"Just answer the question."

For the first time, she looked unsure of herself. "I might have gone there . . . I don't remember."

"Allow me to refresh your memory. He wanted to report who murdered Fiona Winchester. You asked him to do it on your terms and to meet me at the bank. Why?"

"I, um, heard something was going to happen there and I was concerned."

"Why didn't you call the police?"

"And say what to them? Gee, can you come over, because something's going to happen, but I don't know what or to whom? Just that it's at this particular location and time?"

"Perhaps if you told me what it was you overheard?"

"It was the night you appeared on TV about Fiona Winchester's murder. There was talk of it at the restaurant."

"What sort of talk?"

"Nothing specific. Anyway, I left after dinner, and realized about a block away I'd forgotten something. I didn't want to walk all the way from the parking garage, so I parked behind the restaurant and came in the back door. That's when I heard a couple of people in the office saying Earl needed to be dealt with, 'Monday at one.' That was it."

"Who was talking?"

"I don't know."

"Who was at the restaurant that night?"

"The usual. Nick, Jim, Stephen, Stephen's wife, and Earl's wife, come to think of it."

"And you didn't recognize the voices you overheard? Male? Female?"

"The door was closed and the voices were too low. I felt lucky to have overheard what I had. That's what gave me the idea of getting you out there."

"Why me?"

"Because you were the one on TV."

"What made you think it was taking place at the bank?"

"Because Earl is an anal control freak. Good in bed, but anal. He does everything exactly on time—including his orgasm. Exactly at one, he's locking his office door and walking into the bank lobby for lunch. I assumed he'd make it into the parking lot, you know, and you'd see something, be able to stop it." She gave a small sigh, one I interpreted as meaning, no biggie, shit happens. Her next words confirmed it. "Guess I was wrong."

"It seems more likely that I was exactly where I was supposed to be in order to make sure the person sent in to kill Earl did not make it out alive."

She sat up, tilted her head slightly, narrowed her gaze as though the thought had never occurred to her. And then she laughed. "I have to admit," she finally said, "that is rather clever."

"And you weren't involved in it?"

"Apparently I was. A pawn just like you."

I'd reserve judgment about that, I thought, checking my notes, deciding where to go next. "What exactly did you forget at the restaurant?"

"Cocaine."

"That you bought there?"

"Of course. Surely you realize why everyone was so upset to see you at the restaurant the night of the fundraiser?"

"Perhaps if you filled me in . . ."

"I'd heard they'd just gotten in a shipment that night, and that you'd almost walked in on them when they were unloading it in their warehouse out back."

I thought about Stephen Reynard stopping me after I opened the back door, looked out, saw the light on in the little warehouse, the generator running. And then the next day, when someone locked Torrance and me inside that place, there was a film of white dust.

That it was being used for smuggling drugs didn't surprise me. That it was blatantly being done that night while a fundraiser was being held in the restaurant right across the alley, did, however.

"You're certain about this?" I asked Lucia. "There was a shipment of cocaine in that warehouse the night of the fundraiser?"

"I'm positive. I overheard Stephen telling one of his lackeys that the damn stuff wasn't supposed to be there until the next day. Trust me, he wasn't pleased."

Trust? She seemed to be enjoying her part of informant, perhaps too much, and I knew better than to take whatever she had to say as the gospel truth. I suspected that, like Paolini, and everyone else in this affair, she was giving a side of the story that benefited no one but her.

"Who shot at me in front of the restaurant?"

She hesitated. "I don't know."

"Any overheard conversations to give you a clue?"

"None."

"Any conversations in the ladies' room?"

"I don't remember any."

"Something about Tiffany, perhaps?"

Her gaze narrowed. "You mean about the necklace that Nick gave you?"

"Among other things."

"Why don't you ask the woman who was with you when you left? She's the one who told me it came from Tiffany."

Parrish? I remembered her hustling me out when I walked in. I'd had no idea she'd participated in any conversation with Lucia, however. "Do you know her?"

She gave a shrug, but didn't answer.

"Let's go back a ways. Who shot me at the Twin Palms?"

"I don't know."

"You were there. Antonio Foust ran past you and conveniently escaped out the window of the apartment you were in."

"It might have been Tony," she said. "It all happened so fast. I was pretty upset."

"Not from what I recall."

She raised her brows. "Oh?"

"You seemed rather calm."

"Let's just say I found the whole thing to be a bit ironic."

"Meaning?"

"Meaning it happened after you'd gone out with Nick," she said, her tone indicating her displeasure. "Ironic it happened a second time, too, even though it was years later, don't you think?"

"I doubt irony plays into it at all. I might even go so far as to say that Paolini thought you were jealous, though of what, I don't know." I leaned forward. "You do realize I was working undercover? That there was nothing between us?"

"Perhaps not on your side, but I know Nick. He was taken with you."

I didn't like the direction of this conversation, and I tried to determine if it had to do with the fact that Torrance, and Parrish, were sitting out there, listening. Undoubtedly that was in the back of my mind when Torrance tapped on the door, entered and put his hand on my shoulder. I looked up at him, and he said, "This just came in."

It was a note from Rocky, stating that they'd found several long-stemmed roses in a refrigerator where we'd picked up Lucia, along with blank note cards, just like the card on the roses that someone had sent to me.

33

Finding out that Lucia might be the sender of the roses was not surprising. Getting her to admit it in an interview would be. I decided to be direct.

"Did you send me a rose?"

"What rose?"

"A long-stemmed rose, to my office."

"No."

I looked over my notes, tried to see what I'd missed, but could only think about the damn roses. Something off about that. And then it struck me why. When David Cole, the alleged hit man from back east, was chasing me, someone had left the rose on my seat. If it was him, then why? If not, then who? I remember thinking there had been two people in that car, but I couldn't be sure. "Do you know David Cole?"

"Never heard of him."

"You were talking to him that night at the restaurant. Thin guy? Gray hair, beard?" When she didn't respond, I added, "Wore an earring. Some sort of feather?"

"Oh, that was his name?"

"Yes."

"I figured he was a friend of someone's there. He asked if I knew who you were."

"And what did you say?"

"I told him you were the woman with Nick is all. Other than that . . ."

"And you wouldn't happen to know how a long-stemmed rose came to be on my car seat?"

"Not a clue."

"You weren't in his car when he was chasing me?"

She smiled, but didn't answer. I took that as a yes.

"We found roses and cards in the house where you were staying."

"They obviously belong to someone else."

"Whose home is it?"

"It belongs to Stephen Reynard. He's my attorney."

He seemed to be attorney to several suspicious people. "Any idea about a long stem, minus the rose, found in the warehouse behind the restaurant?"

"I have no idea. If you recall, the restaurant was filled with roses. Who knows how it got there?"

"What if I told you we found a print on the rose stem?"

"So?"

"A nice partial latent, lifted from the smooth stem of a rose that happened to have all its petals pulled off. From there, it's simply a matter of matching latents. See who it comes back to. I'm thinking we might even be able to match the stem to the petals found on your brother's lap . . ." I let it hang. There was no print, and I didn't know a damn thing about botany or whether or not petals could be matched to a stem or anything else in that realm, though I'd heard DNA from plants had been used in solving a homicide or two. I also figured chances were good that she was just as clueless.

"All right. I was there. My brother, Louis, had picked me up behind the restaurant. He'd been drinking and when he backed up, he hit my car on the corner of the warehouse, and I pulled off the rose petals and threw them at him, because I was mad. I got out, looked at the scrape he put on the car, and that's when I tossed the stem in the opposite direction and started walking off between the buildings toward the front."

She was good at covering all her bases, I thought. "Was there anyone else back there with you?"

"I think someone may have opened the back door of the restaurant and looked out. I didn't see who, but I heard Louis telling someone he was sorry, that he'd hit the side of the building. When I walked out front, I saw you kissing Nick and then a black car drove up and . . . well, you know what happened next."

"With me, yes," I said. "But not with you."

"I panicked. I didn't know who they were trying to hit. You or Nick. What I did know was that I didn't want my brother involved in all this mess, and I went back to tell him to leave, but he was already gone."

"And where did you go?"

"Nowhere. I simply blended into the crowd and convinced the officers that I'd already given my statement. I told the one that I was Adriana. He believed me.

Which certainly would be one explanation why Lucia's name didn't show up on the report that night. It was the rest of the story I was having problems with. Everything seemed to fit, but a little too neatly, and that concerned me.

"We found some rose petals this morning at one of the homes where I've been staying," I said. "Did you have anything to do with that?"

"And what if I did?"

"Stalking is against the law."

"So is murder. Someone killed my brother. I'd think you'd be going after them."

"What if I suspect you?"

"Trust me. I may not have cared for his lifestyle, but Louis was my brother and I loved him."

Trust you? Right. "Did you kill him?"

"No. When I found him the next day in my car, he was already dead. That's when I took off to stay at the house where you found me."

"Leaving your son?"

"He went with his nanny. He practically lives with her family, anyway."

Thank God for small miracles, I thought. "Any idea who might want to kill you?"

She leaned back in her chair, smiled, and said, "Pretty much everyone."

"How about we narrow it down some?"

"For starters, Earl's wife. She's rather unhappy about the whole affair thing, never mind the kid—couldn't have any of her own, you know. And Stephen Reynard wasn't too happy when I dumped him, for the simple reason that I know everything about his operation. He basically told me that if I told anyone, I might as well pick out my headstone now. And I'm sure if his wife, Adriana, found out about my affair with him, she wouldn't hesitate to have me killed. And there's Nick, of course. He's a little pissed off at me, right now."

"About what?"

"You name it. The kid, Earl, who the hell knows?"

"And when you found your brother dead, and you thought someone was trying to kill you, you called the police when?"

"I didn't."

"Why not?"

"I was worried they'd think I did it."

"So you knew it was murder, not suicide?"

"That's what I think."

"And you loved your brother so much, you were willing to let the murderer go free."

"Of course not—"

"—by hiding from us."

"I told you. You'd think I did it. I didn't want to be arrested."

"I'm wondering if maybe it wasn't more convenient to let us believe it was you who was dead in that car."

"It crossed my mind."

"Why?"

"Because it would get back to Nick, and he would tell the others, and I'd be able to hide out until this whole sordid mess was cleared up."

"Only Nick didn't believe it."

"You know, I think I've answered enough," she said, crossing her arms. "Either book me, or get me an attorney."

I looked at my watch, noted the end of the interview time, and wrote it down. "How about a few phone calls? You can pick out your own attorney."

"You're booking me? For what?"

"Stalking."

"Stalking? But it was just a bunch of rose petals. I was only trying to scare you."

"So you did leave the roses."

She opened her mouth to speak, apparently thought better of it.

I stood, indicating that the interview was over on my part. Since she'd invoked her rights, it meant that any further questioning was out.

I left the room. Rocky was waiting, along with Torrance and Parrish. "I take it you're done with the search?" I asked Rocky.

"CSIs are still out there, but barring any unforeseen great discovery, yeah, we're done."

"So we assume the roses were hers?"

"The stuff's there. Found it in a fridge, like a regular little florist shop. They hers? Or do they belong to that David Cole guy? It'd be nice to find out. Make our job a bit easier. Too bad she asked for her attorney."

Assuming we could get her to tell us the truth, whatever she said, now that she'd invoked, would get tossed from court.

The four of us left the interrogation room, our destination the Homicide office. Funny, but after everything I'd just learned in that interview, the one thing that stood out right now was Lucia's statement about Parrish—the words they exchanged in the ladies' room. Parrish had not mentioned that she had spoken to Lucia in the ladies' room, and now I wanted to know why.

34

"So how do you think it went?" Rocky asked me as the four of us stepped into the elevator.

"I think she's just like her ex-husband. Anything she told us in there serves her and no one else. Just enough to make the lies stick." I looked at Parrish, not anxious to ruin what I thought was a good truce, so I asked in as neutral a manner as I could, "What went on in the ladies' room that she would remember you?"

"I heard her talking about the diamonds to her friend, the owner's wife. I figured it was better to pretend that the whole thing was no big deal, so I acted like I came in to refresh my lipstick, just happened to overhear their conversation, and mentioned that the necklace you were wearing came from Tiffany."

"And what did she say?"

"She said, 'Tell your friend to stay away from my husband . . . or else.' I pretended to leave, then snuck back in. That's when you showed. I did tell Torrance, but with everything that happened, I forgot to tell you."

I glanced at Torrance, who gave a nod. In retrospect, between the drive-by shooting and the discovery of Louise Smith's body, I suppose it was possible that Parrish's contact with Lucia had been temporarily forgotten, and she didn't think to tell me—never mind that at that time we believed Lucia was actually Kyla Greene.

By the time we got back to Homicide, I'd put the matter from my mind. We briefed the lieutenant on the latest, and when we were done, it was well past the dinner hour. Rocky went home to his wife, and, with some subterfuge on vehicles to make sure no one was following us, Parrish, Torrance, and I went to the hotel for the night.

When we got there, Parrish went to the desk to arrange for our rooms, while Torrance showed me to the security room, where the agents assigned to watch over us via closed-circuit TV were stationed. Every entrance and exit was monitored, as was the parking garage and the hallway of the floor on which we were staying. In addition, there were motion detectors, so that anytime anyone went up and down our hallway, the agents were alerted, which meant even if they fell asleep at their posts—and one hoped that they wouldn't—they'd be awakened in time to see someone step off the elevator and approach our rooms.

Parrish met us a few minutes later, handing us each an electronic key card. "The only people allowed on this floor will be our agents. The elevator won't stop at that floor unless accessed by our room keys."

One of the agents, a young, dark-haired man, looked up from his monitor. "Welcome to the Federal Witness Protection Plan," he said. "Service with a smile, and we even deliver room service."

"Do we have to tip?" I asked.

Before he could answer, Parrish, apparently in no mood to joke—go figure—said, "I don't know about you two, but I have work to do. Bank accounts to go over."

"Thanks for the minitour," I told the agent. He gave a nod, his attention back on the screen, and the three of us left, walking to the elevators, while Parrish, in her straight-laced manner, gave me instructions on what I could and could not do. Essentially, I wasn't to leave my room until morning, precisely at 0700 hours, and then, only to meet with Parrish and Torrance.

Torrance seemed particularly quiet, and I wondered what he was thinking about. No way was I going to ask with Miss Straight Lace next to me. Once we got to the elevator, it was a quick ride up to our floor. Our rooms were about midway down the hall, three in a row, with Torrance and Parrish on either side of mine. I didn't like being under such close watch—I liked my freedom. Once I opened my door, however, I was willing to forgive the temporary inconvenience. We were talking first-class luxury, right down to the marble entryway, and plush carpet just begging to be walked across in bare feet.

Parrish and Torrance both waited until I was safely in my room. I managed a quick, "See you in the morning," and then closed the door behind me. Once inside, I set down my suitcase, kicked off my shoes, and stepped onto the carpet, my feet sinking into the soft depths. "Definitely nice."

I walked through the two-room suite, pleased to see that the bathroom was as nicely apportioned—hell, it was larger than my bedroom at home. One look at the oversized bath and the thick Egyptian cotton robe, and I knew what I was doing before anything else—soaking in a tub with no phones and no call-outs.

I started the water, put in some bubbles, a brand in a small fancy bottle with a French name I couldn't pronounce, and knew I was about to experience a luxury not to be repeated for quite some time, courtesy of the FBI.

There was a wet bar, and after turning on some soft music, I opened the refrigerator to see what sort of drinks my tax dollars were paying for. I was surprised to see a nice selection of high-end beers. I grabbed a Sierra Nevada and a wine glass, thinking if I was going to soak in style, my drink would be that way, too. And then I eyed the door between the rooms, realizing that when opened, it would lead directly to Torrance's room, or at least the door on his side, that if opened as well, would lead to his room.

Once again temptation struck . . .
I walked up, unlocked and opened it.
Stared at the closed door on his side.
Just knock. . .
But I couldn't.

I stood there for what seemed like forever, then realized I
did not have the guts to do it. I told myself that Parrish might
be in his room, discussing the case, and no way did I want
her to know I was even contemplating the possibility of such
a thing. Besides, I had bathwater running.

I walked away, not even bothering to shut the door on my
side. Perhaps somewhere deep down, I hoped that Torrance
might open it on his side, come in . . . But I figured I knew
better. He had a will made of iron, and nothing I ever did
seemed to break through it.

I put him from my mind, popped open my beer, poured it
into the wine glass, and set it on the tub's edge, along with
the bottle. I was officially off duty, and to hell with everyone
else, I thought as I undressed, tossing my clothes on a chair.

I stepped into the tub, leaving the door slightly ajar, the
better to hear the music. The water was hot, the beer cold,
and I wasn't sure if it could get much better. And as I sipped
at my beer, giving little thought that drinking on an empty
stomach might not be the best of plans, I began to feel for
the first time in days complete and utter relaxation, even
when my cell phone started ringing. It was on my bed, and
I was not getting out. I ignored it until it stopped. Then the
hotel phone started ringing. This wasn't quite so easy to ignore, since there happened to be an extension in the bathroom. But to hell with it. I figured I'd call whoever it was
later. Right now I was safe. No chance of drive-bys, no
stalkers, no interruptions. I let it ring, and it, too, eventually
stopped.

A girl could get used to this, I thought, draining my glass,
then leaning my head back. Between the heated water and

the beer, I had a slight buzz going, and I let my eyes drift shut, reveling in the feeling of contentment.

Until I heard a noise.

I opened my eyes.

Saw Torrance standing there, leaning against the door frame, his arms crossed. "I don't think," he said, "that I've wanted to take a bubble bath, since I was in grade school—until now."

Oh, God . . .

He made no effort to look away.

I swallowed. Tried to breathe normally.

"You didn't answer your phone, Kate. Either one. I was worried about you."

"I'm sorry."

"I'm not." His gaze moved over every inch of me, and there was no doubt what he could see through what was left of the bubbles. "You remember the promise you made in Napa?"

I nodded. "A rain check," I said, surprised I could even speak.

He smiled. Stepped into the bathroom. My heart started racing when he said, "I'm ready to collect."

35

Torrance took the terrycloth bathrobe from the hook, then walked over to the tub, kneeled beside it. He reached out and caressed my face, his touch sending a shiver through me, despite the warmth of the water. And then he reached around me, drew me toward him, until my face was a mere breath away from his.

"Say the word, Kate," he told me softly, "and I'll go."

I didn't answer at first. I tried to think of all the reasons I should, then all the reasons I shouldn't. Nothing made sense, but it didn't matter. There was only one thing I could think of. "Stay with me."

He took a breath, his shoulders relaxed, and only then did I realize he'd been waiting, unsure of my answer until the moment I'd said it. And as soon as it occurred to me, the thought was lost as his mouth touched mine. It wasn't a kiss born of desperation, hard, unyielding . . . This was different from everything I'd experienced. It was slow, soft, his lips barely touching mine, his tongue gently seeking, exploring . . .

And somewhere in the back of my mind, I was aware that I had stood, water and white suds dripping down my skin, the cold air rushing over me.

Torrance covered my shoulders with the robe before helping me from the tub. He stepped back, his gaze sweeping over me as I stood there, my hand in his. And then he brought me against him, holding me close, touching my stomach with one hand, every nerve in my belly rippling beneath his fingertips as he slid his hand up, caressing . . . until he reached my breast, warm, slick . . .

He brushed his lips against mine, then kissed his way down my neck, farther, farther, until I felt the heat of his mouth on my breast.

My heart raced. My knees grew weak. And just when I thought I wouldn't be able to stand any longer, he lifted me into his arms, and carried me to the bed.

The alarm went off at six, and I woke, feeling Torrance's arms around me.

"Good morning," he whispered.

"Good morning." I gave a sigh of contentment, not wanting to move.

"The shower awaits."

"No. I like feeling you next to me."

He spooned against me, drew me closer. "In the name of conservation, it would be a shame to take separate showers . . ."

My breath caught at the mental image of him soaping my back, and truth be told, we didn't exactly make it out of bed in a timely fashion, which left no time to play once we did hit the shower.

The mirrors were steamed when we got out, and Torrance wrapped himself in a towel, while I slipped on the thick terry robe. He took me into his arms, ran his finger down the neckline of my robe and said, "Did I tell you that Parrish wants us to meet in her room for breakfast?"

"Guess you forgot to mention it," I said, thinking that if we weren't careful, we were not going to be meeting anyone for anything. "Is that why you called last night?"

"Among other things."

"What other things?" I asked, reaching up, brushing my fingers against his unshaven face.

"To see if you wanted to have dinner with me."

I smiled. We had ordered dinner, separately, about fifteen minutes apart, each of us disappearing into our own room when it was delivered, wondering if we were fooling anyone, but not really caring. "Maybe we can do it again, sometime . . ."

"Dinner?" he asked, just before giving me a quick kiss.

"Among other things," I said with a grin, and the next kiss wasn't so quick. Sanity prevailed, and he soon left, leaving me to get ready on my own. I dried my hair, got dressed, and fifteen minutes later, with purse and card key in hand, left for Parrish's room.

Her door was ajar. I gave a quick knock, said, "Good morning," and walked in. Parrish and Torrance were seated at her table, going over paperwork, bank records from the looks of it. There was an assortment of breakfast pastries and fruit on the table, though neither had started eating yet. Parrish looked up, her gaze narrowing slightly as I approached.

Torrance, I noticed, looked the way he did every day, all business, no sign that anything out of his routine had occurred, and I admired his ability to maintain such a façade.

My world had been rocked last night— though in a good way— and I wondered if I was half as good as he was at putting on the purely professional, nothing-going-on-between-us front. I'd asked him once, if we slept together, what would happen when morning came? He'd responded that he didn't know, because we'd never gotten that far. Well, obviously we had now. So what did that mean? Were we an item? Was this a casual thing? I was too tired to think it through, but awake enough to realize Torrance and I still had a few issues to work on. He wasn't one to leave loose ends, and frankly I didn't want any—not that we could solve them right now with Parrish sitting between us, who at the moment was nodding toward an empty chair, indicating I should sit.

She slid a mug my way. "I seem to remember you like mochas," she said, before turning her attention back to the papers she held. "I hope the logistics of your room were okay?"

I paused, noted a rare smile playing at the corners of her mouth. Hell, I thought, recalling our conversation in the elevator, my trouble with some relationships and her parting comment about what could happen when you put two people in an enclosed space . . . Who would've guessed we'd been set up by Miss Straight Lace?

"The logistics were perfect," I replied, taking a seat, earning a look of bemusement from Torrance. Maybe one day I'd clarify that little exchange, but now was not the time.

I picked up the mug, pleased to see it was still fairly hot.

"Mocha okay?" Torrance asked.

"Heaven in a cup," I said, referring to his unspoken question: is the mocha better than sex?

The look he gave me was cynical at best. I gave him my most innocent smile, then asked Parrish, "Did you come up with anything on the bank accounts?"

"I'd like to take credit for it, but in truth we've had a team of accountants going over everything they picked up from the search warrant. Thanks to the account numbers you provided from Fiona Winchester's father, they've come to some interesting conclusions, though they're far from finished."

She gave an overly detailed description of money laundering, offshore accounts, and a multitude of suspicious operations and businesses that seemed to have income flowing into the bank, as well as out of the bank, into various accounts under various names and corporations, including a few belonging to Paolini.

I'm sure I had a glazed-over look when she finished.

"You're wondering what I said?" she asked.

"Precisely."

"The long and short of it is that, thanks to you and the Winchesters, we have our proof that the bank is being used for money laundering. But what is more interesting is that it appears that someone has been skimming money from some of the accounts, putting it in others, moving it around. Sort of a paper chase with numbers. And a large part of it is just plain missing."

"How large?"

"So far we believe almost six million. Which means that Earl Millhouse was stealing from the mob. And it could be that someone took revenge."

36

If Earl Millhouse was stealing from the mob, and got caught, it was certainly a good indication of why there was a hit put out on him. What didn't make sense, however, was the gun that had been used in the previous shootings, mine from the Twin Palms, and Fiona Winchester's.

The question remained, was I brought to the scene as Lucia claimed, to stop what was happening? Or to play executioner of the hit man? I suppose if one could have controlled the pedestrians, kept him from taking a hostage, he might have been killed. Or was it more that I was supposed to be a witness, verify who the suspect was, testify that it was a robbery? And was it really Lucia behind this? Or, as she claimed, someone else? Paolini had said that perhaps someone wanted me to find the gun, but I couldn't imagine this was true unless it was to throw me off the track—perhaps someone trying to clean house by killing off Earl Millhouse and allowing me to find the gun, thereby pinning all the shootings on this hit man, David Cole.

And what about Sophie Millhouse? The wife who had allegedly only recently learned of her husband's infidelity? I suppose it was possible that she'd been so overtaken by grief that the matter of her husband's bastard son was overlooked. While that would certainly be motive on her part for the murder of her husband, hiring a hit man wasn't the usual route taken by the scorned wife—not to say it wasn't done. Divorce seemed to be the more common route.

"I think," I said to Parrish and Torrance, "that we need to pay another visit to Millhouse's widow." I told them my thoughts on this, and miracle of miracles, even Parrish agreed.

Of course there was still the matter of the unknown person after me. Despite the fact that we thought the rose petals were left by Lucia Paolini, and that we had the hired hit man in custody, precautions were still needed and so, once we got back to the Hall, we set up the bait car with Torrance and Parrish. Rocky and I, followed by Bell and Waugh, took off for Millhouse's place.

It was close to nine when we arrived, and Sophie Millhouse answered the door wearing what appeared to be the same sweat suit she'd had on when we'd first talked to her a couple days ago. "You again?" she said.

"Yes. We have some more questions."

She held the door open, indicating we should enter. This time she led us into the kitchen, where she was apparently in the process of eating breakfast. This consisted of a cup of yogurt, half a grapefruit, and a glass, which, though still empty, stood next to a carton of orange juice. "Care for anything?" she asked.

We both declined.

"Sit," she said. "Hope you don't mind if I eat while we talk. My trainer is supposed to be here any minute. If I don't start exercising again, I'm going to fall apart." She poured her orange juice, then went to the cupboard and took out a bottle of vodka, splashing some into the glass. Breakfast of champions, I thought, as she took a long drink, then started in on her yogurt. "What is it you need?"

"You had mentioned the possibility of an affair your husband had with Lucia Paolini?"

"The bitch, yes," she said, then took a spoonful of yogurt.

The bitch? That seemed more like a response that would come from someone who *knew* the affair was legit. In our last conversation, she hadn't come across as so sure. "She ever mention who the father of her son might be?"

Sophie lowered the spoon to her dish, pushing the yogurt away as though suddenly losing her appetite. "She didn't."

"Who did?" I asked, since it was apparent she knew.

"Nick. I was at the bank, and I overheard him and Earl fighting about it. I don't think either of them realized I was there . . ." She shook her head, took a drink, then said, "Do you realize that the only goddamned insurance policy that son of a bitch took out left everything to that kid? I mean, he's just a kid. It's not his fault, but what the hell am I? I was married to the jerk for ten goddamned years, putting up with all his idiosyncrasies so that when he goes and gets himself killed, I'm left with next to nothing. Talk about lifestyle changes . . ."

"How much was the insurance policy for?"

"Five hundred thousand." She took a breath, gave a bittersweet smile. "Life is a goddamned bitch sometimes, you know?" she said, then finished off the rest of her vodka and orange juice. She poured more orange juice, went for the vodka bottle, then hesitated. "To hell with it. You realize that staying drunk these past few days hasn't done shit for my financial status? Makes it hurt a bit less . . ." She pushed the vodka away. Hope for the future.

"Mrs. Millhouse."

"Call me Sophie, please."

"Sophie, then. Did your husband leave any papers? Financial documents, that sort of thing?"

"In the wall safe."

"Would you mind if we take a look?"

"Help yourself. It's a bunch of worthless stuff. At least that's what I've been told." She led us into the living room, swung a painting of a cottage from the wall, revealing a safe.

There were stacks of paper that we went through, and sure enough, it did appear to be worthless, at least to our investigation, I thought, as I sorted through one stack and Rocky the other. He opened an envelope, held it up. "Someone filing for divorce?" he asked.

"What?" she asked, looking confused.

Rocky handed me the papers, and I looked them over. "Apparently your husband was in the process of filing for divorce," I said. "Is that why the house was for sale?"

"As a matter of fact, yes. I didn't want to mention it, because I was worried that someone would think I was involved."

"In what?" I asked.

"His murder. I mean, here he is, dead, and his insurance is to a kid that's not even mine, and he's had an affair . . . Christ, I need another drink . . ."

"You mentioned that someone else went through these papers?"

"Yes. My attorney, Stephen Reynard. He's the one who told me there was nothing worth a damn here."

"He take anything?" Rocky asked.

"A copy of the insurance policy is all. He was going to look it over for me."

I asked, "And you're sure that's all that was taken?"

"I think so. Frankly I didn't really pay attention. I was slightly blitzed, if you recall."

"You mean he came the same day we spoke to you?"

"Right before you got here."

No telling what he walked off with, then. I looked around the home, neat as a pin. "Did your husband keep everything in the wall safe?"

"Pretty much. Except his safe-deposit box at work."

"He has a safe-deposit box?"

"We got it before we had the wall safe put in a few years

back, and then we moved all the papers here. Earl had this pocket watch that was more sentimental than anything else in it. Silly to keep a whole safe-deposit for it."

"You're sure of the contents?"

"Stephen Reynard drove me over there to look inside it. Nothing but the damn watch and a damn copy of the same insurance policy—not that they'd let me take anything but the insurance policy. Apparently there's some rule you can only take three things. A will, insurance, and . . . Oh, yeah, the deed for the burial. They stand over you like a prison guard to make sure, just in case there's something that can be contested. Like the damn watch was worth anything, you know?"

"Do you still have the key?"

"Key? I, um, think so, unless Stephen kept it. Good luck getting in it. I can't even look at the watch until after probate," she said, leaving the room. She returned a moment later. "Here you go. Don't know what you're searching for, but you're welcome to look."

We took the key, had her write us a letter of permission, and with our shadow tailing us, we were at the bank thirty minutes later, showing the clerk not only our identification but also the letter from Mrs. Millhouse. The bank manager was not about to make a move, however, until she looked up Millhouse's signature card to determine if his wife had equal possession of his accounts and safe-deposit as well as being listed as the beneficiary. "Which box did you want to go into?" she asked me.

"There's more than one?"

"Yes. Mr. Millhouse has two."

I glanced at Rocky. "We need a search warrant for the other box."

"You know how long that's going to take?"

"You think they're going to give us the key otherwise?"

The bank manager smiled at Rocky. "Since neither are in Mrs. Millhouse's name, you'll need the warrant for both *and* we'll have to get a locksmith to drill the lock."

"Minor delay," I told Rocky, taking out my cell phone. I called Torrance. "It's Kate," I said, then told him what was going on.

"We'll take care of it. Give me an hour." Nice having a connection with the feds.

An hour later, we had our warrant and an FBI locksmith who, with warrant in hand, the bank agreed to use instead of their own locksmith. At Torrance and Parrish's arrival, the bank manager led us into the vault room. We opened the first box, and found within it, just as Sophie Millhouse had said, a pocket watch.

"Poor Mr. Millhouse," the book manager said. "I wonder if anyone knew they'd be looking in his safe-deposit boxes under these conditions." She walked to the far right of the room, and pointed to the second box. The locksmith took his tools, drilled the lock, opened the door, lifted the box out. He handed it to me and we took it to the counter.

The bank manager moved to the doorway. "We have a private viewing room, but I don't think it is big enough to accommodate everyone."

"This will do," I said. "Perhaps you can stand at the door, make sure no one comes in?"

"Of course." She stood with her back to us, allowing us privacy.

I opened the lid. Inside were several documents that looked like certificates of deposit. And below that, a zippered bank bag, the sort used by merchants to bring in cash and checks. Since it was illegal to keep cash in a safe-deposit box, I was curious to know what was in the bag, and unzipped it.

"Holy shit," Rocky whispered.

My sentiments exactly.

37

Diamonds. If I had to guess, I'd say close to six million dollars worth—since that was the amount of the diamonds being sought by our Robbery Detail.

We took custody of the box, and as I wrote up the receipt that the bank required—describing the contents as just that, "contents"—I wondered who else knew what was in it. My guess was Stephen Reynard, since he'd come with Mrs. Millhouse to look in the other box—perhaps believing the diamonds were in that one? That certainly wouldn't surprise me. Did Mrs. Millhouse know? Did anyone else know? Suddenly the conversation I'd overheard in the ladies' room at Etienne's came to mind. I had thought Lucia and Adriana Reynard were talking about the diamond necklace I had been wearing.

I realized now that I was wrong.

They were talking about the stolen diamonds.

The question remained, who stole the diamonds, and was that why Millhouse was killed?

I met with the bank manager in her office. Torrance was with me, while Parrish and Rocky were standing by in the vault room, waiting for the entourage of marked units that would accompany them back to the Hall. We weren't taking any chances with the amount. "Do you know if anyone besides Mrs. Millhouse and the family friend she brought made inquiries about this second box?" I asked her.

"I do know that Mr. Millhouse accessed it a couple of weeks ago—well, that box or the other, I'm not sure. That's easy enough to check, however. We, of course, followed normal procedure, like we would for any other customer."

"There's no variance on this? Even if he's the head honcho?

"None. He has to be accompanied to the vault with our safe-deposit custodian. He would have known this, of course."

"Was there anyone with him?"

"I honestly don't know. I didn't handle that transaction. Barb did. Would you like me to get her?"

"Please. Before you go, though, we would like to ensure that everything said here, even our visit, remains private. Your lives could very well depend on it."

"I understand," she said. "I'll let Barb know."

Barb was a young woman, twentysomething, with short, dark brown hair and blue eyes. "Let me think for a sec," she said, when we asked her. "I didn't know the woman with Mr. Millhouse, that's for sure, but then, I'm fairly new, so I don't know a lot of people yet. I thought it might have been his wife . . . but now that I think about it, Mrs. Millhouse came in the other day, and I don't think it was the same woman at all."

"Could you describe the woman who was with Mr Millhouse that day?"

"She had short red hair, that was . . . perfect, you know? Every strand in place. I remember thinking, wow, my hair never looks that way, like you know, how wigs are? And she wore large framed designer sunglasses."

I thought of Louise Smith and her red wig . . . "Could you identify her?"

"I don't think so. I didn't pay that much attention. But I did have her sign the access slip, if that helps?"

"It does," I said.

She pulled the slip for Millhouse. "Here it is . . . That's right. It was Jane . . . Couldn't really make out the last name."

"Thanks," I said, then eyed the slip. A lot of good it did. "Doe, Jane Doe."

I looked at the date that Earl and this Jane Doe had accessed the box—the Friday before Earl Millhouse was killed, and just a few hours before our Jane Doe had called me to set up a meeting in the bank parking lot. I was surprised, however, to see that it was not the box containing the diamonds. It was the box that held only the pocket watch. "We need to view the tapes," I told Torrance, since the FBI had taken the tapes right after the robbery. To Barb, I said, "Do you have the access slip from when Mrs. Millhouse came in with her attorney?"

She pulled that and handed it to me.

Sophie Millhouse's signature was on it, as was Stephen Reynard's. "Can you tell me when the other box was accessed?" I asked her, referring to the box containing the diamonds.

She gave me the slip. I read the date. It was last accessed by Earl Millhouse the day after the diamond heist. Undoubtedly when the stolen gems were put inside.

We took the signature cards from both boxes, leaving photocopies and a receipt for both with the bank. Before we left, we again admonished them that our visit and the fact we took the contents of the box needed to be kept confidential.

"You think they're real?" Rocky asked as we drove back. "The diamonds?"

"Hell, yes. And don't lose sight of the amount. There's about six million bucks missing from the bank, and six million bucks in diamonds suddenly turning up. I'm thinking that might have a lot to do with why Millhouse is dead."

"Guess Mrs. Millhouse ain't as destitute as she thought?"

"That all depends on where the diamonds came from,

don't you think? Especially considering they're probably stolen."

"Well, even then, the CDs ought to help—assuming they're not from skimming mob accounts. You think Reynard knew about the diamonds?"

"He knew about something because his wife knew." I told Rocky about the conversation I'd overheard in the restroom. "I can't imagine him being so altruistic that he helped poor, newly widowed Mrs. Millhouse in her search for an insurance policy with her name on it. Whether he knew exactly what he was looking for remains to be seen."

"Maybe we need to go back and talk to him and his wife."

"Definitely. But first we have some diamonds to count."

The FBI's precious-gems expert confirmed that we were looking at the diamonds stolen from the dealers' show. A couple of the larger stones had serial numbers laser-inscribed in the girdle, but the majority of the diamonds had no markings and could easily have been sold without cutting.

Rocky eyed the Polaroid of the glittering stones. "Hard to imagine all these little bits of glass are worth that much."

I looked up as Torrance walked in with the tapes from the bank. "Where's Parrish?" I asked.

"She's still talking to the gemologist." Torrance handed the bank tape to Rocky and he slipped it in the player. It started up, the date and time in the top corner. There were four squares, each focusing on a different section of the bank, all running simultaneously. The bottom-right corner showed the safe-deposit vault room, and next to it a door leading into a private viewing booth for customers wishing to view the contents of their safe-deposit boxes without witnesses.

I looked at the time stamped on the access card with Jane Doe's signature on it. We were over an hour too early. "Fast-forward it," I said. "Thirteen-thirty hours."

Rocky hit the fast-forward button. When he let go, the tape started up just a few minutes before our scheduled time. The three of us watched in silence, until we saw the woman who the bank clerk had described to us. The film was black and white, but there was no doubt we were looking at the same wig, same glasses, and same scarf as was worn by the woman—or rather our Louise Smith—from the parking lot. Whether it was actually Louise Smith, however, was a different question. She walked up to the vault room and waited, soon to be joined by Earl Millhouse and Barb, the safe-deposit custodian. The camera angle made it impossible to tell if it was our transsexual victim, Louise, or someone else dressed like her.

We watched as she stood outside the vault room, her hand resting on the smooth marble wall as she waited for the two to emerge from the vault room, Earl Millhouse carrying his safe-deposit box with one hand, while brushing a speck of lint from his buttoned suit coat with the other. Barb said something to Millhouse, who nodded. He opened the door of the private booth, allowing the wigged woman to enter first. He stepped in after her, closed the door, and Barb moved off. I could see her stepping into the line of tellers, apparently having a conversation about some banking activity, judging from the paperwork the teller was showing her.

I returned my gaze to the viewing booth, noting the time. 1334 hours. The pair had been inside for around a minute, then two, then five. Seven minutes later, they emerged, and, hoping to determine if we were looking at a woman and not a man dressed as a woman, this time I remembered to watch her hands. She brushed her lips with her fingers, but the shot wasn't close enough for me to make a determination, and she took off at a fast clip toward the front of the bank and to the lobby doors.

Millhouse never even looked in her direction, instead hurriedly moved toward the vault room, pushing his suit coat open with one hand to adjust his belt, as he stopped and waited for Barb to accompany him back into the vault room.

"Do me a favor," I asked Rocky. "Rewind it to just before they entered the booth."

Rocky did.

I watched as Barb and Millhouse came out of the vault room. "His suit coat is buttoned. Fast-forward until they exit."

Rocky pressed the control, let go just before they came out.

"Unbuttoned, never mind that she's wiping her mouth."

"Whatd'ya know," Rocky said. "She did him at the bank. Look, you can see his shirt is slightly askew at the belt line. Not what I'd expect for an anal retentive type."

Torrance said, "The question is, was this more than a conjugal visit or was something put in or taken from the safe-deposit box?"

Rocky nodded. "Maybe he used it as a prop to get into the room and have a quickie."

"Not if he knew what was in it," Shipley said. "You don't walk around with millions in diamonds just to get a little bit before lunch."

"Depends on how long it's been," Rocky said.

"Drag yourselves out of the gutter," I said. "At least long enough to realize the diamonds were in the other box."

"So," Torrance said, tapping the TV monitor, "maybe she thought the diamonds were in this one?"

"That seems more likely," I said.

"Regardless," Parrish said, "we have several days of tapes to verify no one else was in the box, assuming we can believe what's on the access slips. If anyone was in there anytime after the diamonds were stolen from the dealers, we'll know."

"All right," Rocky said. "Let's say this woman thought the diamonds were in there. Who is she? Our transsexual, who met us in the parking lot? Jane Doe aka Louise Smith?"

"It would appear that is what they want us to think," I said, as I walked up, rewound the tape until it showed her waiting by the vault for Millhouse and Barb to walk out. I suspected otherwise, and was beginning to think that Louise Smith had been set up in a big way. "Let's get a CSI to go out, print that marble wall right there where she's touching it," I said, tapping the screen. "A surface that slick, there's bound to be some decent prints on it."

Rocky picked up the phone. "Good eye, Gillespie. I'll get one on it."

Thirty minutes later, we got a call from the CSI team who had responded to the bank after looking at the video. A very clear latent was lifted from the wall. Ten minutes after they got back to the Hall, they were comparing the latent lift card to Louise Smith's prints and then to Lucia's booking prints and made a match to Lucia's right index finger.

"What I don't get," Rocky said after we found out the print belonged to Lucia, "is why go to all the trouble with the red wig, scarf, and glasses? What's the significance of Lucia looking like Louise Smith in drag?"

"Damn good question," I said. "Unfortunately, Lucia is not going to tell us, and her brother, Louise Smith, is dead . . ."

"What are you thinking?"

"Maybe we ought to have another chat with Madame Korsakoff. Considering her penchant for selective memory, there might be a thing or two she's overlooked."

"Like she's gonna want to talk to us when we're holding her on a trumped-up solicitation warrant?"

To say that Madame Korsakoff was not enjoying her complimentary stay in our jail was an understatement. "If you're not here to tell me I can post bail," she said, crossing her arms as Rocky and I walked into the interview room, "then I have *nothing* to say to you."

"You know," I said to Rocky. "Some people can't see past the part of 'better here than dead.' "

"Imagine."

Korsakoff gave us an annoyed look. "My freedom is far more important."

"You think that's what Louise Smith thought when they killed her? Or you think maybe she might have liked spending a couple nights courtesy of SFPD, so that she could enjoy the rest of her life doing what she wanted to do?"

"Fine. I get the point. What is it you want?"

"I'd just like to go over the conversation you overheard between Louise and this woman you think was her sister. Maybe there's something you missed? Something you forgot to tell us?"

"I told you everything."

"Well humor us and tell us again. You never know . . ."

"Like I said, this woman I think was Louise's sister comes over and is saying this whole TV appearance thing you made on that old murder is perfect, because of the timing."

"Timing? I don't remember you saying anything about timing."

"Well, I may have forgotten that part, because it really didn't make sense, and besides, it was before she started talking to Louise."

"What do you mean by that, and how do you know it wasn't Louise she was talking to?"

"I gathered she was talking to someone on a cell phone. Arguing, sort of. And definitely not with Louise, because she hadn't come in off the stage yet."

"And what was it you heard?"

She gave a shrug. "Something like, 'the timing's perfect, don't you see? We set it up, and it solves the murder and no one's looking at us. We'll get them back.' Then Louise walks in and the woman asks for her help to get you out to the lot, to help solve a murder, just like I told you."

"Anything else that might have slipped your mind?"

"That's it, I swear. When do I get out?"

"We'll talk to the DA as soon as we get this settled." I glanced over at Rocky to see if he got it all down. He looked up from his notebook, gave a sharp nod, and I stood. "One more question. Did Louise ever wear a red wig for her normal attire?"

"God, no. It didn't go with her skin tone at all."

"They had to be talking about the diamonds," I told the others when we returned to Homicide. " 'We'll get them back,' has got to mean just that. What I'd like to know is who the hell was she talking to on the phone when Korsakoff overheard her?"

"It seems to me," Torrance said, "that if we can figure that out, we'll have the other main player. I'll get a search warrant for her cell phone records, see if we can't find out who was on the other end of that call."

"I'll do it," Parrish said. "You're more familiar with all the players. Better that you stay here and help out."

"So," Shipley said, "you think that Lucia made an attempt to get the diamonds when we saw her dressed up like her brother in drag?"

"I definitely think she was after the diamonds," I said. "But I'm not so sure she was dressing up like her brother."

Parrish, about to walk out the door, stopped on hearing that, and said, "If not her brother, then who?"

"What if Lucia was trying to look like Sophie Millhouse so she could gain access to the safe-deposit box?"

"No way," Rocky said. "Like Earl's not going to recognize that she's not his wife?"

"Nah," Shipley said. "He'd know, especially after she went down on him."

"My point," I said, "is that Lucia is a chameleon. She will take on anyone's identity to achieve her own ends. I can see her using her call girl expertise and past relationship to lure Earl Millhouse into the safe-deposit room for a quickie."

Rocky nodded. "He doesn't even blink an eye when she

shows up dressed as his wife, because he's going to get some. But unbeknownst to her, he doesn't bring out the safe-deposit box with the diamonds, he brings out the other box with the pocket watch."

"Perhaps," I said, "that was when she realized that he was on to her, and she had to find a different way to get the diamonds."

"Like hiring a hit man to take him out in a robbery?"

"And getting us there to witness it, and witness Louise Smith as our potential informant," I said. "They'd have to know we'd be checking tapes. We'd believe Louise was our Jane Doe who signed the access card. They're wearing the same clothes, wig, and glasses. Then she ends up dead, which eliminates her as a witness."

"And eliminates Lucia as a suspect, because her sister/brother was the Jane Doe. It mighta worked, too," Rocky said, nodding to the TV screen, "except that Lucia touched the wall. Not that it does us any good. Lucia bailed. And we don't really have anything here we can arrest her for, unless going down on someone in a bank is a crime."

"I have a better idea," I said as Lieutenant Andrews walked back in the room and stood next to Shipley. "We set up a sting with the diamonds. Have the bank manager, or whoever, call Mrs. Millhouse and say they found a beneficiary card or something that sounds legit, and say that Millhouse and her attorney can have access to the safe-deposit boxes now. Let her open them and see what she does with the stuff, see what happens."

Andrews said, "Please tell me you're not suggesting we let her loose with six million dollars in diamonds?"

"It's only money," I said. "What's a few million?"

"Funny, Gillespie. What's your plan?"

"We put in fake diamonds," I said. "We fill the bank with undercover personnel, see who shows up, then follow them.

At worst, if we lose them, we're out some fake diamonds. At best, we find out where the diamonds were intended to go."

"What if Mrs. Millhouse doesn't know the diamonds are there and she doesn't pick 'em up?"

"She might not know, but Lucia knows, and I'll bet Reynard knows. Why else would he be fired up to play attorney when he hasn't practiced in a number of years? The question is who else knows? Who was Lucia talking to on the phone when Korsakoff overheard her?"

Andrews nodded. "I like the plan."

"Yeah," Shipley said. "No chance for a screw-up."

We hoped.

38

The arrangements were made. We replaced the diamonds with roughly the same amount of cubic zirconium look alikes. We would do nothing in the bank but observe, since we didn't want to put any customers, employees, or undercover officers in danger. We'd watch them go in, watch them go out, then tail them. And in the case of counter-surveillance, we'd bring agents in a couple at a time, some as employees, some as customers, until we had the place infiltrated with enough to cover most any situation—assuming Mrs. Millhoue didn't make the appointment first thing in the morning—something we would certainly discourage.

Torrance and Parrish responded to the bank, where the manager made the call, and according to Torrance, did a splendid job of making it sound as though a mix-up had been made and they should have released the full contents of the safe-deposit boxes to begin with. All Mrs. Millhouse needed to do was to make an appointment for anytime the next business day, appear with her lawyer, sign the release, and the boxes would be hers.

"So what happened?" I asked Torrance when he'd called to tell me.

"Sophie Millhouse said she needed to phone her attorney, Reynard, I presume, then she called back. She made the appointment for tomorrow afternoon. Thirteen-hundred hours."

"The same time her husband was killed."

"Whether the time is hers or Reynard's remains to be seen. Since it's the lunch hour, the bank should be crowded, which will help our agents blend in more. We have a tech in there now, allegedly repairing the cameras, but in reality setting them up so that we can actually monitor the bank cameras from another location. Business will go on as normal. As soon as the diamonds leave the bank, the rolling surveillance will begin. And to make life interesting, we've taken the bank bag and had a locater sewn into the seam at the bottom. They'd have to rip it apart to find it."

"Nice touch."

"Parrish's idea."

Figured. I kept my thoughts to myself, however, because Parrish was the least of my concerns. Nightfall was approaching and I wanted to know what that meant for Torrance and me, and our first night after a somewhat undeclared relationship. I still didn't know where that left us, and I wasn't brave enough to just come out and say something. Definitely not over the phone while we were working a case. If there was one thing I knew about Torrance, he was intensely private, so much so that I often wondered if we were ever to progress past this tentative stage, would he acknowledge our relationship in public? "Are we still booked at the hotel?" I asked—a roundabout way of finding out what he had in mind tonight.

"Yes. Parrish and I will be finalizing the plans with the other agents, so we probably won't be around for dinner."

"I assume we're all going to meet tomorrow?"

"Zero-seven-hundred hours. Do me a favor. Let Andrews know so he can set up a conference room."

"I'll do that now. See you in a few."

That done, Rocky and I drew up our agency's plan for the

rolling surveillance, which we would coordinate with the FBI come morning. It was late by the time we finished and Rocky drove me to the hotel. The moment I got into my room, I opened my side of the adjoining door. Wishful thinking on my part.

I fell asleep going over the plans, wondering if I'd missed anything, and when I answered my six A.M. wake-up call, I saw that the door to Torrance's room was still closed.

Apparently he'd chosen not to open it last night. I told myself it could be something as simple as he got in too late, or something as complex as he didn't want things to progress too quickly, or too steadily . . .

Perhaps what I didn't know wouldn't hurt me, I thought as I dressed for the day. At precisely 0645 hours, my phone rang. It was Parrish. "Hope you slept well," she said.

"Not bad."

"Torrance is here. We have mochas to go."

"I'll be over in a couple," I said.

Torrance looked tired when I walked in. So did Parrish for that matter, and both their good mornings to me sounded less than enthused. Like me they'd been up too late working on the case. "Ready when you are," I said.

Parrish handed me a mocha. "Grab a Danish if you want one. We need to get going."

I skipped the Danish, since I knew Andrews would have bagels if he was providing breakfast for those involved with the surveillance. We left the hotel, with me in the back of the car, listening to Torrance and Parrish debate certain aspects of their plans. Apparently the three of us, and Rocky as well, would be monitoring the cameras from inside a closed room at the bank. Ten minutes later, we were pulling into the Hall of Justice parking lot.

The meeting room was nearly full, agents and SFPD officers wandering in, eating bagels and donuts, drinking coffee. About ten after the hour, everyone was present, about thirty agents and officers combined. Parrish and Torrance presented the operation plan, including copies of photos of the players involved. When they finished, Rocky and I presented our rolling surveillance plan, which would start once our suspects left the bank. Rocky passed out copies while I pointed to a map drawn on the dry erase board that covered one wall. "The bank's main doors face north into the parking lot," I said. "We shouldn't have a problem maintaining our surveillance while they're in the lot, but, as you can see, there are several exits onto two main arteries. We intend to have teams set up on every intersection for a couple of blocks out," I said, pointing to each location as I spoke.

An agent raised his hand. "What about the BART stations? Anybody watching the trains?"

"On the last page, you'll see a list of the BART stops closest to the bank. One is almost across the street. The times are listed for the trains at the bottom of the page, and yes, we'll have officers at those locations. Before we get started, please check to make sure your cell phone, pager number, and call sign are listed correctly on the op plan."

That done, we fielded any questions that arose. Torrance walked up to me as everyone was leaving for their respective assignments. "You ready?" he asked.

"Ready," I said.

"Be careful, Kate," he replied, his voice quiet, his gaze holding mine.

Before I could say anything beyond, "I will," Parrish walked up.

"See you out at the bank," she said, and then the two of them left.

Rocky came up beside me, and together we walked to the car. "You look depressed," he said as we slid into our seats.

"Just confused."

"About what?"

"Torrance. I can never tell what he's thinking," I said, as I turned the key, started the engine. "He's so damn closed."

Rocky eyed me, as I backed out. "And you're just discovering this?"

"Well, no, but I'm wondering if maybe it's dumb to get involved with a man who, well, isn't big on displaying public affection."

"You forgetting your ex? If you recall, Reid had no problem displaying public affection with you—"

"Or anyone else."

"My point exactly. So what the hell brought this on anyway?"

"We slept together."

"About damn time."

"I guess I just thought he'd say something."

"What? You want him to jump up on the table, announce to every officer and agent in there, guess what? Kate and I finally did what we should have done months ago?"

"Funny. That's not what I meant. I just want to know where we stand is all."

"You mean, like are you going steady or was it just a one-night gig?"

"Yeah."

"Torrance doesn't strike me as a one-night-stand kind of guy—if he was, he'd have slept with and dumped you a long time ago."

"Gee, Rocky. For a friend, you know all the right things to say."

"You want to know what I really think?"

"What?"

"If he ever publicly acknowledges that you two are, you know, together, then you better make damn sure that's what you want. I don't think he takes that commitment stuff lightly."

I looked over at him, just before pulling out of the garage. "You're starting to sound a little too philosophical for me."

"You asked."

"That'll teach me."

We arrived at the bank at 0845 hours, parking amid the cars in the center of the lot so as not to stand out. Torrance and Parrish were inside, waiting for us. The manager let us in when we got there, and then showed the four of us to a back room where the FBI had already set up the monitors for the several cameras.

We put on our headsets, then started our radio checks the moment we were ensconced in the room, since each officer and agent would call in as they arrived at their locations. Ten minutes before the bank was to open, several of our officers were still en route and had not checked in, not that we were worried. Our suspects weren't due to arrive until several hours later.

Shipley and Zim were the first to check in, setting up at the lot not too far from the hair salon. Shipley gave his call sign, then, "How do you copy?"

"Loud and clear," I said.

"We have the north entrance in sight. Bank manager approaching from the inside, unlocking the doors for business. Few customers waiting out in front."

I looked in the monitor, saw the manager unlocking the doors, saw the customers, one being an FBI agent. "Tenfour." I glanced at Torrance, who nodded. Before we could do a radio check on the agent, Shipley called in again.

"Got a vehicle matching Reynard's, pulling up into the bank lot now. Two occupants."

"Can you copy a plate?" I asked.

"Negative. Looks like Reynard exiting the driver's side," Shipley said. "Unknown female on the passenger side. Red hair, small build, possibly Millhouse, but can't be sure from this distance."

"Son of a bitch," I said, watching the monitor. "They're too damn early, and if I'm not mistaken, that's a police radio right there at the merchant's window."

Torrance moved up to the screen. "We need to get it out of there before they arrive."

I keyed the mike. "Emergency traffic only," I said, hoping all the officers were close to their locations by now. "Our suspects are here."

Parrish was immediately on the phone, calling one of the agents "working" at a desk. "He can't get to the radio without drawing undue attention."

There was silence, then Shipley saying, "They're walking toward the north entrance . . . going in the doors now."

"We have them in sight," Torrance said.

It was definitely Reynard, and with him a female that from the monitor looked more like Lucia with a red wig than Sophie Millhouse—hard to tell since she was wearing large sunglasses. Regardless, if we didn't do something soon, they'd walk right up to that radio and know we were on to them.

39

Only one thing to do.

I stepped out into the main bank. Slipped out the door. The radio was just a few feet away. I walked over, casually lifted it off the counter, turned it off, then carried it by my side out of view. Unfortunately, I couldn't get back into the room with the others, nor could I move out into the bank without being seen.

I looked around, saw the manager's empty desk and in front of it, a large sign advertising new accounts. Thank God for corporate ads. I sat, just as Reynard and the woman walked my way. My only saving grace was that the manager did not panic at their early arrival. Instead, she took the packet of papers we had prepared the day before, and, as though nothing out of the norm had occurred, walked up to meet them, and guided them to the merchant's window, actually more of a cubicle with a door, which effectively blocked them from seeing me.

"These are the papers Mrs. Millhouse needs to sign?" I heard Reynard ask.

"They are," the manager said.

I could hear the rustling of papers, and guessed that he was looking them over in proper attorney fashion, before handing them to his "client" so that she could sign them.

I glanced at the front door as a woman and a child, and

two men behind them walked in, one man carrying a newspaper. One agent, three unknowns. I shuffled some papers on the desk, just in case anyone was watching, making sure the sign stood between me and the merchant's window. A moment later, the phone rang, and I wondered if I should answer it. Better take it, I figured. I could always put them on hold.

"Bay Trust Mutual," I said.

"What's going on?"

It was Torrance, sounding less than pleased.

"We have a number of customers," I said, keeping it vague.

"I can see that on the monitor. I'd like you to get back in here."

"I don't think that's possible," I said, glancing up when I heard the woman's raised voice—Lucia I realized, playing the part of Sophie. "I'll have to put you on hold."

"Don't you dare, Kate."

I didn't, though it was tempting. Instead, I angled the phone so that Torrance could hear as well, since our pretend Mrs. Millhouse's voice was raised, apparently upset by whatever the manager had told her, something I'd missed when Torrance called.

"Why is it," Lucia said, "that *I* have to make an appointment and sign releases for something that was *mine* to begin with?"

"Just sign," I thought I heard Reynard say, though I couldn't be sure as his voice was much lower.

"Sign. Sign," she said. "My husband leaves me *nothing,* the bank *screws* me over, and *you* want me to sign. I'm not sure I should. Christ. Where'd I put the key . . . ?"

Key? We'd drilled out the lock during the search warrant. "Oh, shit," I said into the phone.

"What's wrong?" Torrance asked.

I whispered, "The key she has won't fit."

"It's a little late to think of that."

"Tell me about it." I was not happy about the slipup. Parrish had gone over everything last night, presumably with Torrance. Regardless of how it happened, placing blame at this late point was useless. I looked around. Saw one of the agents at a desk on the opposite side of the bank. "Do me a favor. Call Charlie. Tell him to bring some papers over here for a signature."

"Will do."

I hung up. A moment later, Charlie's phone rang. He answered it, looked over at me, gave a nod. He hung up the phone, grabbed a stack of forms from his desk and walked over, crossing the bank lobby to my side. He leaned over the desk, as though pointing out where I should sign the papers, and I whispered, "Remind the manager that our customer no longer has the correct key . . ."

"Sure thing," he said. He took the papers to the merchant's desk, said something to the manager as he handed her the papers, his voice too low for me to hear.

"I see," she said. "I'll get right on it. I'm sure the error has to do with her accounting, not a true shortage." She handed the papers back to the agent. "Do me a favor. Go in the back and get the shortage slip and the report from window three, while I finish with Mrs. Millhouse and her attorney."

"Sure," he said, then walked toward the back of the bank and out of my view, undoubtedly to the camera room. He returned a moment later, carrying a manila envelope with his "error report," the key undoubtedly palmed, as he handed it to the manager.

She thanked him, then returned to the merchant window. "Everything looks in order. If you give me the keys, I'll unlock the boxes for you."

She was smooth, no doubt about it. "Follow me," she said, when they apparently handed her the keys. I saw them move off toward the vault room. The moment they rounded the corner, I picked up a folder from the manager's desk, then casually walked toward the back offices, tapping on the door that led to the camera room.

Rocky let me in. "Not bad, Gillespie. You looked real good out there."

"I knew my high school drama skills would pay off someday," I said. "I'm pretty sure that's Lucia out there and not Mrs. Millhouse."

Parrish looked up from the monitor. "We figured as much. By the way, thanks for catching the key."

"You're welcome," I said, moving up beside her and Torrance. They were watching the safe-deposit vault room. A camera had been installed in it just for the operation, and I could see the manager bending down, putting first one key in, then the other, turning it, sliding the box out, then handing it to Lucia, who started walking toward the door, where Reynard awaited her. Suddenly she stopped, turned, looked toward the manager, who was saying something to them.

"What's she doing?" Parrish asked. "Why's she stopping them?"

Reynard and Lucia looked at each other, then back at the wall of safe-deposit boxes. I realized then what it was. "I think she pointed out that they were forgetting the other box. The one with the watch in it."

"Jesus," Parrish said. "We all know they don't want it." A second later, the manager opened that box, and handed it to Reynard, and he and Lucia walked out of the vault room, followed by the manager. They appeared on the next monitor as they stepped up to the viewing booth. The manager unlocked the door, let them in. Unfortunately we had no camera inside, but about two minutes later, the door opened and out stepped Reynard and Lucia, who clutched her straw tote bag as though it carried the crown jewels. I'm sure, in her mind, it did, since the bank bag was locked, and I was confident that if she did look at the diamonds, they'd stand up to a quick scrutiny.

She walked stiffly, the bag's straps over her shoulder, the bag tucked firmly at her side.

"Call it in, Gillespie," Parrish said.

I picked up the radio. "Subject left the vault room . . ." I said as Reynard held Lucia by her shoulder, leading her from the bank.

Shipley was on the air the moment they stepped outside. "I have a visual. Both subjects walking out the north exit to their vehicle . . . Stand by. Some soccer mom's minivan just pulled up, parked next to them. Can't see around it . . . Zim?"

Zim was at the opposite end of the lot. "Yeah, I got them. They're at the car. Reynard's unlocking the door and Mill-house is doing a dance with the soccer mom, trying to get past her into the car . . . Okay. She's in the car. It's backing out . . ."

"I got it," Shipley said. "I'll be taking the point. You with me, Zim?"

"I'm with you. I'll wait until you pull out."

"Don't lose them. They're obviously in a hurry."

I looked at Torrance. "We have a read on the bank bag?"

He looked at a different screen. "It activated the moment they walked out the doors."

"At least that's going without a hitch," I said, as Rocky and I started toward the door. "We'll see you in the field."

Torrance nodded, his attention back on the locator screen. "We'll be out in a few, as soon as Charlie comes in and takes over."

Rocky and I left them, heading out through the bank to the parking lot, and once again I wondered who it was that Lucia had been talking to on her cell phone when Korsakoff had overheard her?

Reynard?

He might be running drugs from his restaurant, but was he a main player? Was he strong enough to hold his own against Lucia?

No sooner had I decided that he was not than I glanced across the street, at the entrance to BART, where I saw Reynard's car slow.

"Son of a bitch," I said.

"What?"

"I think Reynard just dropped her off at the BART station."

Rocky looked over, saw what I saw. The mass of commuters. "Definitely not good," he said.

40

The first thing I did was call Torrance on the cell. I wasn't taking any chances that someone was monitoring our radio traffic, despite the fact that we were using what was supposed to be a secure tactical channel. Radios were lost, stolen . . . And I didn't like it that they had anticipated our response.

It was bad enough that Reynard and Lucia had arrived four hours ahead of schedule. But to have Lucia Paolini appear in Sophie Millhouse's place, then have Reynard drop her off at BART, told me they had spent considerable hours planning how they were going to get the diamonds out of there.

"What happened, Kate?"

"I think Reynard may have dropped Lucia off at the BART station."

"The tracking system showed it stopped moving just outside the bank. We figured the car got stuck in traffic."

"The car's long gone. You have units on it?" I asked.

He checked with Parrish, came back on and said, "Affirm, they're following it, anyway. Stand by, we've got a read on the bank bag . . . They're closing in . . ."

I could hear his radio traffic through the phone, then, "The bag's moving again. They have it pinpointed to the BART station."

I glanced toward the station. The street-level platform was crowded with commuters. Down below would be worse.

"Let's go," I told Rocky.

He was looking at the BART schedule. "Next train's in four minutes."

I informed Torrance as we crossed the street to the platform, let him know what we were doing.

About midway down the escalator, I saw her, walking quickly toward a man, his back to me. I recognized him. Nick Paolini. "She's there," I said, keeping an eye on her as she handed something to Paolini. "She's passing something to him. Green bag."

"I see it," Rocky said. "Looks like the bank bag. Let's split up."

Torrance radioed his and Parrish's arrival, then asked, "What's your location?"

I barely heard him over the echo of the arriving train. "At the bottom of the escalator."

"Ten-four."

Lucia looked up just then. Saw me. I was still too far away, and before we could close in on her, the train doors opened and the departing passengers blocked my view.

"I lost her," I said into my radio, weaving through the crowd.

"Paolini's heading this way," Rocky called in.

"Can you stop him?"

"Affirm."

"Ten-four. I have you in sight," I said, eyeing Rocky as he stepped up to Paolini.

I quickened my pace as I radioed for Torrance and Parrish, informing them to keep watch for the now-missing Lucia. My gaze on Paolini, I saw him stop short when he saw Rocky, then turn, undoubtedly looking for me, knowing I couldn't be far behind. When I walked up, when he saw me, he smiled. "Inspector," he said. "A pleasure as usual."

I ignored the greeting. "Why are you here?"

"I'm waiting for the next train."

"Something about you and your newly acquired desire for public transportation doesn't ring true."

He smiled, though less enthusiastically. "I'm trying to be ecologically minded."

"I doubt it. What did Lucia give you?"

"I have no idea what you mean."

"You don't mind if I pat you down?"

"For what?" he asked, his voice taking on an edge.

"For weapons," I said, giving him the one answer he couldn't refute.

He said nothing at first. He knew the law, probably better than most officers, and I could tell by the look on his face that he was not pleased. He had no choice. We were allowed to do a pat down for weapons—which meant we'd find whatever it was she'd given him. And if it was the diamonds, we'd know in an instant.

Finally he said, "I have no idea what it was she gave me. She simply asked for me to hold it."

"Now there's an original line."

"The truth is always best. What you are looking for is tucked into the back of my waistband." When I nodded to Rocky, Paolini said, "You're not going to do the honors?"

"Not this time. You know the routine. Hands behind your head."

He complied, and Rocky patted him down, handing me the green bank bag, which was, just as he said, tucked in his waistband. There were no weapons—not that I expected any. Paolini rarely carried. He had others to do that for him.

"How did you get here?" I asked.

"Am I under arrest?" he asked, as Torrance and Parrish walked up.

I handed Parrish the bag. She unlocked it, looked inside, gave a sharp nod as people milled around as, some stopping to watch the action.

"Yes," I replied. "You are."

"For what?"

"We'll start with possession of stolen property," I said, as Torrance and Rocky handcuffed him. I looked up, saw several agents and officers coming down the escalator to help with the search for Lucia. A couple officers proceeded onto the train. I figured she wouldn't get far. "Let's take him into the BART office." It was nearby, and we weaved through the myriad commuters, though many had given us more than enough space. Once in the office, the door closed, shutting out the noise of the people and the departing train. I took out my Miranda card and read Paolini his rights as he sat on a chair. "I am aware of my rights, Inspector," he said. "What is it you want?"

"I think you know the answer to that."

He didn't reply.

"Why don't you start with the diamonds? I take it that's what Lucia had that allegedly belonged to you?"

He didn't answer.

"You knew they were stolen when she gave them to you?"

Again, no answer.

"Is this why Earl Millhouse was killed?"

"You are saying it wasn't a robbery?"

I was taken aback. We'd kept it from the press and from our interviews, just as Torrance had asked. But if anyone knew of the hits in this town, Paolini certainly did.

"Answer the question."

"I have no idea."

"It seems to me that you have the diamonds that were in his safe-deposit box. He's dead . . ."

Paolini was quiet a moment. Then, as though resolving himself to his fate, something I'm sure would be altered once his team of attorneys took over, he said, "I bought the diamonds. They may have been stolen before I took possession, but I paid for them believing they were a legitimate purchase."

Yeah. People often buy six million bucks worth of gems on the street. "Who did you buy them from?"

"I'll want a deal."

Torrance said, "We're not dealing on murder. Let's take him to the Hall."

"No," Paolini said. "Here, now, or no deal."

"Deal?" I said. "On what? You haven't given us anything."

"Fiona Winchester?"

I glanced at Torrance. He nodded. "You talk to him. I'll go get the car." He'd need to park it at the top of the platform, which meant we'd have to block traffic on the street. Headaches for the commuters, but they'd get over it.

As soon as he left, the BART officer took a position by the door, which was closed and locked. Rocky stood by me as I said to Paolini, "About Fiona Winchester?"

"Your Narcotics officer, Abernathy, was working for Marcel Etienne and Earl Millhouse. They were running drugs from the restaurant, as your department suspected. When it became an official investigation, and Abernathy couldn't make it go away, Marcel panicked. I'd heard that he got coked up, and that Abernathy assisted him along in that endeavor—by making sure he didn't come out of the warehouse alive."

"And how was Fiona involved?"

"I'm not sure. I believe that she witnessed something at the warehouse, or took something that could incriminate them. Word on the street was that Abernathy gave the gun to Antonio Foust and had her taken out. It was Foust who took a shot at you from the apartment."

"Foust?"

"He worked for Abernathy, who gave him the order. You were getting too close for his comfort."

"The gun," I said, wondering how much of this was true, how much was designed to assist Paolini in his own scheme. "Any idea on where it came from?"

"I can tell you who gave it to Abernathy to begin with, who he was working for. Earl Millhouse."

41

I was surprised to hear that Earl Millhouse had owned the weapon that had been used in three shootings, and that Abernathy, and Foust, had worked for him. "Does this have anything to do with why Millhouse was killed?" I asked Paolini.

"You may find this hard to believe, Inspector, but I have no idea why Millhouse was killed."

Paolini was right. I did have a hard time believing that he didn't know why. But I knew from experience that if I didn't broaden my scope, my focus, I could possibly miss something important. "Do you know who was involved in his killing?"

He remained silent. That told me he did know, even if he was unaware of the motive, something I doubted. But because of his warped, iron-clad ethics, he wasn't about to say. That alone was enough to strengthen my suspicions of Lucia's involvement. Even so, there was still a piece of the puzzle missing, and I strongly suspected that if I could determine who it was Lucia had been arguing with on the phone, and why Paolini wasn't aware of who had placed the hit on Millhouse, then I would solve my case. "Why are you helping me?" I asked.

His gaze met mine, though he said nothing at first. Then, "Lucia's son, Inspector. He might not be my flesh and blood, but if I am in jail . . . ?"

"You're going to jail for possession of stolen property, and undoubtedly money laundering."

"Far better that than murder, Inspector, though I don't expect the charges in either to stick. And there is the matter of my cooperation . . . That I helped you to find Lucia . . ."

"Helped? I would hazard a guess that your help was a way of keeping tabs on what we knew about Lucia and the diamonds."

He raised a brow, but didn't respond, leading me to believe that I was fairly accurate in my assumption . . . Still, there was something that I was missing. What was the phrase that Korsakoff had overheard? "We'll get them back . . ." That implied to me that Lucia and her partner had the diamonds at one time, and apparently lost them to Earl, thereby having to come up with plan B—which was take out Earl and get into that safe-deposit box.

"So *you* were supposed to get the diamonds?" I asked Paolini.

He nodded.

"You paid for them?"

"Not realizing they were stolen."

Right. "How much?"

"Two million dollars."

"To Lucia?"

Again, he nodded.

"Too bad you didn't use a credit card with a double back guarantee. The bank bag was filled with cubic zirconia."

"Trust me, Inspector. I figured that out the moment I saw you."

I barely heard him, because it occurred to me what it was I had overlooked in all this. If anyone could argue with Lucia, it would be Paolini. But he was *not* the arguing type. A man like Paolini made his own laws. That discounted him as my other murder suspect—in this case at least . . . No, it had to be someone else. Someone strong enough to stand up to Lucia, to argue with her . . .

And then I recalled that Parrish was to have written the search warrant for Lucia's cell-phone records, a document that would probably provide us with that very answer . . . "Where the hell is Parrish?" I asked Rocky, wondering if she'd taken off with Torrance.

"Thought I heard her say something about going to the restroom," he said, not looking the least bit concerned.

I glanced at the BART office restroom, the door slightly ajar. Parrish obviously wasn't in there. "You sure that's what she said?" I asked Rocky.

"I wasn't exactly paying attention. I heard the word restroom, that was it." He gave a nod toward Paolini. "You want that we should take him on up now?"

"Yeah," I said, pulling out my radio. Rocky took Paolini by the arm, had him stand, and with him and the BART officer on either side, they escorted Paolini from the office. I followed them, calling Torrance on the radio. "Is Parrish up there with you?"

"Negative," he said. "I'm standing by with the vehicle."

We passed the ladies' room on our way to the escalator, and I stopped. Two things occurred to me. One, when other choices were available, as a woman, I *never* used a public restroom while on duty. Two, I had a hard time believing that Parrish would just excuse herself to use the ladies' room, while on assignment, carrying a bag of diamonds, no matter how fake, and I wondered if Rocky had somehow misunderstood her.

He and the BART officer were about halfway up the escalator with Paolini in tow, and I decided it couldn't hurt just to check the restroom.

I pushed open the door, standing to one side as I looked in. It appeared empty, but the stall doors were closed, and I couldn't tell from my position if they were occupied or even locked. Cognizant that my backup was heading up the escalator with a prisoner, I remained where I was. "Parrish?" I called out.

Nothing.

I hesitated. Why I'm not sure, but something, maybe a slight rustling noise from the far end, caught my attention. I drew my weapon, instinct telling me something wasn't right.

The door to the last stall swung open.

Out stepped Parrish.

She was holding a gun.

And it was pointed at me.

42

Parrish looked right at me. "Put down your gun," she said, her voice never wavering.

I hesitated. There was something terribly wrong with this scenario. And it had nothing to do with me being on the wrong side of her gun.

That was when I noticed her pale face, the sheen of perspiration on her upper lip . . . The signs that told me her heart was thudding as hard as mine . . .

I glanced to my right. Saw the stalls, the doors closed. The last stall, the wider door that Parrish stood in front of . . .

My gaze flew to hers.

"Just put down the gun," she said, hers still leveled at me.

"What are you doing?" I asked, trying to make sense of this.

She didn't answer. Instead, she directed her gaze to the ground, to the front of the stalls, the closed doors. Her head remained stock still. Not a muscle moved.

I glanced in that direction. Saw the single, unexpended round on the floor.

I looked back at her, the apologetic half-smile about her mouth . . .

Jesus Christ.

I heard a train arriving. I keyed my radio as I held it down by my side. Kept the channel open, hoping my conversation could be heard over the train's noise. "You know I can't give up my gun," I said, and I wondered if I imagined her look of relief. "Rule number one."

"Don't make this any harder," she said.

"Harder?" My mind raced. My pulse rushed in my ears. I had to stop this. But how? And then I remembered the conversation we'd had at Torrance's about the FBI Academy.

"You're standing there, expecting me to give up my gun like this is some exercise in Hogan's Alley? Picking out the good guys and the bad guys?"

"I do," she said. "But then the world is *filled* with them. Now put down the gun. *Both* of them. The one I can see . . . and the one I *can't*."

I glanced at the stalls. There was more than one, with the doors closed. It was like playing *Let's Make a Deal,* but pick the wrong door, the wrong suspect, and I'd be dead.

Of course, I was banking on gut instinct. That Parrish had been taken, was being used. That Paolini was not my other suspect. That I knew who the killer was, or rather who had wanted the hit on Millhouse, and who could take on Lucia in an argument. But I couldn't see the bottom of Parrish's weapon, where the magazine should be. I had no way of knowing if it was empty. After all, here she was pointing the thing at me. There could be twelve more live rounds in that gun . . .

If I was wrong, I'd be one dead cop. "You ever play Ring Around the Rosies?" I asked her.

"What?"

I took a breath.

Raised my weapon.

Her gaze widened slightly.

"Ashes, ashes," I said.

She dove to the ground.

I fired.

At the center mass of the last stall.

43

Everything happened at once.

A body slumped to the ground, a gun clattered on the tile. I couldn't see who it was. Didn't have time to look.

"Where's Sophie?" I yelled to Parrish.

"Second stall," she cried, scrambling for the fallen weapon. "Lucia's down! She's dead!"

I spun. Aimed as the door opened. Sophie Millhouse stood there, holding a revolver to her temple, her hand shaking. "Kill me," she said. "Go ahead."

Parrish and I moved to either side of the stall just as Rocky and Torrance burst in. "We don't want to hurt you," I said. "Now drop the gun."

"How did you know it was me?"

"You told me you didn't want anyone to think you were involved in your husband's murder. Everyone else thought it was a robbery."

"But it could have been Lucia."

"Oh, I'm sure it was. That she set it up. She and Jim Greene. Hired David Cole for you."

"Lucia said she could take care of things . . ." Sophie gave a weary laugh. "I'm not sorry he's dead. He'd done things, you know? He liked to pull strings. Make people bend to his will. He was always threatening me. Always hitting me. I wanted it to stop . . . But I couldn't go to the cops, because he said he owned them. I believed him . . ."

I saw the tension in her hand, worried she'd pull the trigger. "Why?" I asked, figuring if I kept her talking, I'd save her life.

"Because three years ago, when I told him I was leaving, that I'd had enough, he—he drove me to this place. This motel. He parked out in front and told me to watch. This girl was walking out and someone shot her . . ." A tear fell down her cheek, and she swallowed past a lump in her throat. "He told me that he bought the gun on the street, and gave it to the guy who killed her, and—and he owned a lot of cops . . . and he'd have me killed just like that girl, because she stole some papers from him the night he slept with her, some account numbers . . ."

She closed her eyes, but the gun remained at her head. Pressed into her skin. Her voice came out a whisper. "He brought home this revolver one night. He said it was the one used to kill that girl. And it had been used on a cop." She looked at me, though I couldn't tell if she really saw me right then, or if she knew I was that cop. "He made me hold it. Then he told me—he told me my prints were on it. That I could never go to the cops, because they'd say I did it. I knew they would. He made sure of that. He told me he always made sure there was someone at the killings, someone who looked like me. With short red hair . . . He said he told the cops I liked roses . . . All those damned roses."

Roses. Short red hair. Lucia. The wig. "But we know it wasn't you," I said. "So put down the gun—"

"No. There's a police report. I saw it. That cop brought it over and gave it to my husband. He showed me. The description of the suspect who shot that girl outside the motel was mine."

"There was no suspect description. No witnesses."

"There was! That narcotics officer showed me the report. Abernathy."

"Buying your silence. The report was fake," I said, thinking about the description. Lucia, undoubtedly. I had wondered why she was present. Why she was always wearing a red wig. They obviously did that to ensure Sophie's cooperation, keep her from going to the police. "So put down the gun. Don't do this . . ."

"But I killed him. I let Lucia set it up."

"What do you mean you let her?"

"She told me she knew he was abusing me. That she could make him stop. She wanted to know where the gun was."

"The gun?"

"This one. The one he used to kill the girl. I told her I couldn't get it, that it was in his safe-deposit box. She said she would get it. Clean it up so my prints weren't on it." She hesitated. "She got it. The gun. She gave it to me. But she said she needed to go back. That she had given him something, and he may have put it in his safe-deposit box. She was mad when I told her I couldn't get into it. That it wasn't in my name."

"She wanted to get the diamonds?"

"You mean the diamonds that Jim Greene stole from the dealers' show to pay back Earl? The diamonds Earl wanted because he was skimming money from the bank? Well, I don't know who got them in the end, but Lucia was a little desperate, because she'd already sold them to Nick. That's why she wanted to get into the box. She said Stephen Reynard would help me."

"Help you?"

"Get into the box." She gave a hysterical laugh. "I told her I changed my mind. But they killed him and I couldn't get into the box. Nothing worked out. The guy she hired got away. She said he wouldn't. That he'd never leave the bank, and he'd have the gun on him from the other murders when he was killed, and I'd be free . . . But he got away . . ." She slumped against the side of the stall. "Then when you got

too close, she sent him after you. And she had him kill her
brother, the one who dressed like a girl, because he knew she
set it up. But I didn't know . . . I didn't know Lucia was
going to do all that," she said, sliding down, her voice getting softer and softer. "I didn't want murder. I didn't want
everyone to die . . . I just wanted my husband to stop hitting
me . . ."

She was on the floor now. Crying. The gun still pressed to
her head.

"Please," I said. "Put down the gun."

"I can't go to prison," she said, closing her eyes.

She bit her lip.

And pulled the trigger.

44

"**A**ny word on Sophie Millhouse?" I asked Rocky as he hung up the phone.

We were back at the Hall in Homicide, and had finished up the debriefing on the operation with all the agents involved.

"Yeah," Rocky said. "She's going to pull through. Apparently she had the gun angled enough that the bullet slid around her skull instead of penetrating."

"Thank God," I said.

Andrews walked in with Torrance and Parrish. "Jim Greene was picked up by the FBI," Andrews said. "He's asked for an attorney."

"Who'd he request?" I asked. "Stephen Reynard?"

"He did until he learned Reynard was also taken into custody."

"Bright guy," Rocky quipped, before eyeing me. "There are two things you didn't go into at the debriefing. One, how'd you know it was Jim Greene, without knowing that Parrish had gotten his number from Lucia's phone records?"

"Because there aren't too many people who could influence Lucia into doing their will, yet he convinced her not to have an abortion and to keep a child she didn't want. That told me he had *some* influence over her, though I wasn't foolish enough to believe that he could ever control her."

"Okay. I'll buy that. But how'd you know that Parrish was holding an empty gun?"

I told him about seeing the live round on the ground, and then using the Hogan's Alley training exercise she'd talked about to covertly communicate with her as to how many suspects were in there.

"Ring Around the Rosies?" he said.

"It was the only way I could think of to tell her to duck, without coming out and saying it."

Parrish gave a grim smile. "Damn good thing I remembered the poem. I should never have gone in there alone, but I thought Rocky heard me, and I never expected to go past the door . . . I never expected to feel a gun at my head when I did."

Parrish had told us that they were both in there, hiding. Lucia had held Parrish at gunpoint, ordering Sophie to take Parrish's weapon, remove the magazine and eject the round. The plan was that I'd walk in, see Parrish with the gun, and Parrish, if she wanted to live, was to get me to drop mine. "I have an idea," Parrish said, "that Lucia expected you to kill me, then she'd kill you . . ."

She crossed her arms, looking distinctly uncomfortable, and Rocky broke the tension by saying, "So Lucia sold the diamonds out from under Earl Millhouse."

"Which meant," Parrish said, "that Lucia and Jim had to do some scrambling to get the diamonds back from Millhouse."

"So why the elaborate hit?" Rocky asked. "And why use the same gun as in Fiona's murder?"

"If I had to guess," I said, "it would be to divert attention from what was really going on with the diamonds. We'd be too busy spinning our wheels trying to tie the hit man, David Cole, to Fiona's murder. Why else go to all the trouble to get us to the bank, positioned to take out Cole the moment he exited?"

"That's precisely what we think," Parrish said, "and what

we told Cole's lawyer. The moment Cole heard, he decided to give a statement. That's when he told us that Lucia changed plans at the last minute. Apparently she phoned him a couple of hours after your appearance on *San Francisco's Most Wanted*. He told his lawyer that he should have suspected something, because suddenly they wanted him to use a specific gun, and commit the robbery/hit the following Monday instead of that Friday as planned."

"And he came after me, because . . . ?"

"He saw you at the fundraiser, recognized you from the bank—and Lucia told him that you were after him, and wanted you taken out."

"At least," Rocky said, "we're spared the expense of her trial."

Some comfort, I thought.

Andrews looked at his watch. "Why don't you all go home, get some rest. We can finish up the paperwork tomorrow."

Parrish said, "I'll bet you'll be glad to sleep in your own bed tonight."

"Yeah," I said, glancing at Torrance, looking for some sign . . . He seemed lost in thought, and I decided I was the last person he was thinking of. "I think I'll walk over to the deli to grab a bite before I head home."

Rocky stood. "I'll go with you."

Torrance didn't move.

Rocky and I walked out the door to the hallway.

"Gillespie!"

We stopped at the sound of Parrish's voice, and I hid my disappointment that it was she calling after me and not Torrance.

"Look," she said. "I just wanted to thank you—"

"Don't worry about it."

"You came through for me. I won't forget it."

She smiled, then. A genuine smile that told me she meant

every word. And I said the only thing I could think of. "You're welcome to come out to the deli with us."

"Thanks, anyway, but I've got some calls to make."

She disappeared back into the office, and Rocky and I walked in companionable silence to the elevators, rode down, then were out into the busy lobby. It wasn't until we were out the front doors, standing on Bryant Street, that Rocky said, "What's wrong?"

I watched the cars zipping past, giving a shrug. "Nothing."

"Bullshit. You've been down in the dumps ever since—"

He didn't say it. He didn't need to. We both knew since when. Since I'd slept with Torrance. "I just wish I could read him," I said, shoving my hands in my pockets. "I guess I thought once we crossed that line that things would be . . . different."

"Yeah, well you didn't see his face when he heard you on the radio saying you couldn't give up your gun."

I suppose I'd assumed they'd heard something—since they showed up in the restroom. Until now, it never occurred to me that it affected anyone else but me, and maybe Parrish . . .

I put it from my mind, told myself it didn't matter. What would happen would happen. All I had to do was ignore the voice telling me I wanted it to happen a hell of a lot sooner.

"Kate!"

Rocky and I stopped, turned. Saw Torrance at the doors of the building. I was too pragmatic to believe that his contact was anything but business. Not here, not on the front steps of the Hall of Justice.

A gust of typical bay wind hit us, and I pulled closed my jacket as Torrance walked toward us. "You invite Parrish to lunch and not me?" he asked.

As usual I could tell nothing from his expression. "She's a guest," I said as he neared us. "You're always more than welcome to come along."

"I wish I could. Parrish and I have a second debriefing at our office." He nodded toward the doors and I saw Parrish up there, waiting.

Once again today, I hid my disappointment, gave a casual shrug. "Maybe some other time."

"Actually, I was thinking of something later . . ."

"Yeah, sure," I said, surprised when he continued toward me, closed the distance between us, and I remembered thinking that something was up. It was broad daylight. There were dozens of people, officers, walking past us, Rocky within hearing distance, Parrish watching us . . . "Tomorrow?" I said, trying to keep a positive spin on this.

But he shook his head. "Not quite what I had in mind." And then he reached out, and before I knew it, took me in his arms, lifting my face up to his. "I was thinking of tonight."

And right there on the Hall of Justice steps, in front of God and man . . . He kissed me.

Acknowledgments

As usual, it is my goal to entertain, mixing some factual police life into the fictional SFPD world I have created for Kate Gillespie. Any errors are mine. With that in mind, I have taken some poetic license with the city of San Francisco, creating a bank where none was, and a new and improved BART station, because the closest one wasn't quite where I needed it.

A number of people have helped me in my endeavors: To my husband, who does far more for me than I can ever say. To SFPD Inspector Sergeant Pat Correa. Thanks for your words of wisdom and encouragement. To my fellow Sacramento investigator, Arndt Gardner, for his input and help with some plotting details in the bank robbery. Thanks to my anonymous neighbor, a bank employee from an anonymous bank in an anonymous town for verifying all my details involving the safe-deposit box. You know who you are. And soon all our neighbors will figure it out. And thanks to all those on EMWA who also responded to my immediate need for info on safe-deposit boxes. To Susan Crosby, my steadfast writing friend, who always offers such sage advice, and points out the tiny things that make a big difference. To my agent, Jane Chelius, who keeps me on the right track. To my editor, Lyssa Keusch, who doesn't hesitate to point out the good stuff, too. I look forward to our next book.

To David Cole and Nancy Rodich-Hodges, whose generous donations to literacy will help someone else enjoy the pleasures of reading. I hope you both like your characters.

Somewhere out in cyberspace is a mystery list called Dorothy L, where there are some very wonderful readers of mysteries. Ginny Richardson, a librarian from Hawaii, was one such reader, and we began to correspond, eventually meeting at a mystery conference. Ginny was visiting her family in California when she was killed in a traffic accident, along with her brother and nephew. I know many of her friends on Dorothy L will miss her. I will miss her. I created the CSI character for Ginny as a way to remember her. Ginny, I hope you enjoy your role.

LAURA LIPPMAN

Edgar Award-winning author of
In a Strange City

**Discover the deadly side of Baltimore
with the Tess Monaghan Mysteries**

BALTIMORE BLUES
0-380-78875-6/$6.99 US/$9.99 Can

CHARM CITY
0-380-78876-4/$6.99 US/$9.99 Can

BUTCHERS HILL
0-380-79846-8/$5.99 US/$7.99 Can

IN BIG TROUBLE
0-380-79847-6/$6.99 US/$9.99 Can

THE SUGAR HOUSE
0-380-81022-0/$6.99 US/$9.99 Can

IN A STRANGE CITY
0-380-81023-9/$6.99 US/$9.99 Can

THE LAST PLACE
0-380-81024-7/$7.50 US/$9.99 Can

And in hardcover

EVERY SECRET THING
0-06-050667-9/$24.95 US/$34.95 Can

"Shots fired!"

"Are you Inspector Gillespie?"

"Yes," I replied. "And you are?"

"Um, Jane. Jane Smith—I mean, Doe."

Right. Jane didn't sound too sure of her name. "You have some information for me?"

"Um, yeah. You wanted to know about the shooting at the Twin Palms?" I wanted to give her my complete attention, I wanted to know where I'd seen her before, but my glance strayed to Bay Trust Mutual and the man I'd seen walking in.

"Keep an eye on the place," I told Rocky. To the woman, I said, "What can you tell me?"

"The man you're looking for is going to be—" She stopped, as we heard two loud pops from inside the bank.

"Jesus," Rocky said.

I grabbed the woman, pulled her behind our vehicle with one hand, drew my weapon with the other.

"Don't move," I told her.

"Shots fired!" Rocky called on the radio. "Bay Trust Mutual!"

Before we could do anything else, the suspect burst through the door.

And ran straight toward us.

Also by
Robin Burcell

DEADLY LEGACY
FATAL TRUTH
EVERY MOVE SHE MAKES